Andrzej Heyduk

The Breslau Conspiracy

ISBN: 13- 978-0-692-02785-1

Revised and updated, July 2014

Here & Now
Press

Special thanks to all my early test readers: Ewa, Janet, Lucyna, Margaret, and Tomasz.

Andrzej

To my first grandson, Oliver Louis Heyduk, who one day will hopefully understand why his Dziadek uses expletives.

Chapter 1

It was one of those dreary Chicago November afternoons which drove thousands of people into bars, even though they wanted to start their weekends in less alcoholic ways. As Michael Riedle looked out of his 'Chicago Tribune' office window down onto Michigan Avenue, he saw people trying to shield themselves from torrential rain and nasty wind blowing ruthlessly from the direction of somewhat disturbed Lake Michigan. He was almost ready to leave and join his friend, Alex Malak, for a couple of early Friday drinks, when he realized that he still had a pile of new mail lying on his desk.

With his raincoat already on, he reluctantly sat down in his rickety chair, worn out by hours of buttock squirming while writing useless articles about the wanton maneuverings of the Chicago City Council, and started leafing through a bunch of letters from disgruntled readers, mixed with meaningless invitations, credit card offers, and good old American junk mail. He was almost done throwing all of this out, when he suddenly caught a glimpse of an envelope with a foreign stamp. It wasn't difficult to spot – in contrast to the US 'forever-en-route stamps', emblazoned with the American flag and nothing else, this postal creation was very colorful and eye-catching. It showed a picturesque ocean bay, and had a large, tropical fish positioned smack in the middle of the stamp. Just above it Michael saw 'Belize' in big letters.

"Hmm" – he said to himself – "someone in Belize must have been really screwed by the Daley clan". Michael didn't know anybody in Belize, nor did he ever get any mail from abroad. As a city desk editor he dealt mostly with mail full of venom and criticism from people who – rightly or wrongly – hated something or somebody in the city of Chicago. The letter from Belize had no return address which – in his experience – was actually quite normal. He opened the envelope, took out a single sheet of lined paper, and unfolded it. Then he stared at the four hand-written lines of text with a mixture of bemusement and bewilderment:

EXTREMELY IMPORTANT
MATTER OF NATIONAL SECURITY
PAPERS UNDERGROUND
51.111704, 17.037590

Michael looked at the envelope again to make sure that it was really addressed to him. It was. He then typed the numbers into an Internet search engine to see whether it would suggest anything. All he got was 'Your search - 51.111704, 17.037590 - did not match any documents'. He shrugged his shoulders, put the letter in his raincoat pocket, and went to see a stiff shot of whisky with Alex firmly attached to it.

Perhaps he would have taken a closer look at the letter, had he had a brilliant career of an important investigative journalist, someone like Bob Woodward, someone of international renown. But his life seemed to have been hopelessly committed to the task of chronicling all the minute details of life in Rush Street. Single and in his 50's, he was more or less resigned to the fact that he would retire as the 'bard' of municipal bullshit. It therefore seemed to him extremely unlikely that any matter of national security, be it in Chicago, Kalamazoo or Belize, would somehow land on his desk.

At dusk Michael showed up at the Green Mill jazz bar on Broadway, once a hangout to Al Capone and Charlie Chaplin. The place was packed with rain-soaked city rejects from all walks of life. Alex was already there, waving to him over the din of live music and heavy boozing.

Michael didn't have a lot of friends, but Alex was definitely one of his best. He didn't quite remember how they first met, although he did recall that the connection between them had been instant and enduring, partly because they were so different and had dramatically divergent personal histories. Michael was a native of Chicago, very much like all of his ancestors, all the way back to his great grandfather Alois who at the ripe age of 16 boarded a ship in Hamburg and sailed to the US in search of a better life. The Riedle family eventually settled in the western suburb of Berwyn which was then full of Czech immigrants bearing thoroughly unpronounceable names. It was there that Michael went to school, moved to his own apartment just off Cermak Avenue, married, and got divorced. Then he moved to Wisconsin where he dabbled briefly in theater, only to eventually come back to study journalism at University of Illinois at Chicago – the school with undoubtedly the ugliest main building in college America.

Once he got his diploma, it seemed his career would immediately take off – he was somewhat brash, adventurous, inquisitive, not to mention insolent. But, having worked for a number of minor newspapers, he finally landed a job at the 'Tribune' where he got stuck forever at the city desk.

His friend Alex had an entirely different story to tell. Born on the wrong side of the Iron Curtain, in communist People's Republic of Poland, he trudged along for years with the rest of his fellow countrymen, mostly apathetic and despondent about the spiritual and material misery around him. He graduated from college, and - yes – it was all free. But in return he had to listen for hours to the mandatory 'Marxist philosophy' lectures. Alex never had any real job back in his country – he dabbled in all kind of things, but in the early 80's he realized that his life was going down the drain and that the so-called post-war division of Europe would not change in his lifetime unless there was a Third World War. So at the age of 30 he decided he needed to make a dramatic change – he fled his native land and showed up in Chicago as one more representative of the 'huddled masses', washing up on American shores. And since he had been enough of a nuisance to the communist authorities, the Department of State graciously awarded him a political asylum in relatively short order. But then things got complicated and muddled.

Alex became a US citizen, but drifted aimlessly in his new country, never quite sure about what to do and why. Eventually – like Michael – he got stuck in a relatively meaningless job – he used his self-acquired computer skills to babysit a network at a Morton Grove rubber factory. Unlike Michael, he was often hesitant and cautious. He also inherited from his past a deeply seated mistrust towards any governmental authority: be it police, city council, the White House or Morton Grove Fire Department.

Michael fought his way through a sea of half-inebriated humanity to reach Alex's table. His friend was sipping his first scotch and had already ordered Michael's favorite drink – vodka martini, both shaken and stirred. He was also staring at the screen of his laptop, which he almost never parted with.

"Come on, Alex, shut this thing down" - said Michael cheerfully - "we need to concentrate on forgetting this week, as usual".

"Why? Did you have a work-related nervous breakdown? Or perhaps the Chicago garbage collectors went on strike again without consulting city desk first?"

"Just shut up and drink. I actually haven't done anything particularly useful for the past few days, but I managed to piss off a bunch of people. How about you?"

"Well, the network is up and running, bits and bytes are flying, and everybody is deliriously happy".

"Fantastic. You are such an equal opportunity savior of humanity".

It was not unusual for Michael and Alex to tease each other about their respective jobs and ethnic backgrounds. Quite often their verbal exchanges would be deemed by external observers to be seriously politically incorrect. However, they never engaged in such 'pleasantries' in the presence of other people.

Michael went to get another round of drinks. When he returned to the table, Alex was once again glued to his laptop.

"Hey, since you are so hell-bent on making love to this heap of useless circuits, perhaps you could check something for me."

"Sure. What do you need to know?"

"Well, I got this weird letter today..."

"From your ex?"

"Hell no! From Belize."

Alex was very rarely flustered by whatever Michael happened to be saying to him at any particular time, but in this case he didn't quite manage to hide his surprise.

"From Belize? You must have been hiding something from me. I know where Belize is only in rough approximation, but apparently you actually know people there."

"You're such a jerk. Of course I don't know anybody in Belize. That's the damn point. The letter is from some anonymous Belize dude, and it's bizarre, not to mention kind of cryptic."

"Well, do you have it? Can I see it?"

Michael stuck his hand in his raincoat pocket and fished out a somewhat crumpled envelope. Then he handed it to Alex with distinct reluctance, as if he expected some dire consequences to immediately follow this simple transfer of paper. Alex looked at the letter for what seemed to Michael like a few minutes. Finally he smiled and threw the letter on the table.

"Come on, Michael. This has to be some stupid joke. Are any of your illustrious colleagues on vacation in Belize?"

"No. And I know it sounds stupid, but what the hell are these numbers?"

"No clue. Did you google them?"

"Yes, but I got nothing."

"OK, let me try again."

Alex started a session of googling, yahooing and binging, which was all to no avail. Michael saw that his friend drew a blank. They both sat helplessly in the midst of live jazz music and loud clanking of all kinds of glass vessels. Finally Michael picked the letter off the table and squashed it with his hands into a nice, tight, Belize ball.

"Enough of this" - he said - "You're right – some idiot at the 'Tribune' is probably laughing at me as we speak. Perhaps they wanted to test my knowledge of geography."

"Oh shit!" - exclaimed Alex with surprising urgency.

"Oh shit what?"

"I know what these numbers are. They are geographical coordinates – you know... like latitude and longitude."

"What are you talking about? Coordinates are these things with degrees, minutes and seconds. The numbers here are totally different."

"Yes, yes, but there is another notation, digital something or other. I remember seeing it somewhere. Give me this piece of paper again. I'll try to find some conversion page for this crap."

"How do you know all this?"

"It's always a great pleasure for any Polack to aid a feeble-minded Kraut." – said Alex with a very wicked chuckle.

Undeterred by the ethnic slur, Michael gave Alex the ball of paper. His friend spent the next few minutes punching furiously on the laptop keyboard, muttering sweet Polish nothings to himself and looking at what seemed to be an endless succession of websites.

"I got it!" - he said finally with obvious triumph in his voice - "There is an FCC site which can convert what they call 'digital notation' into the usual degrees and minutes."

Alex looked at the letter again and started keying in the two numbers. He then looked at Michael as if to ask for his permission to hit the 'Submit' button. "Shall I do it?" - he asked.

"Go for it."

"OK, I got it. Write this down. According to this thing latitude is 51° 6' 42.134 N and longitude is 17° 2' 15.324 E – and of course I have no idea what this means."

"Well, now it should be easy – we just find out where this place is, don't we?"

"Right. So... I am going here... and then.... bingo."

What happened next greatly perplexed Michael. Alex was looking at his laptop screen with a combination of surprise and puzzlement. He remained totally silent for such a long time that Michael just had to assume something important had just transpired.

"This doesn't make any sense." - said Alex finally, his voice clearly shaken.

"What's wrong? What location did you get?"

"It's Wrocław."

"What the hell is Vrots... or whatever?"

"It's the city I lived in for 30 years."

Chapter 2

Easter Sunday night, April 1st 1945, was not a joyous occasion for the inhabitants of the ancient city of Breslau. Not that many of them were left anyway. Three months earlier, just before the Red Army completely encircled what the Germans called 'Festung Breslau'[1], tens of thousands of people were ordered to leave the city and march west on foot in bitter subzero temperatures. Most of them perished – there were thousands of corpses lying in the snow along the roads stretching from Breslau all the way to Hirschberg, Liegnitz and Görlitz.

At exactly 6 pm on Easter Sunday the Soviets began heavy, sustained artillery and aerial bombardment of the city, which lasted for nearly 12 hours. Soon the center of Breslau was being consumed by a ferocious firestorm, which engulfed everyone and everything. In the morning of April 2nd one could hear church bells ringing. However, the bells did not need any human cooperation in order to spring to action – the intense heat from all the fires on the ground produced 'thermal tornadoes' which leapt furiously towards the sky and had enough force to move and sway even very heavy objects. Breslau was dying a fiery, desolate death.

Lieutenant Heinrich Grabbe, a soldier of Waffen-SS, never witnessed anything like it before, even though he was a veteran of the dreaded Eastern Front and saw firsthand the sheer savagery of this war. At 9 am on Easter Monday he emerged from a crypt underneath Adalbertkirche in Dominikanerplatz to survey the damage. What he saw was beyond description. To his

---

[1] 'Fortress Breslau'.

right there was the vast building of the main post office with huge flames and thick smoke shooting out from nearly every window. Right in front of him he could see heaps of smoldering rubble – just 24 hours earlier in the same spot there were three small curved streets with rows of neat houses and small stores. And there were people – some dead, some half-dead, and some alive but dazed, scared, confused and resigned to die.

Although lieutenant Grabbe was a soldier and was supposed to follow orders, he no longer knew who was in charge and why. Technically the city was in the hands of Gauleiter[2] Karl Hanke and General Hermann Niehoff, but the chain of command was often broken. Grabbe tried to tidy up his tattered, filthy uniform and started walking north, towards Neumarkt, one of the main squares of the city, which was only a few hundred yards away. He didn't really know why he chose to walk that way. He stayed in the middle of the street, because fires were raging everywhere and buildings were collapsing all around him. When he reached Neumarkt, he realized that he might have picked the wrong spot to go to. In a sense the square was no longer there. Only four houses encircling Neumarkt were still standing while all the others were either on fire or completely annihilated. A thick cloud of smoke, soot and ash hung over the entire area filling every nook and cranny with an acrid stench of death and destruction. It was a sunny, relatively warm spring day, but all lieutenant Grabbe could see was the fiery twilight of the final defeat.

Instinctively he started walking towards one of the two remaining houses which stood at the entrance to a narrow street called Messergasse. As he started traversing the square, zigzagging his way around huge bomb craters, he realized that he was totally alone – there were some bodies and body parts all over the place, but no other living soul was present. Right in the middle of the square there were mangled remnants of an antiaircraft artillery position, which attracted merciless Soviet bombardment the night before. Grabbe reached the building and stood in front of its main door hesitant and confused – he wasn't

---

[2] Party leader of a regional branch of the NSDAP (more commonly known as the Nazi Party).

sure what to do next. This was Neumarkt 15 where before the war people drank beer and chatted endlessly about daily trivialities. The house was still adorned with large lettering 'Krähe-Stübel', but the intricately painted sign on the front wall – 'Brauerei Schwarze Krähe' - was reduced to just 'Br warze K' because of dust and crumbling paint.

For a while Grabbe considered getting inside the house to see whether there was any water or beer left, but suddenly he heard the sound of a car engine. He looked to his left and saw an approaching black limousine racing towards him at a relatively high speed. The vehicle was covered with dust, its front bumper was grotesquely bent, and one of its little swastika flags on the hood was gone. And yet Grabbe knew immediately that this car had to carry a high-ranking officer. He wasn't mistaken.

The limousine screeched to a halt right in front of him and out emerged an impeccably dressed general, accompanied by two men in civilian clothes. One of them was carrying a black leather briefcase. In comparison to Grabbe's bedraggled appearance, the trio looked like they had just left an elegant restaurant and were looking for a good spot to have a nice dessert before retiring for brandy and cigars. The two 'civilians' were wearing standard issue Gestapo garb – long black leather coats, black hats, ominous faces.

"Please identify yourself." – barked the general at Grabbe.

"Yes, sir. I am Lieutenant Heinrich Grabbe, Waffen-SS, Besslein Regiment."

"What are you doing here and where is your unit?"

"I have no idea, sir."

"On both counts?"

"Yes, sir."

"Listen to me carefully. I am general Horst von Stirlitz. I will walk into this house with these two gentlemen and will remain there for about 15 minutes. I need you to secure the entrance to the house during this time. Absolutely nobody gets in and, if you have to, shoot any possible intruders. Is this understood?"

"Yes, sir."

Grabbe assumed his position at the front door as soon as the three men disappeared inside. He had no idea what was going on, but he couldn't help thinking that 'securing' this place was a somewhat silly task since there was absolutely nobody around, except for a scraggy-looking dog which suddenly appeared on top of what just a week earlier had been a Neptune monument adorning the center of the square. All the fires were still raging around the square and it was safe to assume that Russian aerial attacks would soon resume.

When general Stirlitz emerged from the house, his two companions went back to the waiting limousine, got in, and slammed the doors shut. The general faced Grabbe and looked straight at his face with steely earnestness.

"I have an important job for you, lieutenant."

"Yes, sir."

"Here is a briefcase. Inside you will find two sealed envelopes and a letter with instructions on how to get these envelopes to gauleiter Hanke. I am ordering you to follow these instructions very strictly. Do you think you can do this?"

"Yes, sir."

"This is a matter of utmost importance, so I really need to know that I can rely on you."

"I won't fail you, sir."

"Good. But that's not all. As soon as you safely deliver these letters to Hanke, I need you to get in touch with any Brennkommando[3] you can find and order it to burn this house to the ground."

Grabbe failed miserably at hiding his puzzlement.

"Yes, sir... but everything is burning around here anyway."

"I know. Don't worry about it. Just make sure that this house is totally gone as soon as possible."

---

[3] Special units equipped with flame-throwers whose task was to burn down large swaths of houses along strategically selected streets in order to make an additional barricade against the advancing Red Army units. Brennkommandos in Breslau worked with ruthless efficiency, first forcibly removing people from their apartments, then throwing residents' furniture and personal belongings out onto the street, and finally setting fires.

"Understood, sir."

"Heil Hitler!"

"Heil Hitler!"

The general got back into his limousine, which immediately sped away down Messergasse. Lieutenant Grabbe fulfilled his promise and executed perfectly the first part of the general's order by delivering the sealed letters to gauleiter Hanke in a matter of hours. Unfortunately he had a major problem with the second part of the order since 15 minutes after emerging from Hanke's headquarters he was killed by a powerful bomb blast in the vicinity of the Breslau University building. He was therefore in no position to know that his death didn't matter that much, at least with respect to obeying orders – on the very same day the house in Neumarkt 15 was hit by Russian artillery shells which reduced it to a heap of smoking debris. As ordered by general Horst von Stirlitz.

Chapter 3

It would be an understatement to say that Alex was intrigued by what happened at the Green Mill jazz bar. He spent the following day constantly mulling all kinds of possibilities in his mind. It was certainly possible, although not very likely, that all of this was some sort of a monumental coincidence – his friend Michael just happens to get a mysterious letter from an anonymous person in Belize and this letter just happens to reference geographical coordinates of his home town in Poland. "If this is a joke" – thought Alex – "it would have to come from someone who knows that I am Michael's friend and that I used to live in Wrocław."

The problem was Alex couldn't think of a single person who would meet these criteria. He actually wanted the letter to turn out to be a stupid hoax, because all the other alternatives were not only exceedingly baffling, but downright scary. He spent his Saturday pacing restlessly and searching the immense expanse of cyberworld for clues. It was quite easy for him to pinpoint precisely the spot identified by the coordinates: the northwest corner of Nowy Targ, a large square in downtown Wrocław. He knew this place quite well – it was only half a mile away from his college where he studied for 5 years. But he was at a loss as to why this particular location might be of any significance to anyone. He found some photographs and maps, printed them out, stuffed them in an envelope, and headed to Berwyn to see Michael at his place. Before leaving Green Mill the night before, they not only had had a succession of additional drinks, but also had agreed to meet on Saturday evening to discuss the Belize letter while totally sober. It was almost a miracle that both of them actually remembered what they had agreed to do.

"So, did you do any research on this?" – asked Michael as soon as he and Alex sat down in a large room full of the usual assorted crap, which always 'decorated' Michael's apartment.

Alex wasn't yet ready to start talking about details.

"Listen, Michael, before we go on, I would like us to assume that this isn't a practical joke."

"Really? Why?"

"It's simple. If it is, then there is no point talking about it. We can have a few beers and on Monday we'll laugh about it as soon as the 'joker' reveals himself."

"All right. Assumption made. What do we do next? I know now that this town of yours is in the southwest corner of Poland".

"Correct. And the coordinates point to a spot at the edge of a square in the city center."

"Anything peculiar about it?"

"No. It's been a while since I was there last, but I remember that there is a small supermarket at this location. Unless they demolished the building, it looks like this."

Alex took out one of the printouts from the envelope he brought with him and shoved it in front of Michael.

"Ugh, what the hell is this?" – asked Michael with obvious disgust while looking at a black-and-white picture of a grey box pretending to be a viable piece of architecture.

"It's a perfect example of the so-called socialist style of building things. When the communists took over after the war, they started rebuilding the city with 'prefabricated' concrete slabs to speed up the process and cut down the costs. The end result was total ugliness. This shit is now all around the square."

"What happened to the less ugly shit that used to be there?"

"Damn, I knew it."

"You knew what?"

18

"That you would need a brief history lesson. So, here it is. Before the war my city was at the southeastern edge of Germany and was called Breslau. The square in question was called Neumarkt and it was surrounded by beautiful 18th and 19th-century houses. However at the very end of World War II the city was designated as 'fortress', just before being completely encircled by the Ruskis. Between February and May of 1945 it was almost totally destroyed by constant bombardment while a bunch of insanely fanatical cousins of yours defended it to the bitter end. Did you know that Breslau surrendered well after Hitler killed himself, only three days before the end of the Third Reich?"

"No, I didn't."

"Well, now you do. Neumarkt – or Nowy Targ as it's known now – basically ceased to exist. Only two buildings were spared and the rest is gone forever. What they built there after the war is a disgrace and I think there are some plans to demolish the prefabricated stuff and start over once again."

"OK, so how come the city is now in Poland?"

"Have you heard of Stalin? He took over a part of eastern Poland and persuaded the Allies to give Poland some parts of eastern Germany. And now instead of Breslau we have Wrocław".

Michael fell silent for a while. Alex had no idea what his friend was thinking about, but he was afraid it wasn't anything rational. Their mutual history suggested that every now and then Michael had the tendency of parting with reason and embracing irrational emotions instead.

"This may be a long shot, but do you know what was there before?" – he said finally.

"Where?"

"Before the war. What was there at exactly the spot identified by the coordinates?"

"Oh, that's not a long shot at all. Look at this."

Alex gave Michael another printout from his envelope. It was a photograph of a relatively large building with some German signs over its main door.

"It used to be a small brewery and a bar." – explained Alex – "The German 'Brauerei Schwarze Krähe' means Black Crow Brewery."

"So what if something got hidden underground there before the war?"

"Don't be silly! What makes you think that? And even if it was, it probably is no longer there. A more likely scenario would be for someone to hide something before they started rebuilding after the war. None of which explains anything about this damn Belize letter which – I am hoping – is someone's lame attempt at being funny."

"You know what all of this means, don't you?"

"Please, Michael, I really don't want to know."

Alex expected the worst and he got it.

"I have to go there." – said Michael.

"To Belize?"

"No, to Poland."

Alex stared at him in utter disbelief. Then he got up from the couch, went to the kitchen, took out a beer out of Michael's fridge, opened it, and gulped down half of the bottle in just seconds. When he returned to the living room, he found Michael looking at the letter from Belize. In some strange, convoluted sort of way he felt sorry for his friend who was obviously obsessing about a document that might turn out to be a totally meaningless piece of garbage.

"Look, Michael, I know this whole thing puzzles the hell out of you, but don't get carried away. We know absolutely nothing about this letter and its author – for all I care, he can be an elevator operator in the 'Tribune' building who got seriously annoyed with you for not saying hello one morning."

"Oh, yeah? And how would this master of elevators know about Breslau and its decimally coded coordinates? Coincidence? Luck? Give me a break."

"All right, I take your point. But, please, you cannot just get up and fly to Europe to excavate a store in the middle of a densely populated city in search of some phantom 'national security' papers."

"I know, I know... But it almost doesn't matter anymore, because I just have to go there regardless. If we don't go, this thing will bother me for the rest of my life."

"Hey, wait a second. Just wait one damn second. Did I just hear you say 'we'? I'm not going anywhere, Michael, and the sooner you realize it, the better."

Michael looked almost hurt, but kept his feelings to himself. It was his turn to grab a beer from the kitchen. When he returned, both of them sat in total, uncomfortable silence for a minute or two. Then Michael got up and starting walking slowly in circles, with the beer bottle in his hand.

"I need your help, Alex" – he said almost plaintively – "You are a native speaker of Polish and I can't tell 'kielbasa' from 'Lech Walesa'. All I am asking is that you fly with me over there to have a look. I will gladly pay for your ticket."

"Well, thanks a lot for your generosity, but that's not the issue. I have no idea what you're scheming, but let's get things straight. Since the letter says there are papers underground at that location, you land in Wrocław, you go to the supermarket in Nowy Targ and ask for permission to dig a big honking hole in the store floor, just below the shelf full of frozen pierogis, on the pretense that some friend of yours had lost a few documents there half a century earlier. Is that your plan? Because if it is, you're nuts."

"Who said anything about digging? This place might have a cellar or a basement."

"True, but this would not be the cellar of yesteryear, full of mysterious mementos of past plots of national security import, but a new cellar, put in place by the heroes of socialist revolution to store cabbage, potatoes, and bigos."

"What the hell is bigos?"

"Never mind. And another thing – how do you explain the fact that the dude in Belize chose **you** for this incredibly dangerous mission of digging up a supermarket in Eastern Europe? Why not some big reporters from Washington or New York who actually might have had a bit of previous experience in international intrigue and not exclusively in finding out if Mayor Daley had a secret liaison with a nubile hooker from Guatemala in a forsaken warehouse just off Belmont Avenue?"

At this point Michael abruptly stopped walking in circles, sat down, and looked at Alex as if he was about to say something he might regret later. Then he sighed and said it anyway.

"I think the author of the letter picked both of us".

"What? Oh my god, you can't be serious."

"Well, just think about it. What if someone wanted to get in touch with a journalist who either himself was a Polish-American and could attempt to retrieve the stuff in Breslau or who was an American reporter in close touch with a Polack like you who could help him? Remember, you yourself wanted the assumption that this wasn't a hoax, and I'm working on that assumption. So, someone wanted people to go and find these papers, read the information contained in them, and somehow act on it. Now, I have no idea why this person wouldn't do it all by himself, but there's a bunch of possibilities: language barrier, travel restrictions, old age, bad health or whatever."

"OK. But how would he make a connection between the two of us?"

"I don't know. But nowadays almost everything is possible. You should know – after all, you're the prince of cyber world".

Michael's last sentence gave Alex a bit of a pause. He thought about something for a few seconds and asked his friend if he could use his laptop. Michael brought his machine from another room, but before giving it to Alex he wanted to know what exactly was going on.

"What are you going to do? You are usually most dangerous when you have such things at your disposal."

"Well, I need to settle this here and now. So, first tell me if you ever wrote a piece for your newspaper in which my name and ethnic background would be in some way featured or mentioned".

"Why?"

"Because if you did, the connection between us would've been automatically added to Internet search engines."

"OK, let me think... No, I don't remember ever mentioning you".

"Are you sure?"

"Yes..."

"How about that one piece you wrote years back about our St. Patrick's drunken sing-along in Michigan Ave.?"

"No, I spared you major shame by omitting your name altogether... But wait, there was also this Taste of Chicago thing."

"What Taste of Chicago thing?"

"Well, I think I did mention you about two years ago when writing about it. And, as far as I remember, I used your name and alluded to the fact that you were a Polish friend of mine. But that was almost like a side note, added to the description of some weird Polish dishes."

"Great. So now, give me your laptop and let's pretend that we are this mysterious person in Belize who is trying to recruit his 'Breslau crew' on the net. What search terms would he be after?"

"Obviously he wouldn't know our names. So how about 'USA', 'Wrocław', 'Polish', 'Poland', 'reporter', 'journalist'... Well, let's also throw 'Chicago' in there."

"OK."

Alex went to work. It took him a while, but after a few minutes, having paged down a bunch of times on the list of search results, he found a reference to the 'Chicago Tribune' article about the Taste of Chicago. It was obvious that if someone wanted to search for a journalist and his connections to 'Polish stuff', he or she would certainly be able to do it. This posed a dilemma for Alex who really wanted to discourage Michael from any further craziness. He decided to procrastinate.

"Michael, I am willing to consider all options, but let's wait till at least Monday and see whether all of this isn't a wild goose chase. After all, the possible 'joker' could also have used the same information on the net to make sure that we get totally fooled."

Michael grudgingly agreed, but it was obvious he was already convinced that this whole thing was no joke.

Chapter 4

The Joseph Strauss International Airport in Munich made a big impression on Alex. It was spotlessly clean, efficient, and full of perfunctorily pleasant Germans who made sure that every passenger passing through felt well taken care of, even though he probably wasn't. The coffee was excellent, the beer was outstanding, and the old Bavarian specialty called 'Weisswurst', served almost everywhere, definitely deserved rave reviews. It was also very surprising that – in contrast to Chicago's O'Hare – a visit to a men's room did not pose any immediate threat of contracting nasty diseases.

It seemed a bit strange to Alex that he was actually on his way to Wrocław to inspect rows of produce and cans of spam in a non-descript supermarket. Having argued with Alex for days about the possible meaning – or lack thereof – of the Belize letter, he finally relented and agreed to go to Poland for just one week 'to have a look'. He decided to treat this escapade as an unexpected vacation – they both had plenty of vacation time at their respective companies, so there was no problem with scheduling their trip. Alex was sitting in a large, open terminal hall waiting for the final flight to Wrocław while Michael decided to just walk around and look at all the airport stores. The airport was full of smartly dressed European businessmen who looked like they knew exactly why they were doing what they were doing, which was sipping strong coffee and yelling into their cell phones in a multitude of languages.

Faced with two hours of waiting time, Alex reached for the table in front of him and fished out the first English-language newspaper he could find. It was 'International Herald Tribune' which offers all Earthlings the 'essence' of world news as seen with American eyes. He looked at the front page. It was full of dramatic developments concerning Major League Baseball playoffs, sex scandals, and someone's failed drug test. He was just about to put the newspaper back on the table, when he caught a glimpse of a small news item in the lower right-hand corner of the page: 'Belize Man Found Dead'.

"Oh, fuck" – thought Alex expletively – "that's all we need". He looked around to make sure that Michael wasn't anywhere to be seen. Then, with a lot of apprehension, he started reading the news:

Authorities in Belize confirmed that yesterday, November 15th, the body of 88-year old Charles Whitmore was discovered in his own house in the capital city of Belmopan. The cause of death remains unknown. Mr. Whitmore has lived in Belize for over two decades and was repeatedly accused of being Karl Krugman, an assistant to the Nazi war criminal Heinrich Himmler. However, these accusations have never been definitively substantiated. The investigation into the cause of his death continues.

Almost without thinking Alex tore out the appropriate fragment of the front page and put it in his pocket.

The flight from Munich to Wrocław lasted just over an hour. Michael seemed pensive and didn't say much while in the air, leafing thoughtlessly through airline magazines. Alex, on the other hand, was worried. He decided not to say anything about the Belize death to his friend, because he feared it would just fuel Michael's wacky theories ignited by the letter. But he also couldn't stop wondering about the possibility that the man who had died in Belmopan had something to do with the fact that he was just minutes away from landing in Wrocław with Michael at his side.

"Don't you think it's all a bit peculiar? – he said to Michael.
"What?"

"Well, here we are. A German and Pole, living in America, going to a city claimed by both of our ethnic brethren, in pursuit of some mysterious crap which most likely is going to turn out to be just that – crap."

"Hey, I live in Chicago and I'm a journalist. I like crap."

The weather in Wrocław was surprisingly good – it was sunny and unseasonably warm. Michael and Alex took a taxi to Hotel Qubus, which was situated just a mile away from their 'point of interest'. Their incredibly garrulous driver managed to squeeze his entire biography into a 20-minute oration, replete with quasi-conspiratorial references to all kinds of places they were passing by. Michael didn't understand a word of it while Alex just nodded his head every now and then to feign unwavering interest.

"Get used to this." – Alex whispered to his traveling companion – "People will just blabber stuff in Polish and you'll have to listen and pretend that you not only understand, but also care."

It was early afternoon by the time the two of them checked in, showered, and had lunch at the hotel restaurant. Although tired and jet-lagged, they decided to take a stroll around the city center. Alex had an ulterior motive in doing that – he wanted to 'accidentally' wander into Nowy Targ Square hoping that just the sight of the drab building, housing the supermarket, will discourage Michael on their very first day in Poland. He first took him to see two magnificent squares constituting the heart of Wrocław: Rynek and Plac Solny. Both were ancient 'market squares' and as long back as early medieval times were lively centers of commerce. Nowy Targ used to be an integral part of this 'mercantile trinity', but all of that ended with the nearly complete destruction at the end of the war. Rynek and Plac Solny had been meticulously rebuilt and Michael marveled at their beauty and vivacity while walking around. Alex pointed out various interesting details, told his friend about many an hour spent around this area in his school years, and generally played a guide to this accidental American tourist. But he knew this wasn't going to last for long.

Having shown Michael 'the good', Alex decided it was a very opportune time to show him 'the bad and the ugly'. He took him north towards the main university building, but then they turned right into Nożownicza Street, which used to be Messergasse before the war, and started walking towards Nowy Targ which was just a few hundred yards away. In minutes they stood at the intersection of Nożownicza and Nowy Targ, gaping at the large, nearly totally empty space in front of them.

"Holy shit, you were not kidding when you told me this place was a bit dingy."

"I warned you. That big building over there, on the other side, is one of the two remaining pre-war structures. The other one is this little house right behind you. All these other pseudo-houses were built about 4 decades ago. As you can see, there is nothing in the middle of this square other than a bunch of parked cars."

Michael looked at the dreary walls pockmarked by years of neglect and realized that not even a sunny day was able to help this place in any way. Then he grabbed Alex by his arm, turned right, walked a few paces with him and stopped in front of a row of storefronts.

"So, is this it? – he asked.

"Yes. Where it says 'Sklep spożywczy PSS Społem Centrum'."

"This is the name of the supermarket?"

"Yes."

"Damn. I think 'Jewel Osco' beats the shit out of that one".

"Very funny... This is a pretty small place, almost like your decrepit 'neighborhood' excuse for a supermarket in Cermak."

"Shall we go in? It looks quite busy."

"We'd better not, because we don't know how many times we'll have to be in this store. Are you sure you still want to go through with this?"

"Absolutely."

"Well then, we need to first find out if this place has a basement."

"And if it does?"

28

"We'll call Kazik, of course."

Chapter 5

Back at the hotel Alex looked something up in the telephone directory, dialed a number, and started spewing out long sequences of consonants while Michael was sitting and drumming his fingers, irritated by the fact that he had no idea what was going on.

"Well?" – he asked impatiently as soon as Alex was finished.

"I was just talking to someone in the store. The store manager wasn't there, but she is 'pani Basia' and she will be there tomorrow afternoon."

"Her first name is 'Pani'?"

"No, moron. Her first name is 'Basia'. We stick 'pani' or 'pan' in front of the first names of people we haven't drunk enough vodka with to be on less formal terms. Anyway, pani Basia will be there tomorrow and the place does have a basement."

"How did you find that out?"

"I pretended to be one of their suppliers and asked them if they had additional refrigeration unit in the basement?"

"You know, sometimes you are cleverer that your ethnicity would suggest".

"Danke, meine kleine Liebchen."

"What?"

"Nothing. We need to see Kazik, although he is 'pan Kazik' to you."

Earlier, on the way back from Nowy Targ to the hotel, Alex tried to explain who 'pan Kazik' was and why he might turn out to be extremely useful. Still, Michael had his doubts since he didn't quite understand the usefulness of knowing someone who was a plumber unless the plan was to lay a bunch of large diameter underground pipes leading directly from the hotel basement to the subterranean parts of the store. Alex took another stab at explaining.

"Kazik is an old friend of mine who works for the city as a plumber. My hope is that he can help us get into the basement without raising any suspicions or attracting attention."

"How?"

"I don't know yet. We'll ask him, but perhaps we can all be plumbers for one hour and inspect the cellar on some kind of a 'plumbing' pretense."

"Great, sounds like right down my alley. How come you even have a plumber friend?"

"Well, he isn't really a plumber."

"What?"

"He is, and apparently quite good at it, but he also has a university degree in German and holds a PhD in philosophy."

"Alex, stop fooling around and just tell me who this dude is".

"I just told you. At some point in his life he decided that it was going to be better for him to carry big wrenches and work on city contracts rather than to read Heidegger in German to a bunch of slumberous students. Anyway, you'll meet him tomorrow – he is joining us for breakfast in my room at 9 am."

"Does he speak any English?"

"No. He only knows 'thank you' and 'fuck you'."

"Perfectly adequate, I guess... But what did you tell him? Why would he even help us?"

"I had to tell him the truth – well... sort of. All he knows is that you're this crazed American reporter who dreams of fame and fortune and who thinks there is some incredible Teutonic holy grail underneath a shitload of sauerkraut and pickles in Nowy Targ. He will ask no questions and he will go away once we do what we need to do. He'll also help us if the unthinkable happens."

"Meaning?"

"Well, if by some inexplicable convergence of god's will and pure coincidence we do find something down there, it will most likely not be in Sanskrit or Swahili, but in German or Polish. If it is in German, he'll be able to translate whatever we'll find."

"But..."

"Don't interrupt me. I have one more thing to say, and it's important. I came here with you, because you're my friend and you were very insistent. But I need to make a deal with you. If we get to this basement and find absolutely nothing, which is my expectation, I want you to promise me that we both quit immediately and go home. I can take you to a good restaurant for dinner to reminisce about our adventure over some juicy hunk of Slavic meat. Heck, I can even take you to Cracow to see a few dead Polish kings. But after that, it's home, baby. Is that a deal?"

Michael thought about this for a while. What Alex didn't fully realize was that his friend had decided – even before they left for Poland – that the letter from Belize could not have been an astronomically unlikely coincidence and that it was therefore about something very important, but intangible. Yet he had no choice. He knew very well that without Alex he would be totally helpless in Wrocław. So he agreed to the deal and awaited Kazik's appearance the next morning.

Pan Kazik was right on time. He walked into Alex's room shortly after 9 am the next day, talked gibberish with him for a while, was properly introduced to Michael, and then sunk his teeth into bacon, eggs and a toast. He was a short, somewhat pudgy man in his late 60's or early 70's, wearing some sort of professional overalls with a big badge hanging proudly on his chest. Although Michael had absolutely no idea what was going on, he did notice that pan Kazik also brought with him two additional badges and two additional sets of identical overalls. Michael correctly sensed that his career of a Polish plumber was just about to begin. He didn't have to wait long for confirmation.

"OK, here is the plan" – said Alex – "this afternoon Kazik will call the store manager and tell her that a city crew will visit her facility to fix something in the basement. She'll most likely agree to any particular time, so we'll set it for tomorrow at 9 am. Kazik says we'll have about half an hour – anything longer might raise questions. You and me will dress in these overalls and will have official badges."

"Really?"

Michael picked one of the badges and stared at it for a while.

"This is ridiculous. How can anybody pronounce this name?"

"What? Wojciech Szczęsny? It's easy. Anyway, you won't have to pronounce it."

"What if someone asks me something?"

Alex turned to Kazik and asked him – "Kaziu, a jak go o coś zapytają?"

"Damy mu w garść jakąś rurę, żeby wyglądał na durnego pomocnika." – replied Kazik.

Michael looked at both of them with growing irritation, which he found increasingly difficult to hide.

"We'll give you a piece of 'rura' so that you look like a dumb apprentice".

"Great. And what, may I ask, is a 'rura'?"

"A piece of pipe or - in slang - a very sexy girl".

"Which one do I get?"

"The pipe."

"Fantastic."

Chapter 6

If Michael were a military man, he would have dubbed their mock plumbing trip to the store with some exciting name, such as 'Operation Big Rura', now that he knew what 'rura' was. But he wasn't. In fact he never wanted to have anything to do with any military stuff in his entire life and this strange mission in a foreign land reminded him too much of a bad movie about some special forces exploits. On the day of their trip with Alex and Kazik down to the sauerkraut-and-pickles vault in Nowy Targ he woke up feeling both excitement and trepidation. On the one hand he was looking forward to perhaps finding out what the cryptic letter from Belize really meant. But unfortunately he also felt like an idiot – chasing a potentially silly hoax half way around the world.

The arrival of Kazik at their hotel at 8:45 in the morning did nothing to alleviate his fear of slipping into abject silliness. Their co-conspirator drove up to the front lobby in a minivan adorned with all kinds of incomprehensible lettering and a big picture of a leaking faucet positioned on both sides of the vehicle. Once in Michael's room, they put on their plumber garb, pinned their respective badges to their chests and started on their way to the supermarket. The trip to Nowy Targ took just a few minutes. As soon as they pulled up to the front of the store, Kazik presented Michael with a 4-foot plastic pipe and talked to Alex briefly.

"OK, Michael" – Alex said - "just carry this on your shoulder and keep your mouth shut. If anybody says anything to you, just try looking utterly stupid. I know you have it in you".

They walked into the supermarket with fake confidence. Kazik was carrying a very professionally looking leather bag full of plumbing paraphernalia while Alex was entrusted with an electronic device whose exact function was a total mystery to him, but which had all kinds of impressive, blinking lights and gauges. The store was pretty small and had just a few shelves running down the length of the interior. At the very back there were two checkout counters at one of which they immediately spotted pani Basia. It wasn't that difficult, because she was a matronly woman in her 50's whom Victorians would diplomatically call 'buxom'. She turned out to be a very friendly character who greeted Kazik warmly, exchanged some pleasantries with him, and proceeded to lead the entire crew to an unobtrusive door in the back wall of the store. Thankfully nobody said anything to Michael who carried his 'rura' proudly, trying desperately not to knock anything over with it. Basia opened the door and told Kazik to feel free 'to go down there'. They went down a short flight of steps, basked in flickering fluorescent light, and finally found themselves underground at the approximate coordinates spelled out by the Belize letter.

What immediately struck Michael was the fact that the cellar didn't look like it was hiding the great mysteries of the Third Reich. It was a pretty small, cramped space with metal shelving running along all four concrete walls. In one corner there was a large industrial refrigerator making noises suggesting its impeding end of useful life. Right next to it stood a small metal desk with all kinds of papers stacked on top of it. The shelves boasted a collection of cans and packages, all waiting to be some day sold to the customers upstairs.

"Now what?" - asked Alex.

Michael seemed to be a bit lost for words, but recovered quickly.

"Well, I'll take the left half of this place and you take the other. Let's look carefully at all the shelves and for any objects behind them. Also make sure you pay attention to any signs of something having been stashed away in the walls or under the floor".

"Not to mention in the refrigerator" - said Alex mockingly.

Michael ignored him and continued.

"Obviously we are looking for documents, so things like sheets of paper, envelopes, binders, folders, etc."

They both began their search while Kazik sat down at the desk and started leafing through the papers. He also opened each of the four drawers and examined their contents. As Alex expected all along, they found nothing. No cryptic papers, no hidden doors, no safes masked by rows of cleverly aligned canned carrots. Alex asked Kazik about something and then reported back to Michael.

"All these papers on the desk are just some inventory crap and invoices. Sorry, Michael, but I'm afraid this has been a total waste of time."

Michael stood in the middle of the basement and seemed to be immersed in some internal deliberations, most likely involving swearing. He looked like someone who was waiting for something dramatic to happen at any moment. Nothing did.

"Let's get the hell out of here" - he said abruptly and started immediately on his way up the stairs.

As soon as they reached their hotel they shed their plumber's gear and had a goodbye drink with Kazik, thanking him for all his help. Once he departed they went for a stroll around Rynek and ended up in a small bistro where they decided to have a very early lunch. Michael was unusually reticent, sitting glumly over his sandwich.

"Lighten up, Michael. We tried and we drew a blank. As I promised, I'll take you to Cracow and then we'll go home."

"OK."

"OK?"

"What else do you want me to say? I'm sorry I dragged you all the way over here for nothing... It's just that I find it very odd that I would get this letter from some mysterious person, with precise coordinates, and yet there is nothing there."

"That's not so odd. If this isn't a prank, it's quite possible that some documents were really hidden there at some point. But that entire area changed dramatically and repeatedly since the end of the war. The papers could have been burned, torn to shreds by a bulldozer, or simply rotted into nothing. It is not easy for any document to survive over 60 years in some damp nook underground."

"Wait a minute. Why do you assume that the documents, if they ever existed, would have been hidden over 60 years ago?"

Alex stared at his friend for a few seconds, sighed, and made a decision he knew he would regret.

"I guess I need to level with you, Michael." - he said - "I think the papers, if ever there, would have been stashed away around 1945."

"What? How the hell could you possibly know that?"

Alex reached into his pocket and took out a folded piece of paper. He carefully unfolded it and handed it over to Michael.

"I tore this out of a newspaper at the Munich airport while you were walking around." - he explained.

Michael studied the text intently, re-reading it a couple of times. But, contrary to Alex's expectations, he didn't seem upset or angry, nor did he show any signs of resorting to immediate physical violence. He just sat there in silence for a while.

"Why didn't you show me this back then?" - he finally asked in a calm, somewhat subdued voice.

"Well, I didn't want to give you additional fodder for wild speculations before we even started the search in Nowy Targ. And think about it - the news from Belize doesn't change a damn thing. If we go totally bonkers and assume, just for the sake of the argument, that the old geezer who died over there had really been involved with some top WWII Nazis and that he is the author of your letter, so what? He's gone, the trail is cold, and there are no papers".

"Do you think he was snuffed?"

"How would I know? But it's a moot point. We'll never know what he meant, if he really wrote the letter. In fact, we have absolutely no idea what exactly happened."

"But why do you think something might have been hidden at these coordinates in 1945 and not - say - 1942."

"It's just a guess. In 1945 the entire Reich was in a state of growing panic and the collapse of Nazi Germany was imminent. I'm sure there was a lot of last minute document burning and hiding at that time, and Wrocław was a very good candidate for this sort of activity, because it remained in German hands until the very end and it was well beyond the reach of allied bombers.

They finished their lunch, sipped some coffee for a while and - for a change - talked about other things, like places to see in Cracow, ways to get there, etc. They agreed they would travel by train next morning. Michael was beginning to behave more like a tourist than a disgruntled treasure hunter, which was a great relief for Alex.

"Hey, can you do me a favor?" - asked Michael as they were leaving the bistro.

"What is it?"

"Can we walk back there to take one last peek?"

"Back where? To the store? Are you nuts?"

"No, just to the square. I just want to see it again briefly in all its charming ugliness. No silly exploits, I promise."

"OK then. Let's go."

It took them only 10 minutes to reach Nowy Targ. This time they walked all around it, looking at all the drab houses. Finally they sat down on a bench, which stood directly opposite the biggest building in the area and one of only two that survived the war.

"So how come this big thing wasn't destroyed by the Ruskis?" - asked Michael.

"I have no idea. It's almost a miracle, because they bombed the hell out of anything standing here".

"Why here? Why not in Rynek or somewhere else?"

"Well, to some extent your distant Nazi cousins caused this disaster themselves by placing antiaircraft artillery here and hiding people in the underground bomb shelter."

"What bomb shelter?" - asked Michael looking at his friend with sudden interest.

"Oh shit!" - thought Alex sensing that their trip to Cracow might be off.

Chapter 7

Michael was clearly intrigued by the news that during the war the Germans had built a big bomb shelter under Nowy Targ. He immediately started attacking Alex with questions about its construction, location and all kinds of other things. It was obvious that he regained hope of continuing the search for hidden documents, although his friend had no idea how and tried valiantly to discourage him.

"So where exactly is this shelter?" - pressed on Michael.

"As I already told you, I don't know. All I know is that there are two entrances to it. One is over there, across the street from the supermarket, and the other one on the opposite side of the square. But what difference does it make, Michael? Your letter places the documents under the store, not in a bomb shelter a hundred yards away. Jesus, just lay off it and let's get the hell out of here."

"Please, Alex, hear me out. What if before the war the basement of this beer place was adjacent to the shelter. Or perhaps there could even be a door from one to the other. Someone hiding something down there could have placed it roughly at the coordinates, but the actual stash could have ended up on the shelter side, and not in the basement."

"And what if Lee Harvey Oswald had help from little green Martians to blow away JFK? Or what if the Cubs win the World Series next year? My god, Michael, we can have all kinds of 'whatifs', but please try to remain in the world of at least some plausibility".

"There is nothing implausible about what I've just said and you know it. But if you no longer want to help me, that's fine. Just tell me what happened to this shelter since the war."

Alex thought briefly about his options, and concluded they didn't look too good. He didn't want to just dump Michael and return home by himself. But he also didn't want to prolong the madness spawned by the Belize letter. It was obvious that the only way to drag Michael back to his boring desk in Michigan Avenue was to somehow solve the 'shelter issue'. Alex had an uncomfortable feeling that it would take descending underground again to accomplish that.

"All right, I'll tell you what I know, which is not a lot." - he said dejectedly - "After the war the shelter was abandoned for many years. Then they had some sort of a club or disco in it, but the place got flooded and was again abandoned. I think currently it's just padlocked, although there is talk of digging it all up and building an underground car park there."

"Is it possible to get inside?"

"It's padlocked and I don't happen to have the key. But even if you could get in, the place is probably in an awful shape. I don't even know whether there is still electricity down there. But what the hell, come on, I'll show you."

Alex got up and started walking across the square towards the supermarket serviced by the three 'plumbers' earlier the same day. Michael followed him to a staircase leading down to a door with a big padlock on it. The staircase ran north-to-south, parallel to the store, but was located on the other side of the street encircling the square. They stood at the top of the stairs and looked down. It was not a pretty sight. There was a lot of assorted trash down there and the air suggested occasional presence of late night beer drinkers with bladders filled to capacity. The door was adorned with a red sign saying 'Wstęp wzbroniony' which Alex obligingly translated for Michael as 'No Entry'.

"So, are you sure you want to break your way into this dump? - he asked.

41

"I don't know, Alex. But look how easy it would be to check whether it's possible to cross this street underground and get to the store basement wall. All we would have to do would be to go down, take the first possible right corridor, and head straight west for about 50 yards."

"What if there is no corridor to the right?

"Well, the issue is solved then, isn't it? No way to get there, nothing to look for... Will you go with me?"

"You know, Michael, I am relatively good at fixing computers and networks, but my prowess in break-ins is extremely limited. I mean the Watergate burglars were masters in comparison to me. Additionally, the last thing I need is an extended accommodation in a Polish prison cell."

"Oh, come on. Trespassing is probably just a misdemeanor."

"Wow, you really know how to reassure people."

They argued about their prospective career of common criminals for a few more minutes while walking back to the hotel. Finally Alex agreed to call pan Kazik once again to seek his opinion on how to break the law in a foreign land without being caught. Pan Kazik wasn't amused and advised them to go to Cracow as scheduled. But, in his infinite generosity, he also agreed to give them two good flashlights and a set of about ten keys that - he claimed - opened almost any padlock in the entire universe. However, he categorically refused to have anything to do with actually using the keys himself thus telling them that this time they were on their own.

Alex knew he had no good way of extricating himself from what now seemed inevitable. He agreed to go with Michael, having first warned him that immediately after his return from the 'shelter mission' he would start packing. Their plan was very simple - they were going to go back to Nowy Targ very early in the morning, around 4 am. Alex knew the place would be totally deserted at such an early time. Michael would go down the stairs and try Kazik's keys on the padlock while Alex was supposed to stay above, watching the territory. Neither of them had any clue as to what was going to happen if they actually managed to open the door.

But opening the door was not their only problem. In the evening, as they were eating dinner in a quiet Italian restaurant, a well-dressed tall man approached them and asked them in heavily accented English if he could briefly join them to ask them a couple of questions. Alex was both surprised and annoyed.

"Excuse me, sir" - he said almost angrily - "but if you are trying to sell us something, we're not really interested."

"Oh, no no. You misunderstand." - replied their unexpected visitor - "I am captain Zygmunt Trzepizór of the ABW".

He took out a very impressive badge out of his breast pocket and shoved it in front of Alex's face.

"What the hell is ABW?" - whispered Michael to Alex.

Alex gave him a look that could mean only one thing: 'shut the fuck up'. Then he turned back to captain Trzepizór with a blatantly fake smile on his face.

"I'm sorry, sir, but you probably are confusing us with someone else."

"I don't think I am. You are Alexander Malak and your friend is Michael Riedle. Right?"

"Right, but... "

"Please don't be concerned. This is just a formality".

"OK, so what can we do for you?"

"Well, we got an anonymous phone call from someone claiming that you came to Poland in order to smuggle out a batch of historical documents".

"What?"

"I know it sounds strange, but we have to follow up on such things. I hope you understand."

"Wait. Are you saying someone called you and identified both of us as potential smugglers by name?"

"I'm afraid so."

"But we have no historical documents. We're just tourists. You can search our rooms if you want to".

"That will be quite unnecessary. I am sure this was just a prank call, but I had to ask you these questions just in case. Otherwise I can't close this incident. I'm sorry I interrupted your dinner. Have a great evening".

Captain Zygmunt Trzepizór stood up and departed as quickly as he appeared, leaving Michael and Alex in the state of shock. Throughout this entire scene Michael was speechless, not knowing what was going on and why. When he finally regained his capacity to produce phonemes, he could only think of one series of them.

"What the fuck has just happened?" - he asked.

The problem was Alex had no idea. He explained to his friend that ABW was a Polish equivalent of the FBI, but that only increased Michael's anxiety. Both of them were very worried about the fact that Mr. Trzepizór knew them by name and claimed someone else knew them by name too. On top of that, whoever this anonymous caller was, he or she apparently had some inkling as to what Michael and Alex were up to in Poland. But how? And why?

Initially Michael's inclination was to forget about the whole thing and jump on the first plane back to the safety of his city desk in Chicago. On further reflection, however torturous it might have been, he realized that someone's interest in their doings was the first clear indication that the letter from Belize and their trip to Poland possibly bothered some unknown people or forces. And if so, maybe these phantom documents underground, whether they still existed or not, had some major import. "All the more reason to persevere" - he thought. To his utmost surprise Alex voiced very similar sentiments.

"Well, shit - something is pretty fishy about all this. I didn't emigrate from Poland all these years ago to now be intimidated by some captain who could have invented the whole story."

"Do you think he did?"

"No. But I say we proceed as planned and to hell with all of this. I don't think they're watching us, but even if they are, they can't really do anything to us for breaking into a smelly dungeon. I'm more worried about the possibility of this anonymous caller watching us."

Alex and Michael set their alarm clocks for 3:30 am. When they got out of the hotel a few minutes later, they realized the weather took a turn for the worse - it was much colder and a light drizzle was blowing into their faces. They didn't want to take a taxi to Nowy Targ, not to attract anybody's attention, so they walked along deserted streets, glancing back furtively every now and then as if expecting a cohort of ABW agents right behind them. But there was nobody around, save for a few stragglers trying to get home after a late night party. They entered the square a few minutes later and saw absolutely nobody in their immediate vicinity. As planned, Michael went down the stairs leading to the shelter door and started trying Kazik's keys in succession while Alex was standing at the top of the stairs fidgeting aimlessly with his fingers and looking increasingly nervous.

The padlock gave in on the fourth try. Alex joined Michael at the bottom of the stairs and they both opened the door, which gave off a loud, metallic screech. They were greeted with pitch-black darkness and a foul, moist smell of things silently rotting and dilapidating. They lit up their flashlights, closed the door behind them, which produced the same hostile screech, and peered into the inky nether world while pointing their beams left and right. Alex noticed a large, industrial switch on the wall to his right. He flipped it and on came the ceiling bulbs - dim, murky, uninviting, but still very much functional.

They were in.

Chapter 8

It was obvious that the ex-bomb shelter under Neumarkt was a totally forsaken place. Michael and Alex saw a relatively large room, which looked somewhat like a reception area with some sort of a counter at the back wall. However, there was a lot of trash strewn all over the floor and the concrete walls looked like they were just about to say 'go away' in German. To their left there were three steel doors, presumably leading to some other chambers of this cavernous space. They were all closed and Michael had no interest in them since going through any of them would take him away from the supermarket basement. To the right there was nothing but empty plastic bottles, and semi-crushed cardboard boxes. But right past all of that Alex saw a small opening in the wall, which was neither a door nor an entry to a side corridor. It looked almost like a haphazard hole in the concrete through which Alice in 'Alice in Wonderland' might have to crawl to avoid having her head cut off by the vicious queen.

Since this seemed to be the only possible way to go right, Alex and Michael fought their way through trash and - having reached the opening - shone their flashlights into darkness. Unfortunately they saw nothing. This posed a major dilemma for them. The diameter of this gap was certainly just large enough to accommodate a grown man or even a bunch of heavily built drug smugglers running dope under the US-Mexico border via a well-crafted tunnel. But there was no light in there and no way to know how long this thing was and where it was leading. Alex kind of knew what was going to happen next, and it did.

"Alex, you stay here, and I'll try finding out where this goes to".

"Err... at the risk of sounding a bit forward, are you fucking crazy? It's a hole in the wall with no stinking lights in it. For all I know, it might be going straight down into hell."

"I have to do it. Besides, it can't be any worse than Lower Wacker Drive. If it goes for about 50 yards west, I'll be at the supermarket basement. If not, we'll have bacon and eggs later this morning just before jumping on the train to Cracow."

"Well, how will I know what's going on once you're in there?"

"You won't. But I'll either shout to you or simply come back. If I do shout, just follow me in, even if you can't make out what I'm saying."

"Great. Do you also have any advice on what I should do if you neither shout nor come back?"

"No clue. Just call your friendly captain Ziggy Stardust or something".

With these brave and possibly last words Michael fired up his flashlight again and started crawling into the opening. Alex could see him, or rather the flickering light, for the next minute or so. Then suddenly the light disappeared and all was dark and quiet. Very quiet. Alex heard nothing but some hungry rumblings in the pipes running along the ceiling and a sound of dripping water somewhere deep in the putrid guts of the shelter. He waited for what seemed to be an eternity, but absolutely nothing was happening. After a while he even started thinking about the best way to contact captain Trzepizór to inform him that he lost an American citizen in WWII bunker which was off limits to begin with. His somewhat pessimistic ruminations were nevertheless abruptly interrupted by a hollow, sonorous sound, which in this particular environment sounded like an explosive belch. Although Alex could not identify a single intelligible word in this underground pronouncement, he assumed that it met the definition of Michael's shout. "Well, here goes nothing" he said to himself and followed in Michael's footsteps. As soon as he started his crawl, he was surprised by two things. First, the tunnel was not straight and had many sudden turns, but maintained its general westward direction. Second, as he moved forward, the opening was becoming bigger and bigger, so that eventually he could simply get up and walk. It took him about five minutes to get to the spot where his friend was... At the bar.

The passage opened up completely changing into a more or less regular corridor at the end of which Alex saw light. A few moments later he walked into a room where he saw Michael sitting on a wobbly bar stool. Obviously this place was once a small pub. There were a few round tables, dusty chairs, some empty bottles, and lots of assorted trash. There was also a bar counter made of old wooden barrels crowned with a crescent countertop. That's where Michael was. As Alex walked across the room, he picked up a couple of bottles and looked at their labels.

"Well, one thing is certain." - he said - "This wasn't a pre-war hangout for Nazi generals".

"Why do you say that?"

"The labels on the bottles suggest late 70's or early 80's. This must have been a post-war hangout for communist drunks."

"Hm... It's strange. At some point someone made the passage from the shelter entrance to here. And without the passage this bar seems to have no doors or entry points."

"Yes, it does... or rather did. Look over there".

Alex pointed his finger at one of the walls where a faint but distinct outline in the concrete could be seen.

"I think there used to be a door there, but for whatever reason it was permanently blocked. So I think the bar was in operation for some time, but then it was abandoned, and its entrance sealed. Later someone dying for a drink dug his way from the shelter entrance to here."

"Seriously though, why would anybody do it?"

"Who knows. After the war the shelter was worked on a number of times, so maybe this passage is the result of some construction effort, which was never completed. Anyway, the sealed door is on the north wall, so the west wall is behind the bar counter. We must be sitting right by the supermarket basement."

"I agree. It's quite possible that before the war this was a part of the brewery you mentioned earlier. You know, the Crow something or other. Unfortunately I don't see anything interesting around here. I already looked behind the bar and all along this wall - just empty bottles and some unrecognizable crap."

"Yeah, and all of this crap seems to date back to the times of People's Republic of Poland, not Third Reich."

Alex and Michael, both sitting on high stools, kept sweeping the room with their eyes in search of something unusual or out of place. Every now and then one of them would stand up and walk to something he saw to examine it closer. Finally they both gave up and sat silently for a while.

"What about the barrels?" - asked Alex.

"What about them?"

"Well, shouldn't we look into at least one of them?"

"I tried to move this one, on the left, before you joined me. They are very heavy - probably filled with something to make them steady".

"Right, either sauerkraut or cut up victims of a serial killer. Anyway, we don't have to move them. Let's see if we can rip the countertop off. That way we'll get access to the lids."

The task of dislodging the countertop turned out to be relatively easy. They gripped the opposite ends of it and started pulling it up while at the same time trying to rock it left and right. After a minute or two of this work they heard a dry crack and the top came off, falling to the floor with a thud. Alex and Michael looked down on the barrel lids and then stood motionless and stunned as if they just saw Adolf Hitler himself.

"Holy shit!" - said Alex finally.

His terse comment was justified to the extent that each barrel lid was adorned with the same, black Gothic lettering: 'Brauerei Schwarze Krähe'. There was also a little black logo on each of them and two small wooden handles on each side of the lettering. Michael hesitated for a moment, thinking perhaps that his life might change forever in some totally unpredictable way once he looks inside. Then he placed his hands on one of the lids and tried pulling it up. It came off easily with a little squeak and disclosed that the inside was full of sand. Alex stuck his hand in and fished around for a few seconds.

He knew they were in for some hard labor.

"Michael, we probably need to knock all these barrels over to empty the sand."

"Yeah, I was thinking the same thing. You realize it could be a wasted effort. The barrels might've been lying around after the war and were simply used to build the bar counter many years later".

"I know, but I don't think I can drag your sorry ass out of here unless we do it. So let's get on with it. Let's turn this place into French Riviera, minus the sea and the sun."

There were six barrels to empty and knocking each of them over was not an easy task. After they managed to tip the first one, it crashed loudly to the floor spilling half of its sandy load. They used their hands to empty it to the bottom, sifting constantly through the sand in search of anything that might not be just filler. After the third barrel was emptied, they felt sweaty, tired and disappointed.

"Actually, do you think this sand is German or Polish?" - asked Alex, his voice oozing sarcasm.

"I'm afraid it might be Polish, because it's so damn obnoxious and tiring to work with." - shot back Michael.

The fourth barrel fell down and spilled very much the same stuff on the floor. But this time when Michael's hand reached the bottom, he felt something that was definitely neither sand nor wood. It felt like cardboard. Michael extracted something like a flat package consisting of two relatively thick sheets of cardboard tied together by a piece of string. It certainly didn't look like a top secret 'national security' document. Instead it could be taken for a hastily prepared Christmas present by someone who could afford neither a ribbon nor a proper box.

Michael ripped off the string with obvious impatience and soon was holding in his hand a large manila envelope. He saw immediately that this was no ordinary envelope.

Alex came up to him and they both stared at their finding. The first thing that struck their eyes was an embossed seal with a black swastika in the middle. Right below the seal there was some German text. Neither of them could speak German, but Alex knew what 'Geheime Reichsfache' meant: 'Top Secret State Affairs'. On the other side of the envelope they saw a few intricate signatures and another, smaller seal, guarding the envelope's flap.

They almost certainly found what they were looking for. And the Cracow trip was now certainly off.

Chapter 9

Alex was mad at himself for not taking anything with him to put the envelope in. The reason he didn't was relatively obvious - he never really expected to find anything on their trip to the bomb shelter. But now they have, and he had to do something to hide and protect the envelope. He ended up stuffing it unceremoniously under his jacket. Excited and tired, they started on their way back through the tunnel leading to the entrance. They were about half way there when they heard something very disturbing - the metallic screech of the door. Apparently someone has just entered the bomb shelter. Seconds later they heard voices and then there were distant shapes pointing their flashlights towards them. They both instinctively dropped face down on the dusty floor and almost stopped breathing.

They could hear some sort of an argument among the intruders, though it was impossible to make out what they were saying. It seemed they were standing in front of the opening in the concrete wall, very much like Alex and Michael were a few hours earlier, discussing their options. Whatever their options were, they did not include getting into the tunnel, because after a few minutes they left, switching the light off and slamming the door behind them. Alex and Michael remained lying down in pitch darkness for at least a minute.

"Do you think they're gone." - whispered Michael almost directly into Alex's ear.

"I think so."

"Who the heck were they?"

"Czechs."

"What?"

"I think they spoke Czech."

"How do you know?"

"It's almost like Polish, except they use twice as many consonants. Could be Slovaks too."

"So what did they say?"

"I have no idea. It's a different language."

"Bullshit. It's all this Slavic crap. You all understand each other, but pretend not to."

"Right, very much like you understand the hillbillies of Mississippi or a bouncer in a night club on the south side of Chicago."

Having thus exhausted their rhetorical skills, they switched the flashlights back on and started on their way again. In just a minute or so they found themselves at the entrance door. However, Alex looked at his watch and realized it was now 7 am.

"Damn, this is going to be difficult" - he said.

"What?"

"It's rush hour now and people will be all over the square when we walk out. And I don't know if you noticed, but we look like we have just worked our shift at a labor camp in Kolyma".

"What's Kolyma?"

"Part of Gulag, you idiot".

"All right, all right. So what do we do?"

"Well, I can try calling for a cab on my cell. If the driver parks right outside of the supermarket, we can make a relatively quick dash for it."

Alex's plan worked astonishingly well. The cab was ordered and when the driver arrived, he called Alex. As soon as this happened, they both emerged from the dungeon, somewhat blinded by the early morning light, and took a sharp turn left to cross the street and enter the waiting car. "Hotel Qubus, please" - said Alex in Polish. The driver - thankfully - did not seem to care that his passengers were shedding a lot of sand and were somewhat dirty. They rushed past the reception area and went straight up to Michael's room.

They both showered, put on the hotel bath robes, and sat there for a very long time digesting what has just happened and looking every now and then at the swastika-adorned envelope which Alex put on the little table by the phone. Then they ordered breakfast and still sat there for even a longer time.

"Are we going to open it?" - asked Michael hesitantly.

"No, we need to get Kazik here first, because we probably need to know what these seals say before we break them."

There was a moment of awkward silence.

"Hey, Michael... I'm sorry I doubted all of this meant anything. It's still possible that the envelope contains a shopping list for Himmler's last supper. But I do admit it looks much more serious than that. So I'll call Kazik and we'll find out. Remember that he will first have to translate all of this stuff into Polish and then I'll do the English translation."

"Fair enough, Alex. When?"

"Now."

Alex wasn't kidding. Pan Kazik showed up in Michael's hotel room about two hours later, wearing his highly professional plumber's uniform. He was told what to do and he didn't ask any questions, which actually surprised Michael a bit, because he was increasingly worried that Alex's Polish friend knew more than he should, and yet never expressed any surprise and never sought additional explanations. Kazik sat down at the little table, carefully looked at the envelope, turning it over a couple of times, and then asked for a pen and a piece of paper. It took him just a few minutes to translate whatever there was on the outside of the envelope into Polish. He then shoved the sheet of paper towards Alex as if to say 'now it's your turn'.

Alex went to work scribbling his translation on the same piece of paper. Then he grabbed the paper, stood up and looked almost like someone who was ready to deliver a major policy speech on the political convention floor.

"OK, here it is" - he said - "The writing under the swastika seal says 'Top State Secrets - Highly Sensitive Material' and below that there is some handwriting which might be just an accidental smear or some last minute note. The seal on the other side has an embossed sentence meaning 'Any unauthorized breaking of this seal is punishable by summary execution'. Below - written in capital letters - is 'Reichsmarschall of the Great German Reich' followed by three signatures that are totally impossible to make out. And that's it."

Michael looked at Alex with thinly disguised puzzlement.

"Who the hell was Reichsmarschall?" - he asked.

"I'm not 100% sure, but I'd say it would be Herr Hermann Goering, the fat buddy of Adolf".

"Do you think one of these signatures is actually his?"

"Don't know, Michael. They are more or less illegible."

"OK, then. Time to open this thing."

As soon as Michael said that all three of them once again looked at the envelope and stood motionlessly for a few seconds looking hesitant and almost apprehensive. Could it be that the promise of 'summary execution', to be meted out to the unlawful breaker of the seal, would still somehow be in force? It seemed totally and ridiculously implausible and it yet gave them a somber pause. Finally Michael broke the spell, picked up the envelope, ripped up its flap, and took out two yellowish sheets of paper. Tossing the envelope aside, he placed both sheets on the table and they all congregated around them.

The first sheet looked like a quickly typewritten note with a signature at the bottom. The other one seemed to be a bit more complicated document, divided into a couple of sections. Kazik, having studied the documents briefly, said something quietly to Alex.

"What is it?" - asked Michael who, as usual, didn't know what was going on.

"Well, Kazik can more or less dictate the short text to me right now, but we need to give him a copy of the other one so that he can work on it overnight and come back with a translation".

"No!" - exclaimed Michael.

"Why the hell not?"

"We're not sure what all of this means and we're not making any copies. If he has to come back here later to translate it, fine. Otherwise, let's get to work."

Alex was somewhat taken aback by this sudden outburst, but he played along, sensing that his friend was growing increasingly uneasy about something. He asked Kazik to dictate to him the shorter text, again writing it down in English. Then he read it out loud:

> *Three copies of this document have been prepared. One has been placed underground at coordinates 51° 6' 42.134 N and 17° 2' 15.324 E. The other two were delivered to gauleiter Karl Hanke for distribution as specified in special directive no. 06219. Please act accordingly and maintain all precautions for level 1 security,*
>
> *Heil Hitler!*
> *General Horst von Stirlitz*
> *Breslau, 31 March 1945*

Alex and Michael looked like they had no idea what all of this could possibly mean which was understandable because they really didn't. So they decided to deposit Kazik in front of Alex's laptop and ask him to start working on the other translation while they went on to have a quick pow-wow in the other corner of the room. Michael was very eager to ask the first, relatively useless question.

"What do you think?"

"Not much. I have no idea what it means, but I know who this Hanke character was."

"Who?"

"He was the last commander of this city before the Red Army came. In terms of Nazi fanaticism, on the scale of 1 to 10 he was probably 15."

"OK, but he was just in command of one city. Why would he be entrusted with some highly classified documents? Two copies of it too."

"I was wondering about this myself. He was, as far as I remember, trying to work his way up the rungs of the fascist ladder and was very well liked by the 'fuehrer' himself, so perhaps he earned enough trust to be given some important assignments. But for now we don't even know what these assignments might've been, so let's wait for Kazik."

"What about the other guy? The guy who signed this thing."

"General von Stirlitz? Never heard of him".

"And what about the Czechs?"

"What?"

"What about the Czechs that showed up in the shelter?"

"Michael, give me a break. I have no idea who they were. Could be some tourists seeking thrills under Nowy Targ".

"At 7 am in the morning? In a place that's normally padlocked?"

They could have carried on this discussion forever, were it not for the fact that Kazik made a subtle grunting noise suggesting he was done with his translation. Alex went up to him and they whispered for a while among themselves.

"Michael, Kazik is leaving" - said Alex.

"Why?"

"His job is done. There's nothing further he can do for us and he wants to get out of here. He also seems to be a bit disturbed about all this, which I don't quite understand. So let's just let him go."

"OK."

Kazik embraced Alex briefly and said goodbye to him. Then he turned to Michael and shook his hand in a somewhat awkward manner.

"Thank you for all your help" - muttered Michael.

Kazik smiled sheepishly and left the room. There was a bit of a pause and then Alex did what he knew he had to do - he sat down in front of the laptop and started translating Kazik's Polish text into English. Michael didn't really know how to kill this nail-biting time, so he paced around the room for a while and then poured himself a drink. His friend kept totally silent, obviously very intent on the job at hand. After about 15 minutes Alex sat back, sighed and motioned to Michael. They both sat at the little table and stared at the laptop screen, reading the document to themselves.

Top secret - Level 1 security

Operation "Black Eagle" in force as of 15 May 1945 if no other option available.

1.   Cell Distribution
Duvall, WA - Reinhardt Kloss
Lithia, FL - Wolfgang Trier
Ballwin, MO - Erich Loewe
Fort Wayne, IN - Karl Brunner
Lancaster, PA - Richard Steinholz
Galveston, TX - Heinrich Kaltenspiel
Bethany Beach, DE - Joseph Niebsch
Louisville, CO - Andreas Stolzhammer

2.   Action triggers

GWV
XHDFQ BXFQU VFMCK UNSMM AORCX AYXDH ERUMI
XEYID UQUPM KVILX VRZGV ZGNOQ NIUUS BDAEC ISTKG
LECRP VOCSV XOGBC UAADY RRNTS WZIGO NFBAJ BMFSY

BUCWK JVVBX GXJSG HBPVB FGUNZ QNNOP WEPIO
GSSWE MFMEG YYROO VQMLZ UHEAP OVMJI EOMWE
LGNCY

Reichsfuehrer
Adolf Hitler
1 March 1945

Chapter 10

"Well, that's just fucking great." – began the discussion Alex, showing his customary flair.

"What?"

"Come on. You've read this thing too. The last part is some gibberish, probably a code of some sort, and the first part looks like a postwar vacation assignment for some selected Teutonic yokels."

"Vacation? In Fort Wayne?"

"All right, you have a point. However it doesn't change the fact that this document is practically useless and doesn't give us any information."

"Well, I think it does. It seems like the listed people were sent to all these places at the end of the war to perform some task."

"Wonderful. Except we have no idea whether they actually went there and what they were supposed to do. And even if they did, it was over 60 years ago and they are all dead."

"Did you notice a couple of strange things about this document?"

"Yes, that it is made of paper and carries German text".

"Oh, stop it. I'm serious. Adolf himself signed this thing and yet all the people listed are not identified by any military ranks or other official functions. Also these American towns are either very small or at best medium-sized – no big cities."

"That's a very astute observation, Michael, except we have no stinking clue about what all of this could possibly mean."

"Well, let's take stock of the situation."

"Yeah, let's. I like taking stock".

The derision in Alex's voice was beginning to seriously irk Michael who decided to embark on a preemptive strike.

"Listen, Alex, I know you feel that this whole escapade is stupid. But since you agreed to come here with me and since we invested a considerable sand-digging effort to get to this piece of paper, and since the letter from Belize turned out to be about a real document, why don't you humor me a bit longer. Come on, man – don't you want to know what it's all about?"

"It would be nice to know, but I rate our chances pretty low. But go on…. Taking stock, I mean."

"All right. So, some old fart in Belize, who had unconfirmed Nazi past, finds me and indirectly you on the Internet and decides to send a letter pointing to geographical coordinates in Breslau a.k.a. Wrocław. Judging by the brevity of this correspondence, I'd say he was expecting to die, either by natural causes or otherwise. And he did. His letter takes us here where we find a document signed by Hitler, apparently sending a bunch of Krauts over to the US on some top secret mission. We have no idea what this mission was and if it was ever completed, but the Belize letter seems to suggest that finding the document was in some way a matter of national importance. So perhaps, whatever the initial mission was, it still somehow matters."

"OK, I like it so far."

"You do?". Michael couldn't quite cover up his astonishment.

"Yes, it sounds fairly logical and doesn't rely on a bunch of wild assumptions."

"Great. I'm glad you think so. But there are also some loose ends. First, the damn 'action triggers' in the document are coded and they may be the key to understanding what this bunch of Germans was supposed to do in the US. Second, there were three copies of the document one of which was placed underground in Nowy Targ. But why? Also, the remaining copies were given to this fanatical Hanke dude who presumably was supposed to give them to two individuals. The question is did he do it and who those individuals were?"

"Wait. If we assume that the guy who croaked in Belize had really been an aide to Himmler, then one of the copies was probably for him. How else would a simple adjutant even know about the existence of this thing?"

"Good point. So let's assume that Hanke did deliver one copy to Himmler and we don't know what happened to the other one. Which is a pity."

"Why?"

"Because whatever it was they were doing, the two guys getting the document were probably in charge of setting things in motion. Looks like the copy underground was some sort an insurance policy just in case the other two copies somehow never made it to their addressees"

They both stopped for a while, considering their further arguments. Alex was still sitting at the little table with the laptop in front of him while Michael was walking nervously around the room wishing it were a much bigger pacing space.

"Of course we both know there are other loose ends, right?' - asked Michael.

"Yes. Obviously someone else is interested in what we're doing here, if we believe Mr. Trzepizór. The way he asked his questions seems to indicate that these 'mysterious forces' are aware of the fact that we went to Poland and they know why. However, they may not know anything about any details, like the coordinates, the actual document, etc."

"I agree. And then there are the Czechs".

"Oh my god! Will you forget about the fucking Czechs! They don't fit into any of this crap."

"In a sense, I hope so. But it just seems very weird that they would show up at 7 am in an underground shelter which is normally not even supposed to be seen by anybody".

"OK, then - let's assume the Czechs are a loose end. Moving on, what do we do next?"

"First, what do you think this code stuff is?"

"You give me too much credit – in my professional capacity I usually don't deal with WWII deciphering. Only broken hard drives."

"Any chance we can have someone decode this for us?"

"There is a 'cipher' museum somewhere in the States. Maybe we can call them after we return".

"We're not going back yet".

"What?

"We're not going back yet, because we need to find out more about this Hanke character. We've been here only for three days, so we can stay for a couple of days more. Do you know anything else about him?"

"Not a lot. He was really nuts in some ways, very much like most of you guys. At the end of the siege of Breslau he decided to reduce a large area of the city on the other side of the river to rubble to build a landing strip. He thought this would allow the defenders to get help via air. Ultimately only one plane took off from there. His."

"He escaped?"

"Yeah, skipped town at the very last minute, but apparently got captured and killed by Czech partisans".

As soon as Alex said that, he realized he was going to hear something painfully stupid. Michael didn't disappoint him.

"Really? So there **is** a Czech connection in all of this after all".

"If you mention the Czechs once again, you'll never make it back to US, because I swear I'll just smash your skull in. What the hell do you mean? What connection? Hanke flew to Prague or somewhere around there over half a century ago and now his Czech 'emissaries' are back in Wrocław looking for Nazi treasure in a rotten bunker? Give me a break!"

"All right, all right. I'll shut up now."

"Listen, there is a great university library in this town and I'm sure they have all kinds of documents relating to 'Festung Breslau'. I'll go there today after lunch and we'll see what we can come with up on Hanke. In the meantime, I strongly suggest you start packing. But first of all, let's stick the original document somewhere safe – I suggest the hotel safe."

There were no further arguments from Michael. Alex put both the original envelope and the two sheets of paper into a larger white envelope with a hotel logo on it. He sealed it and was ready to go. They both felt a bit hungry, so they went down to the reception, asked for their stuff to be placed in safe-keeping, and then headed for the hotel restaurant where they had lunch which would probably do justice to a couple of more hungry people. Immediately after the meal Alex went to the library, leaving Michael to take care of their travel arrangements back to the US. They were supposed to get together in Michael's room at about 6 pm.

Michael called Lufthansa to find out about the best connecting flights from Wrocław to Munich and then back to Chicago. As he was talking on the hotel phone, he realized his cell phone was ringing which surprised him a bit. Obviously no one in Poland would be calling him on this number other than Alex, but they parted company just a moment ago. He ditched his Lufthansa call and answered the other one.

"Hi, Michael. What's cooking baby? – someone said.

He knew this voice very well. It belonged to his colleague from 'Chicago Tribune', Rick Weigert. It was already past 8 pm Chicago time, so Michael assumed Rick was not calling him from the office, but from his home. Mr. Weigert was a mildly annoying individual, who usually sat just a couple of cubicles away from Michael and who had the unfortunate habit of trying very hard to be friends with everyone even though nobody was really interested, primarily because of Mr. Weigert's lack of attention to matters of personal hygiene. He also betrayed constant and ebullient optimism, which irritated the hell out of his immediate and decidedly more pessimistic environment.

"Rick, what are you doing calling me over here? I'm sure it's not because you miss me".

"Of course I miss you. And so does the FBI?"

64

"Yeah, right. What do you want?"

"Well, we've had a little bit of an incident over here? You got a small package at the Tribune which was put on your desk."

"Great. You can go ahead and open it. It's probably my latest shipment of rainbow-colored prophylactics".

"That's the problem, Michael. It opened itself. By blowing up."

There was a very long pause. Finally Michael recovered well enough to continue.

"You mean it was a bomb?"

"Yes... at least to some extent?"

"What the hell is that supposed to mean?"

"Well, the FBI guys who showed up here told us later that it was such a small device that it couldn't really have killed or maimed anybody. And it didn't. It just blew all kinds crap off your desk, which is probably just as well. They think it was some sort of a warning. Anyway, they want to talk to you as soon as possible. I have a phone number for this special agent, Kim Swanson. You're supposed to call him as soon as you get back. So how is your vacation going anyway?"

"It was going great until you called." – barked Michael.

"Oh, come on. Don't worry. It's probably some guy you pissed off by writing something about him. Come home, talk to the spooks, and everything is going to be OK".

"All right, Rick. I should be there in a couple of days... Hey, would you happen to know where this package was sent from?"

"Sure. And that's kind of weird. It was sent from Belize".

Chapter 11

It was getting late and Michael was beginning to show early symptoms of frantic anxiety. The phone call from Chicago shocked him in a number of ways. He realized that his trip to Poland in search of the mysterious documents mentioned in the equally mysterious letter was somehow 'monitored' and was not to someone's liking. There were clearly some forces engaged in all of this, and he had absolutely no idea what these forces were and what they were capable of doing. He was feeling helpless, somewhat lost, and - to some extent - frightened. Minutes and hours kept ticking away. It was already 8 pm and Alex was nowhere to be seen. Michael tried his cell phone, but there was no answer. He walked around the room for a while, watched consonantal Polish television, not understanding a single word of it, and then walked some more. Finally he broke down and poured himself another 6-dollar drink from the in-room bar.

The source of his growing anxiety was not only the fact that his friend was very late or that someone in Belize thought it wise to send him an explosive 'warning', but that things seemed to have progressed past the point of his control. Stuff was happening, and he didn't understand it, nor did he have any idea what to do next. His first thought after hearing from Rick was to rush back to the US, talk to the FBI about his mundane 'vacation' in Poland, and then forget about the whole thing. But then he realized, to his chagrin, that it might be too late. Someone might already know where they went and why, and could possibly be even aware of the fact that he had this weird document in his possession. And if so, some things could have been set in motion which would preclude him from just lying his way out of this mess.

He had two other problems. First, he was still very much a newspaper reporter, well accustomed to sniffing out secrets wafting through the gaping chambers of the Chicago City Hall. It would be very difficult for him to just let go of a story that taunted him with potential historical significance and a lot of appetizing improbabilities. He sensed there was something very important about all of this and that he was very much on the right track, even if the track right now seemed to lead to a dead end. Second, it wasn't particularly easy for him to decide whether to share the news from Chicago with Alex - assuming his dead body was not floating in the river yet - or to keep quiet about it. He thought about this for a while and then decided that he would reconsider the issue once Alex told him all his news.

For that he had to wait one more hour, because Alex came back to the hotel shortly after 9 pm. He seemed to be excited about something and Michael was in no mood for excitement.

"Sorry I'm late, but I ran into an old friend of mine and we chatted for a while."

"Let me guess. He is a city garbage collector who also has a PhD in biochemistry?

"Hey, easy... what's wrong with you? He actually is a historian, but it doesn't matter. I kind of asked him if he knew anybody who would know anything about WWII era ciphers and he gave me a phone number for professor Peter Smart of Aberdeen University. Apparently he is a damn good mathematician and some kind of a genius with coding and decoding stuff. It's too late now, but I'll call him tomorrow to see if we can get anywhere with this coded 'triggers' mess."

"Great."

"Michael, is there something wrong?"

"No, go on. What did you find out about Hanke?'

"Well, it's a very convoluted story and no one really knows for sure what the hell happened to him. Without a doubt he flew out of Breslau on the night of May 5th 1945, just hours before the city surrendered to the Russians and virtually minutes after learning that Hitler had appointed him chief of SS and German police. He was apparently trying to get to Prague, but his single engine plane developed some sort of a problem and he was forced to land in what today is called Pszenno, but then it was known as Weizenrodau, near the city of Schweidnitz, about 50 kilometers south of here".

"You mean he never got to Prague?"

"No one knows for sure. In other words, Pszenno is the final known and documented stop for Hanke. Apparently he did manage to take off again and fly into what today is the Czech Republic. Some of the documents I read at the library claim that he eventually reached Prague and attached himself to - wait a second, I have it written down somewhere - yes, he attached himself somehow to the 18th SS-Freiwilligen-Panzer-Grenadier-Division 'Horst Wessel'. I have no clue what this unit was, but these guys supposedly tried to fight their way back into Germany, but were cornered by Czech partisans and surrendered. At that point Hanke was possibly wearing a uniform of an SS private to conceal his identity".

"OK, so he was caught by the partisans who didn't know who he really was. Why did he die then?"

"Here the story gets a bit murky. The documents I studied suggest that he was captured in Neudorf, today Nová Ves, just south west of the city of Chomutov. And, by all accounts, he was shot in the back while trying to escape. But the details of his escape are in essence a total mystery. There is one report that suggests that he slipped out of a POW camp and reached the house of one Karel Pohradniček where he stayed briefly before being discovered and shot".

Michael took some time to digest all this information, which was a bit difficult, because he couldn't quite shake off the news from Chicago. He eventually calmed down enough to ask Alex a simple, but very important question.

"If this Karel's place was the last stop on Hanke's way to hell, what happened to the two envelopes, or one if he'd given one to Himmler's man before?"

"Obviously, I don't know. He could have handed off this stuff to someone while on his way to Prague. However, I find it improbable, because he had strict orders to deliver the documents to specific people. So, I suspect he had one or both of them when he was captured unless he got rid of all of this before he flew out of Breslau."

"If he took the papers with him, then what?"

"He could've stashed them somewhere, like in the house he stayed in briefly. I did find out that the Pohradniček family still lives in the same house, though Karel is long gone. His descendant is the owner now and her name is Frantiska Pohradničkova."

"How the hell did you discover all that?"

"There are no secrets on the Internet. I have the actual address and phone number, but that's useless anyway. I don't think we're going to be calling Frantiska and asking her in our non-existent Czech if someone was shot in the back in her yard over 60 years ago and if he left some papers at their house."

"How far is this place from here?"

Alex was clearly startled by this question and he immediately suspected something weird was being hatched in Michael's distressed head.

"Why?" – he asked almost in panic.

"Don't get mad at me, but..."

"You know I will."

"OK, but perhaps we could rent a car and drive there. Just a day trip."

"What? Why would we do that? Michael, you need to come back to reality. Are you seriously suggesting that we show up at this Pohradniček place and casually ask for information about Hanke? Give me a fucking break! I can already see this: 'Hello, Frantiska. Hey, sorry to bother you, but do you remember that German schmuck killed here a while back? Did he happen to leave some papers with you before he kicked the bucket?' And of course we'll be conversing with her in fluent Czech."

"I don't know what we should ask of her and how, but I need to do this."

"Well in that case, why don't we just call her?"

"No, Alex. I need to be there and see her... There is also something else I need to tell you."

Alex somehow knew that all along. He sensed that in his absence something important happened to Michael. But he was certainly not prepared for his story about another shipment from Belize. They both sat in silence for a while, mulling the events of recent days in their heads.

"Michael, what do you think this means?" - asked Alex after a while.

"I'm not sure. But let's go back to the story we constructed earlier. It seems that someone got to my correspondent in Belize. Someone who didn't want him to say anything to anybody about the papers in Wrocław".

"Agreed. So let's assume that Herr Karl Krugman sends a letter to you, but then is visited by this someone and meets with an untimely death. If that's the case, this mysterious person, or people, must have known that Krugman knew something which was supposed to remain a secret."

"Right, but here's the thing. If they needed to send me a warning of some sort, like 'lay off this thing now', it kind of suggests that they didn't have any concrete information about the content of the Belize letter or my intentions. They just knew Krugman sent something to me.".

"Not necessarily. They could have known exactly what was sent, but they were just telling you to ignore it".

"Right. Yet somehow I have a feeling that they don't know whether I managed to retrieve the papers or not. And, I know you'll hate me for this, the Czech visitors underground could have been trying to find out."

"I hate you".

"Listen, I have no idea why they were Czech, but we don't know anything about the people we're dealing with."

"OK, so why didn't they crawl through the same damn hole we did to check things out".

"For the same reasons you thought I was nuts to go in there".

They both kept quiet for a few moments, convinced they were thinking about the same thing.

"300 kilometers." - said Alex eventually.

"What?"

"It's 300 kilometers from here to this Czech place. About 5-hour drive. Tomorrow morning you go and rent a car, and I'll call this Brit who is supposed to be a cipher genius."

"OK...there is one more thing." Michael's voice was suddenly hesitant.

"Yes, I know. Someone sent you a warning, which you ignored. If this guy did a hit job in Belize, you might now also be a target."

"And by extension - you."

"I know."

Chapter 12

Alex didn't quite know how to approach his impending telephone conversation with professor Peter Smart. He had absolutely no idea who this man was and Mr. Smart obviously didn't even know Alex Malak existed. But it had to be done. So, having had an early breakfast and having exhausted all the possible excuses for not calling Aberdeen, Alex dialed the number he got from his friend he had met at the library.

"This is Peter Smart. How can I help you? - said the voice on the other end of the line. Alex was a bit taken aback by the rolling r's of Mr. Smart's Scottish accent.

"Yes, Mr. Smart. My name is Alex Malak. I'm terribly sorry to bother you, but I was given your name and phone number by professor Adam Cygan of Wrocław University.'

"Ah, yes. How is the old lad these days?"

"He's doing great. Sir, I understand you are an expert on all kinds of ciphers and coded messages. Is that right?"

"Well, Adam always gave me a wee bit more credit that I deserve...". Professor Smart chuckled, which made Alex even more uneasy than he already was. But he had to go on.

"Well, sir, the reason I'm calling you is that I happen to have this WWII era coded message, and, being a bit of a history buff, I'm dying to know what it actually means."

Alex hated himself for lying, and at the same time congratulated himself for being extremely cunning.

"World War II message? Well, that should be easy. Does it start from a three letter code followed by a bunch of other capital letters?'"

Alex was briefly incredulous.

"Yes, it does." - he said hesitantly - "But how would you know it, sir?"

"Oh, that's easy. It's the Enigma code - used by the Germans throughout the war and actually broken later by the Poles. The Germans basically didn't use anything else to code their messages back then."

"So, do you think you can decipher my message for me?"

"You don't need me for that, Mr. Malak" - said professor Smart almost condescendingly - "There are now 'virtual' Enigma machines on the Internet. You feed them the code, and they come out with the text. It's a bit funny, really... so many people died because of this code, and now it's an Internet curiosity."

"So this virtual Enigma is generally available."

"Oh yes, certainly. I can give you a web address you can use to do that."

"That would be great. Thank you".

It was still relatively early and Michael, who was supposed to rent a car for the trip south didn't show up yet, so Alex went to work. He fired up his laptop, copied the coded message from the translated text and fed it into the virtual Enigma machine he found courtesy of professor Smart. The electronic beast 'thought' for a while, and then offered the deciphered message:

Nummer eins schweren globalen Rezession Nummer zwei Stufe eins Bereitschaft Nummer drei Stufe eins Bewaffnung Nummer vier Jessie Owens Syndrom ausführen nicht später als zwei Jahre nach alle Voraussetzungen erfüllt sind

"Shit" - thought Alex. He irrationally expected the deciphered message to be in English and he was disappointed that it wasn't. The German text stared at him and he stared back, noting that the message had absolutely no punctuation, so it was difficult to make out whether it was one, long sentence, a bunch of short points or total Teutonic gibberish. He was also greatly intrigued by one phrase he immediately understood – 'Jessie Owens Syndrom'. It seemed very odd to him that the name of the famous black American athlete would be a part of a top secret, ciphered Nazi message.

Since he didn't want to get Kazik involved again, Alex sought help from the Internet once more, pasting the text into Google's 'translation engine'. He was well aware of all the limitations of machine translation, but he thought the text was simple enough for a dumb machine to handle. He was right only partially. The resulting text was all screwed up:

Number one number two serious global recession level one readiness level one number three number four armed Jessie Owens syndrome run no later than two years after all requirements are met

He spent the next 30 minutes carefully comparing the original with the translation, noting words that were clearly missed or put in wrong places. He also checked a few German words on various online dictionaries. The final version made grammatical sense, but not much more:

1. *Serious global recession*
2. *Level one readiness*
3. *Level one armament*
4. *Jessie Owens syndrome*

Execute not later than two years after all requirements are met.

Once again Alex gaped at the fruits of his labor, seriously doubting the usefulness of his efforts. But he didn't have enough time for further musings, because Michael burst into his hotel room and seemed very eager to visit the Czech Republic.

"Quick" - he said - "The car is in front of the main lobby. Let's hit the road".

Alex grabbed his laptop and they went downstairs to the awaiting Fiat 500 which looked like a Ford Fiesta struck by something flat and heavy from the back to shorten it dramatically, so that people could be extremely uncomfortable while inside.

"What happened? Did they run out of sardine cans on wheels?" - asked Alex.

"Leave me alone. That's the only thing they had. But it will do. You said it was a five hour drive, didn't you?"

Yes, I did. But perhaps you missed the point about the mountains".

Alex crammed himself into the tight space behind the wheel and they started on their way, first heading due south, and then veering a bit west, as the road started weaving through the mountains. They were entering what used to be called Sudetenland. This was the first time during their trip that they had some time to actually look around, pay attention to the sights, relax, and enjoy the scenery. Their Italian marvel whined desperately as they were getting higher and higher into the mountains.

"When will we reach the border?" - asked Michael.

"You probably won't even notice it. Remember, this is European Union, no more border controls."

After about two and a half hours of driving they did cross into the Czech Republic and started going downhill. It was a very pleasant, sunny day and the fall foliage was covering all the hills. They stopped and had a snack in a small village café full of somewhat surprised Czechs, immersed in their local chitchat over strong coffee. This wasn't a route traveled frequently by Americans or - for that matter - by any foreigners. Back on the road, they started approaching Prague, but they knew they had to turn sharply west before reaching the capital city. They didn't really talk very much, juggling their own thoughts about their adventure and the mission at hand. Alex mentioned that he had the coded message deciphered, but Michael suggested they would talk about it once he could actually see it.

"We are getting close. Let's stop in this little town to freshen up a bit" - said Alex pointing to a road sign saying 'Trpomchy 5 km'".

"This is the name of the town?".

"Yes.".

"Jesus, I don't know how these guys untwist their tongues every day before going to sleep. And what sort of a sorry ass name is 'Czech Republic'? Why not Czechland or Czechistan? What's wrong with these people? They hate vowels, perhaps even more than they hate the Germans or the Ruskis, and they call their own country some weird two-word name. And now we're on our way to see a woman called Frantiska Pohradničkova. I'm beginning to long for names like John Smith or Susan Jones."

"Or like Newt Gingrich, Barack Hussein Obama, Rod Blagojevich, and last but not least, Chicago's very own compulsive postage stamp licker, Dan Rostenkowski".

"Oh, stop it. You know what I mean."

"No, I don't. Stop bitching about foreign lands. It's not your country or your language so who cares how difficult it is for you. They certainly don't. They could as easily complain about Chappaquiddick.".

"All right, all right. Speaking of languages, are you sure you can't communicate in Czech?"

"I keep telling you, Michael, Czech is a different language, very much like English and Dutch - related, but different. When someone speaks very slowly, I may be able to understand about 10%. And then there are various tricky parts."

"What do you mean?"

"I'll give you a classic example. In Czech 'Láska je nebeská' means "Love is heavenly", but in Polish almost identically sounding sentence - 'Laska jest niebieska' - means 'The walking stick is blue'".

"You're kidding." Michael was genuinely surprised.

"No, I'm not. And it can also mean 'The hot chick is blue'."

"I thought 'rura' was 'hot chick'."

"Laska, rura - same thing. Very attractive woman. And the same sentence can also mean 'The staff is blue'."

"What staff?"

"The one in your pants, you dickhead" - said Alex laughing at his friend's linguistic confusion. And he made fun of Michael all the way to the gas station in the town of Trpomchy, which was probably just as well - they needed some levity in the trip that turned out to be much more serious than they could ever have imagined. Alex, in his usual impish way, would not let go of his trump card.

"So, do you know" - he asked - "that there is a Czech sentence which contains absolutely no vowels?"

"Go away."

"Here it is" - said Alex, scribbling a few words on a piece of paper:

Strč prst skrz krk.

Michael looked at it, gave his friend a wicked stare and then smiled.

"OK, I know you're dying to tell me what this means."

"Right. It means 'stick your finger through your throat'. And perhaps anybody willing to pronounce this should be ready for some throat piercing."

"I agree. Thank you for making my trip to Czechistan so incredibly enjoyable."

The village of Nová Ves turned out to be a very picturesque, almost idyllic place, situated at the bottom of a group of hills. Alex and Michael had no trouble finding the address they were looking for. They pulled up in front of a house at the edge of the village. It looked like a typical, European farmer's house with a few embellishments, like colorful flower baskets hanging under each of the windows, and green shutters, which looked almost Mediterranean. There was a Jeep parked in front the front door - a clear sign of globalization.

They walked up to the house and rang the bell, not knowing what to expect. And they certainly didn't expect a middle-aged man who opened the door and eyed them with intense suspicion.

"Hello... Frantiska...err... doma?"

Alex thus exhausted his knowledge of Czech, but his heroic effort brought the desired result. "Počkejte prosím chvíli" - said the man and went back into the house. They could hear him talk to a woman:

"Kdo to je, tatínek?"

"Některé hloupé Američany."

"Did you understand any of that?" - whispered Michael.

"Yes, I think he introduced us to someone as 'some stupid Americans'."

"Great."

In just a few seconds a young woman emerged from the house.

"Ale laska!" - thought Alex in Polish.

"What a 'rura'!" - thought Michael in Pinglish.

Their reaction to the emergence of Frantiska was understandable, because she was a beautiful woman in her late 20's - long blond hair, blue eyes, long legs, voluptuous lips, and all the proper concave and convex attributes of femininity. But the fact Frantiska was so young also meant that she could not have possibly had anything to do with events dating back to WWII.

They stood there totally transfixed until Frantiska spoke.

"Dobrý den, co můžu udělat pro vás?"

Chapter 13

Alex felt like a total jackass, which was not a sentiment he was unfamiliar with. He looked at Frantiska with a really dumb expression on his face and it probably didn't go unnoticed. She was still standing in the open door, in all her enticing splendor.

"Well... yes... We're sorry to bother you." – he mumbled cautiously - "Do you speak English?"

Frantiska hesitated and looked at both of them again.

"Yes, a bit. But is difficult for me." It was obvious that she wasn't comfortable with speaking anything but Czech. Alex bravely persevered, sticking to a bunch of lies he had concocted earlier with Michael.

"My name is Alex and this is my colleague Michael. We are American historians from Chicago and we were wondering whether it would be possible for us to ask you a few questions."

"Historians? Why questions for me? I don't understand."

"Could we come in for a second? I promise this will not take long."

"Yes... fine. Please after me."

Frantiska led them through the door into a modest living room with a wide, panoramic window through which they could see an open field and some hills at a distance. She motioned for them to sit in two armchairs positioned at a low table.

"Perhaps you would drink some tea?" - she said haltingly.

"We would... I mean, yes please. That would be great."

She left for the kitchen.

"Something is not right." - said Michael in a hushed voice.

"What?"

"Obviously she's too young to know anything about what we're interested in. And who is this grumpy guy?"

"It's her dad. She called him tatínek."

"Great. So who was Karel, the dude who was supposedly here when Hanke showed his face in 1945?"

"I don't know. Just calm down... Here she comes."

Frantiska returned with two glasses of rather thin tea and a bowl of sugar. "Prosím... please" - she said, giving each of them a small tray with some biscuits. They started sipping their tea and munching on the snacks, but Alex knew he needed to start the conversation as soon as possible and get it over with. He was pre-emptied.

"My name. You know it. How?" - asked Frantiska with telegraphic precision. The silence that followed her question was almost painful. Michael spoke for the first time during this entire encounter.

"Please, don't be alarmed. We did some research before we came here. You see, in May of 1945 something important happened in this house, and..."

"I know." - said Frantiska.

"Excuse me?" - said Alex.

"I know. My grandfather often tell me this story when I was little. This man came, German. He was escaping or something and he gave my grandpa envelope to keep for him. He tell him he would be back to get it."

"And then he was shot." - said Michael, eager to push the story along.

"Shot? Oh, no, no. He gone and never come back. Grandpa didn't know what happen to him."

"So what did he do with the envelope?" - Alex sensed they were close to what they came for.

"He burn it."

"What?"

"Before the Russians come, he had to burn it. He was afraid Soviets would think he was Nazi. Envelope had stamps with swastikas."

An eternity of awkward silence ensued. Then Alex put his tea down, stood up, walked up to Frantiska and shook her hand."

"Frantiska, thank you very much for your time. You've been very helpful. And, by the way, did this German leave just one envelope with your grandpa?"

"Yes, I think so."

"Was your grandpa's name Karel?"

"Yes, how you know?"

"Oh, as my friend said, we studied all of this before coming here."

"It's funny."

"What's funny?"

"Other people also asked about his name."

Michael, who was already half way out of the house, suddenly froze, turned around, and looked at Alex with undisguised consternation. Then he took a few steps back into the house and faced Frantiska.

"You mean someone else was asking you about your grandfather? When was that?"

"Yes, few days ago. Two men came from Praha, from some ministry. They said they need to look through my grandpa's papers because of tax reasons."

"And did they do that?"

"Yes, they were here for an hour and then gone away."

"And did they take anything with them?"

"No, they tell me all was just a big mistake. But they asked me, like you, if my grandpa's name was Karel."

"Did they ask you any other questions?"

"No."

Michael and Alex thanked Frantiska profusely for all her help, jammed themselves back into their Fiat Uno and took off. As they followed the same route backwards, each of them brooded over what had just transpired. Although they couldn't have possibly known it, their thoughts were more or less the same. It was apparent to them that the 'ministry' men who had visited Frantiska's house had nothing to do with any governmental agencies, but were sent to find out if - by some remote chance - Karel kept the envelope given to him by the 'German'. And the German was almost certainly Karl Hanke.

"Let's call it a success and go home." - proposed Alex after about 20 minutes of driving.

"Well, it is a success, because we now know that only two copies of this damn document survived the war. One was in the barrel under Neumarkt and the other was delivered to Himmler and perhaps ended up in possession of this Belize guy."

"No, I don't think Krugman had this document in Belize. If he'd had it, he could've simply given it to someone to act on. It seems obvious he was aware of its contents and of the fact that a copy of it existed under Nowy Targ, but the last time he actually had access to it was probably back in 1945."

"Are you saying we are the proud owners of the only remaining copy?"

"Yes. Who knows what Himmler did with his copy. Could have eaten it for lunch out of fear."

There was a moment of silence as they started weaving their way back into the mountains.

"I'm sure you know I'm worried about something else." – said Michael.

"Yes, I know. The Czechs."

"Right. Aren't you?"

"I have to admit I am. Someone is really trying to put a lid on all of this, which makes me worried. And I'm beginning to think that Mr. Trzepizór's anonymous informant had something to do with the crew who ended up in the shelter under Nowy Targ."

"I'm glad you've finally seen the light."

"Yes... and that's unfortunately not the only light I'm seeing."

"What the hell do..."

"Shut up!" Alex turned his head towards Michael and rolled his eyes in an almost comical way, pointing to the back window of the car.

"What is it?" - asked Michael.

"This black Audi has been following us since we left Frantiska's place."

"Oh, come on, Alex. You're getting paranoid. There is no good place to pass us around here, so he's just trailing in the back."

"Oh, yeah? Well then, let's do a little experiment".

Alex waited for the next gas station. As soon as he saw it, he abruptly pulled into it. The Audi passed by and disappeared round the bend. They dithered aimlessly for a while, buying a few extremely unhealthy snacks, and then started back on the road.

"See" - said Michael - "nothing to worry about."

"Don't jump to conclusions. The experiment is not over yet."

And it wasn't. They drove on, passing two little villages. After a while the black Audi rejoined them, following them about 200 yards back. Never too close, never too far away. Michael was getting alarmed.

"What the hell do we do now?" – he asked.

"Nothing. Let them follow us. Let's see how far this goes."

"Can't we just lose them?"

Alex looked at his friend with utter disbelief.

"Lose them? You obviously watched too many James Bond movies. We are in a spaghetti can called Fiat 500 and they are in an Audi. Losing them in this piece of crap is like losing a Harley on a moped or a Ferrari in a Trabi."

"What's a Trabi?"

"Shit, for a reporter you really show obvious gaps in your knowledge about all the curiosities of 20th century civilization."

"Maybe. But remember, I am on city desk in Chicago. I know where to go on Milwaukee Avenue to see huge rats, and I bet you don't know that. I also know where to get the best Korean hookers in Evanston."

"Good for you. Anyway, let's just see what happens. I wonder if this guy is going to cross with us into Poland or is this some sort of Czech affair only."

They drove for a couple of hours, each of them looking furtively at the rear view mirror every now and then. The Audi was there all the way until it suddenly split off at a motorway interchange just south of Wrocław.

"Perhaps he wasn't following us at all." – suggested Michael.

"Maybe. Nothing we can do about it."

Back at the hotel they had a rather hasty dinner over which they decided it was too late to arrange for travel back to the US the following morning. They would stay in Poland one more day. They also discussed an issue, which Alex brought up while feasting on his dessert.

"I don't know how you feel about, Michael, but I think we should take the original document we found under Nowy Targ back to the US."

"I agree. We have a complete translation on your laptop, but it may still turn out that the original is somehow important. The problem is that the spooky guy, Ziggy something or other, clearly knew that we might want to take some documents out of the country. And who knows, perhaps the black Audi had something to do with all that. Do you know why taking these papers with us would constitute smuggling?"

"Well, if the rules haven't changed, you need a special permission to export anything that dates back to 1945 or earlier."

Michael thought about it for a while and then asked a question which to him was quite logical, but which totally confused Alex.

"What's the nearest foreign airport?"

"What?"

"Don't panic. I'm not plotting anything outrageous. It seems to me that if this rule is in force in Poland, and there are no border controls within EU, we could go somewhere in Germany and pass their controls before flying to the US. I doubt Ziggy has regular conversations with his German counterparts about two American schmucks traveling with two pieces of old paper."

"OK, but what if the Germans have a similar rule?"

"That's possible, but at least they won't expect us to have such documents."

"Hmm, you may have a point. The closest airport would be Dresden. It's only about 200 km away. We could get there in a couple of hours via the motorway."

"No, no. Assuming someone is keeping an eye on us, we need to do something more cunning. Is there a train from here to Dresden."

"I'm sure there is."

"Great. I'll call Lufthansa to rebook our flights. Then a day after tomorrow we'll call a cab and ask the driver to wait for us not at the lobby entrance, but by the side door. We'll do express checkout, grab our bags and go to the railroad station without anybody at the hotel knowing about it."

Alex gave him a rather strange look. "Aren't you a bit too conspiratorial?" - he asked.

"Just cautious."

"All right then. Let's call it a plan."

Chapter 14

Having made all their preparations for going back home, Alex and Michael had most of the day at their disposal. In the morning they got their treasure back from hotel safekeeping, ate a quick breakfast and decided to take a last look at Wrocław. Alex took his friend to Ostrów Tumski, an island on the Odra River where the city started about ten centuries earlier. There, walking down narrow cobblestone streets framed by old houses and even older churches, they talked about the events of the last few days. Alex admitted that he had never actually expected to find anything at the location specified in the Belize letter. Michael, in his turn, confessed that he also had doubts, but that he somehow felt obliged to 'check things out'. Neither of them ever imagined that they would be sneaking out of Poland via Dresden with a cryptic document signed by Hitler. And of course neither of them had any idea what all of this meant.

They walked past the monumental Gothic cathedral and sat down on a bench in a tiny park in front of a red brick seminary building. Absorbed in their thoughts, they didn't say a lot, enjoying their serene surroundings. But they also knew they really needed to talk.

"When we get back to the hotel" - said Alex finally - "I need to show you the deciphered part of the document."

"OK, Alex. But you've already told me that it looks like the message sets a number of conditions for triggering some action off."

"Right. And I don't understand these conditions. But isn't it very strange?"

"What?"

"OK, let's say that in the dying moments of the Third Reich some of your more screwed up compatriots concoct a plan to do something in the US and they set conditions to trigger the whole thing. Why would these conditions be met only now, after so many years, and who would be in a position today to actually do whatever the plan wanted them to do? I mean there would have to be people, or some groups, all over the country to set things in motion."

"I have no idea. You know, I almost feel like the old geezer in Belize, who apparently knew about the whole thing and was against it, kept silent for over half a century, because he expected that those conditions would never be met. And then, once he realized we were at the 'trigger point', he panicked and sent me his letter."

"That's an interesting idea, but we have no way of knowing what actually happened. I'm also totally confused about some of these triggers, but we should probably discuss this while looking at the message."

"OK, let's go back to the hotel."

"Wait, one more thing. How are we transporting the documents?"

"What do you mean?"

"Well, are we trying to hide them in our luggage or what?"

"I vote for stuffing the envelope in your carry-on bag. No hiding. If they find it and take it, let them. The only thing they can do is to confiscate this thing."

They walked leisurely back across the Old Town towards their hotel. Their route took them once again across Nowy Targ where pani Basia was still busy selling groceries and exchanging pleasantries with her customers. Alex remembered almost nostalgically that just a few days earlier he had taken Michael to see this place to discourage him from further pursuits. It seemed like it had happened a century earlier.

In the evening they made some last arrangements for their departure the next morning, and then they sat down in front of

Alex's laptop to look at the decoded message. Having read it a number of times, they discussed it at length to finally agree that it was relatively easy to understand all the triggers except the last one. They had no idea what 'level 1' meant, but that wasn't particularly important at this stage. Michael started another session of speculation.

"It definitely looks like the people listed in the document were sent to the US not so much to do something immediately, but to start some sort of preparations for future events. Perhaps they were told to sit low, recruit people, train them, arm them, and wait."

"Yeah, except by the time all the conditions had been satisfied, all of these people would have been either dead or talking exclusively to Alois Alzheimer."

"True, but they might have been able to hand their future mission to younger people."

"Oh my god!" - blurted out Alex suggesting strongly that his mind accidently tripped over something important. Michael waited patiently.

"All of this reminds me of that story the other day about a botched Nazi plan to sabotage America. Remember? The Brits recently declassified some documents which revealed the details."

Michael looked puzzled, although he did remember seeing some news about this. Alex, as usual, found the relevant story on the Internet in just a few mouse clicks. He pulled the laptop closer and they both read quietly:

"In June of 1942, Hitler, who was increasingly worried about American involvement in the war, started planning Operation Pastorius which was supposed to sabotage the American war effort. In a relatively short time a group of eight German saboteurs was put together and they were transported to the US East Coast on a submarine. Four of them walked on shore in Long Island and four south of Jacksonville, Florida. They were armed with the knowledge

of how to create bombs out of everyday items like dried peas, razor blades, etc. However, Operation Pastorius was fatally flawed for a number of reasons.

First, the men to whom the mission was assigned got drunk in a Parisian bar the night before deployment and told everyone that they were 'secret agents'. Second, the Germans picked a poor leader, George John Dasch, who, almost as soon as he landed, wanted to give up. Third, the German U-Boat, carrying the saboteurs, ran aground and was almost stopped by the US Coast Guard. Fourth, the men walked ashore wearing bathing trunks and Wehrmacht hats."

Michael looked at Alex, Alex looked at Michael, and then they burst out laughing. Their mutual merriment lasted a good minute before it gave way to the usual reciprocal ethnic ribbing.

"Now that's what I call German precision" - said Alex sarcastically.

"Well, perhaps some of the saboteurs were Polish." - countered Michael.

"Yes, I'm sure Hitler had a bunch of Polish spies in his bunker, just in case. Anyway, Operation Pastorius was obviously a ridiculous flop, but you can't deny it confirms that the Nazis were plotting all kinds of things against the US. The guys in Wehrmacht hats were sent early in the war, but think about it - maybe the mission organized at the very end, in the face of total defeat, was long-term and much better planned."

"I sure hope so, because if the people sent in 1945 were of the same caliber, we're wasting our time."

"Right. But let's suppose that at least some of them were successful in implanting themselves in their assigned American towns and in completing successive stages of their orders. Their 'heirs' today, if the warning from Belize is to be believed, apparently think that all four triggers are now flipped. I also found on the same website some info on a bunch of really bizarre plots cooked up by the Germans at the end of the war. This included plans to contaminate alcoholic drinks with methanol, inject sausages with poison, and prepare poisoned Nescafe and sugar."

"Damn, I'll never eat a hot dog again."

"That's not all. Another elaborate plan involved supplying agents with special headache-inducing cigarettes that could be given to an assassination target. When the person complained of a headache, they would be offered an aspirin laced with poison."

"Great, but what does all of that prove?"

"Nothing. But it suggests a lot. One captured French Nazi intelligence agent apparently told his interrogators he had attended a conference in the final weeks of the war whose purpose was to plan a violent campaign that would sow chaos across Western Europe and eventually lead to the state of civil war in which Fourth Reich would emerge. That campaign was to involve sabotage, assassinations and even chemical weapons. So at the time it was reasonable to believe that after the Allied victory there would remain a dangerous postwar Nazi underground which would continue a secret war."

"And you seriously think this underground exists right now in the US and is just about to spring to action?"

"You're asking me? This entire trip was your idea, so deal with the consequences. I'm telling you what I've just read. Going back to our own screwy situation, as the conditions specify, the world is in relative economic chaos, people are generally pissed off, and the would-be hitlerites have 'level 1' armament and readiness, whatever the hell that means. Now, they also must think that the fourth condition has been met."

"Yeah, and that one baffles the crap out of me."

"You know who Jessie Owens was, don't you?"

"Yes, but that doesn't help me. Do you think Owens had anything to with all this stuff?"

"No, that's just unimaginable. He really irritated Hitler by winning four gold medals at the Berlin Olympics and beating the 'perfectly Aryan' German dudes in the process. And although Owens then refused to criticize Adolf, I still think he would never have had any contacts with the Nazis. After all, they viewed him as 'Untermensch' or 'sub-human'."

"Who else was sub-human?"

"What, you don't know your cultural heritage? I was sub-human. More precisely vast populations of Eastern Europe, like Jews, Gypsies, Poles, Russians, Serbs, Belarussians, Ukrainians, etc. They also hated racial sub-humans like blacks, Latinos, Indians. Let's see, who else? Oh, yes, all the mentally challenged people, invalids, and Mitt Romney."

"What?"

"They apparently hated Mormons too."

Michael chuckled.

They both felt a bit tired and decided to go to sleep. The departure from Wrocław in the morning turned out to be completely uneventful. They got to the railroad station early in the morning, caught an InterCity express train to Dresden and spent their time on board dozing off in their totally empty compartment. They never even noticed that after a while all the signs by the tracks changed from Polish into German. The train pulled into the Dresden Hauptbahnhof at around noon. From there they took a cab to the airport and waited for about two hours for their flight to the US. And then it was time to go through security, which for flights to any destination in the US was particularly stringent.

Alex watched as Michael walked through a full body scanner and then was asked a couple of questions by a German security officer dressed in a light green uniform. He waited briefly until they handed him his carry-on bag. It was all done in just a minute and Alex was next. He too went through the scanner to be confronted by the same officer.

"Hello, sir" – said the German.

"Hi."

"Can you please tell me where you are going?"

"Sure, returning to Chicago from a short European trip."

"Business or pleasure?"

"Pleasure."

The security guy handed him his laptop bag, but was still holding the larger bag.

"Can you open this bag for me, please?" – he asked.

"Shit." – thought Alex and looked desperately at Michael who was sitting about 20 yards away watching his friend intently. He opened the bag and put it on a low table by the German officer. It was inevitable that the large envelope with swastikas all over it would immediately draw the officer's attention. And it did. He took the envelope out, looked at it with keen interest, looked inside, without taking the papers out, and then turned to Alex.

"What is this?"

"Just some old documents. I'm a history buff and I thought this was interesting, so I bought it."

"Where did you get it?

"I bought it in an antique shop in Poland."

"Please wait."

The officer took the envelope and walked a few yards to his colleague, presumably a superior. They talked in hushed voices while pointing to the envelope every now and then. Then one of them got on the phone and talked to some remote power of German security for a few minutes.

Alex was getting increasingly worried and he also noticed that Michael stood up and started walking nervously up and down the terminal. Finally both officers came back to Michael.

"Sir, do you know that it's illegal in Budesrepublik to display swastikas or any other war-related German symbols?" - asked the senior guy.

"No, actually I didn't know that. But I'm not displaying anything. It's just my private stuff I'm taking back home."

They both looked at Michael for a while and then they put the envelope back in his bag and gave it back to him.

"That's all right, sir. Just don't waive this thing around. Keep it in your bag."

"No problem."

"Have a good trip."

"Thank you... Danke."

Alex rejoined Michael. "Let's get the hell out of here." - he said, almost running towards their gate.

"What happened?"

"Nothing. They saw the envelope, examined it, talked about it, and let me go."

"Just like that."

"Yes."

"That's kind of odd, don't you think?"

"I don't know. Let's just go home."

Chapter 15

All was relatively quiet at 33 thousand feet above the Atlantic. Michael ate his cardboard dinner early into the flight, had two glasses of wine, and then decided that the best way to kill the next few hours was to go to sleep. Alex tried to follow suit, but couldn't. He was strangely restless and anxious, constantly thinking about their peculiar adventure of the past few days. He got up a couple of times just to walk up and down the aisle to kill time, and then he would sit down and call for another glass of wine just before getting up again to walk up and down the aisle. Finally he decided that the best way out of his predicament was to plug the earphones in, courtesy of Lufthansa, and listen to some radio channels.

He flipped through all kinds of things, including the Hot Latino Tunes Channel and the Ya-Ba-Da-Ba-Doo Oldies station. Finally he heard the calming voice of the BBC World Service announcer talking about all the miseries of contemporary world with measured, impeccable, perfectly intoned English. An ideal inducer of sleep. Except it wasn't. Just minutes into the broadcast Alex heard the news which warranted his yanking the earphones out of his ears and giving Michael a violent elbow to his ribs.

"What the hell?" - moaned Michael.

"Sorry. I need to tell you something."

"Really? I thought we were crashing and you wanted to say your final good bye."

"Krugman was poisoned."

"What? How do you know?"

"I just heard it on the news. Apparently it was ricin."

"Ricin? The preferred toxin of the KGB?"

"Yes, but they didn't say how it was introduced into his organism."

"What difference does it make? The guy was snuffed, like that poor Bulgarian bastard Markov[4] on Waterloo Bridge in London."

"They say they are still investigating."

"Right. I wish them luck. The Scotland Yard still doesn't know who killed Markov."

"Well, you're right about one thing. It doesn't matter how he was killed. He was clearly murdered, just a few days after he sent his letter to you."

"Yes, and that makes me feel very comfortable. Perhaps we should hijack this plane to Havana and spend the rest of our lives drinking mojitos with Castro."

"Calm down and shut up. The last thing we need is trouble on this plane."

Chicago greeted them with cold and drizzle. Since it was Saturday, they decided to go to their respective homes and reconvene at Michael's place on Sunday afternoon. They were both greatly relieved to be back, but they also felt they needed to discuss what, if anything, to do next. Additionally Michael dreaded the fact that he would have to call FBI on Monday. He has never had any earlier contacts with federal authorities and was not very happy about the fact that this was just about to change.

When Alex showed up at Michael's apartment Sunday afternoon, he found his friend lying on a couch with a half-eaten Chinese takeout in his hand. He looked a bit disheveled and definitely not very well rested.

"What, you stayed up all night? - asked Alex.

"No, but I didn't sleep well. I've been doing zilch since I got up."

"I'm shocked. You doing jack shit? Unbelievable."

---

[4] Georgi Markov was a Bulgarian dissident who in 1978 was killed in London by KGB agents with a ricin pellet placed on the tip of an umbrella.

"I've been thinking though".

"Oh no, that means we're probably in more trouble than just 24 hours ago."

"You may jest for as long as you want to, but I think we **are** in some sort of a deep doo-doo. Or at least I am."

"Why?"

"Well, I'm going to talk to this Kim Swanson guy from the FBI early this week. And what, do you think, I should tell him? Especially if he asks me about our wonderful vacation in Poland. Remember that lying to federal authorities is a crime."

"Oh, hell, you're just full of shit. Yes, it is a crime, but only if you are under oath. I think you'll be asked a couple of informal questions about whether you know anybody who might want to blow your head off, and that will be it. And you can definitely lie."

"But should I?"

What followed was a lengthy and rather convoluted discussion about the virtues of occasional lying, especially when faced with people endowed with some governmental oomph. Alex was dead set against saying anything to anybody about their European adventure, at least for some time to come, until things get 'cleared up' and somehow settled. But, when pressed by Michael, he was unable to specify in any way what clearing up or settling might mean in this context. They finally decided that Michael should say as little as possible during his FBI interview. They also agreed that the envelope retrieved in Wrocław should be stashed away somewhere - their final choice was a storage locker at Union Station. It was 9 bucks a day, but they didn't expect to keep this stuff over there for more than a few days. Michael was to take the envelope to the locker on his way to work on Monday morning.

Once all of this had been decided, they each grabbed a beer, slumped into armchairs, and started on the subject that was really weighing heavily on their minds. Alex was first to voice his concerns.

"Listen Michael, regardless of what all of this means, and it may still mean absolutely nothing, don't you think we are being somehow watched, monitored, or whatever."

"Yes, I do. And I also think there is something sinister about it. But the only thing we can do is to wait and see what happens."

"No, we could also go to the FBI, or use your interview with them, to tell them all we know and then we could just slide back into our meaningless but safe everyday lives."

"I have to admit I did think about this option. But it's too early for that. Let's just wait and see where all of this takes us. It's not like we can influence anything from now on.

"I disagree. We can do one thing which might help us get to the bottom of all of this. We need to find out what's all this stuff about Jessie Owens."

"Why?"

"Well, I think all the other conditions, whatever their details, were satisfied. Assuming that's the case, the final trigger is this talk about the 'Owens syndrome'. Krugman sent you his letter presumably because he realized that things were just about to start happening and ..."

"Wait" - said Michael turning abruptly towards his friend - "didn't we at some point speculate that Himmler's buddy had kept quiet for such a long time, because he thought that it would've been virtually impossible for all the triggers to actually ever happen?"

"Yeah, we did. So what?"

"So, what did recently happen in America that absolutely nobody thought was possible for decades to come, or ever?"

Alex stared at Michael for a few seconds as if asking if he was really serious about what he was suggesting.

"You mean... you think... No, that's just silly."

"I don't think it is. For the first time ever we have a black president. But I think this 'syndrome' thing is not specifically about black people in the White House. It might be more generic.

Like you said earlier - there were all these 'inferior people' in Nazi ideology".

"You mean, if Joe Lieberman had ever gotten elected, the final trigger would have been set off too."

"Yes. Absolutely. Think about it. Since the end of WWII up until Obama's win we've had zero 'non-standard' presidents. Just a steady stream of white Presbyterians, Quakers, Episcopalians, and even one Catholic.

"But this is just nuts. You are in effect suggesting that this would-be Nazi plot, hatched back in 1945, sent German agents to this country with orders to wait until such time that they are armed to the teeth, we are all pissed off about what's happening about economy and stuff, and a racially 'deficient' personnel is at the helm. OK, so let's say all of this is in place. Now what?"

"Don't know. How about the ultimate revenge? The catastrophic destabilization of the US? Or even a Nazi takeover?"

Alex thought about it for a while and then said something that puzzled Michael.

"We have two and half months left."

"What?"

"If what you say is true, we are two and half months away from the second anniversary of the current president's taking the oath of office. And the German document clearly said – *'Execute not later than two years after all requirements are met'.*

"So something can happen tomorrow or 5 days from now or whatever."

"It can."

Chapter 16

On Monday Michael showed up at work in the morning, having first made a trip to Union Station to entrust the swastika-adorned envelope to a storage locker. He was greeted suspiciously warmly by all his colleagues, which he attributed to the fact that most of them were probably thrilled to death by FBI's interest in his 'case'. None of them had any idea what that case was, and Michael wasn't sure about that either.

He went through all kinds of perfunctory maneuvers usually necessary after some vacation time. He caught up with reading his mail and was relieved to see no further shipments from Belize, or - for that matter - any other foreign lands. He exchanged gratuitous pleasantries with all the people he intensely disliked, including Rick who seemed really keen to find out what the hell was going on. But since Michael himself didn't really know what the hell was going on, Rick's curiosity had to go unsatisfied.

"So, what the hell is going on?" - asked his Editor-in-Chief, Melvin Burke, when he confronted Michael in his cubicle.

Melvin was a grumpy old man who didn't like anything or anybody in particular for no apparent reason. He was well past his retirement age, but he insisted that 'Chicago Tribune' would immediately collapse were he to suddenly quit. This view stood in stark contrast to the general conviction of his staff that he was a feeble-minded idiot and an obnoxious prick who needed to go and plant oriental herbs in his Peoria garden, far removed from the Windy City and journalism.

"I'm not sure, sir." - said Michael cautiously.

"Well, talk to these FBI characters as soon as possible. We don't want any trouble around here."

"I understand. I'm calling them today."

"Good. And by the way, Riedle, stop taking vacations and start doing your job, will you?"

"Yes, sir."

It was obvious to Michael that any procrastination with respect to talking to federal authorities would not work to his advantage. So the first thing he did after lunch was to dial the number left for him in his absence by the people who meticulously examined his desk after it had been 'cleaned' by a minor bomb blast.

"This is FBI. How can I help you?" - said cheerfully a woman on the other side of the line. Michael hesitated, but had no other option but to continue.

"Yes, I was given this number to get in touch with special agent Kim Swanson."

"And can I have your name, sir?"

"Michael Riedle."

"Please wait a moment."

The moment dragged on for over a minute, but finally the woman returned and informed Michael that Kim Swanson was unavailable, but would be happy to meet him on Tuesday at 9 am in the Dirksen Federal Building.

"Will you be available at that time tomorrow, sir?" - asked the woman, not shedding any of her initial fake cheerfulness.

"Yes, that's all right. I'll be there. Where should I go once I get there?"

"Go to room 335 on the third floor and tell them who you need to see. They'll be able to help you."

The Dirksen Federal Building in Dearborn Ave. was one of those non-descript edifices of sheer governmental bureaucracy which inspired fearful awe in almost anybody walking in there. It housed the ICE, formerly INS, for those abject foreign individuals who were trying to stay in the US for good, even though they knew they had almost no chance. It housed the CIA, although nobody knew on which floor and for what reason. And it housed the FBI, on the third floor, where Michael was just about to enter room 335. Curiously enough, the door to this room had no markings or explanations other than the actual number. On Monday evening Michael called Alex to tell him that his 'hour of doom' had been set for 9 am the following day. Alex wished him luck sensing he might need it.

Inside room 335 there was a small desk with a morose looking receptionist behind it. Michael informed her about the purpose of his visit and was led through a side door into a tiny chamber with nothing but a table and two chairs in it. There were no windows, no wall decorations and no other furnishings of any kind. "I wonder how many people get beaten up in here daily" - thought Michael. The glum receptionist told him to wait and went back into the front room. Left to his own resources, Michael sat down in one of the chairs facing the door and waited nervously for agent Swanson to show up.

He expected all along that his interlocutor would be some old, rude, federally full of himself type who would use intimidation as his primary weapon. He was wrong. Special agent Kim Swanson was a tall, very attractive woman in her late 30s with pitch-black hair, cut very short. She was wearing a mini skirt and a tight, somewhat daring blouse, which revealed assets almost certainly not mentioned on any of FBI's inventory lists. She walked up to Michael with a big smile on her face.

"Very nice to meet you, Mr. Riedle." - she said in a deep, mellow voice as if she was Ingrid Bergman just stepping off the Casablanca movie set. Michael was a bit stunned, so he didn't say anything and just shook her hand while entertaining a few chaotic thoughts about sexual entrapment. She sat down in the other chair, facing him across the table. A moment of awkward silence followed as she opened a folder full of papers and got her pen ready.

"OK, let's start. This is not going to take long. I just need to ask you a few questions. Would you like a glass of water or something?"

101

"No, thank you."

"All right. As you know, in your absence you received a package which contained an explosive device."

"Yes, I know."

"Can you think of anybody who would want to do you harm or who might bear some kind of a grudge against you?"

"Not really, but in my line of work it's not unusual for people to hate me in one way or another because of something I wrote."

"Do you know anybody in Belize?"

"No."

"Have you ever been to Belize?"

"No."

"So you are not aware of any reason why anyone in that country might want to send you anything?"

"As I said, I don't know anything or anybody in Belize".

Michael was painfully aware of the fact that he just started skirting the outer perimeter of lying to a federal agent. He was therefore relieved to hear that Ms. Swanson decided to change her line of questioning.

"I understand you took some time off and went on a European vacation with a friend of yours."

"That's right."

"Prior to that, did you get any threats, verbally or otherwise?"

"No. But please remember that almost any of my readers could have been pissed off – err, I mean irritated – by almost anything I write."

"I understand, Mr. Riedle, but we don't think that's the case."

"What? Why?"

"Well, the investigation still continues, but we have established that the package sent to you contained a highly sophisticated device which had almost no lethal power, but had to be constructed by professionals and not any of your disgruntled readers."

"Sophisticated in what sense?"

"Sophisticated as in military or terrorist expertise sense."

Michael pretended desperately to look surprised.

"So, what are you saying?" – he asked.

"Well, this seems to be an almost classic case of sending you some kind of a warning. So we're trying to establish who would want to do that and why."

"I'm sorry, but I have no idea."

Agent Swanson paused for a while scribbling something in the stash of important looking sheets of paper.

"So why did you go to Poland?"

"Oh fuck!" – thought Michael. He forced a smile and a totally phony expression of ease.

"Well, it's the native country of my best friend and he thought it would be a great idea to just wander about his 'home territory'. It turned out to be a great trip".

"Did anything unusual happen when you were there?"

"No, other than the call from my co-worker Rick about the Belize package."

At this point Kim's cell phone rang. She stood up, motioned to Michael to stay put, and left the room. Michael looked at his phone and saw three SMS messages from Alex, but he couldn't read them, because Kim was back.

"OK, Mr. Riedle, just a couple of additional questions. Are you absolutely sure that you have no idea who could have possibly sent you this package?"

"I have no clue."

"And nothing happened during your European trip?"

"Right."

"Fine. You know what, I'm going to give you my card with all the contact numbers. If you happen to remember something, please give me a call."

Michael knew special agent Kim Swanson didn't believe him. He took her card and she looked him straight in the eye with just a trace of a smile on her face. He felt like she almost said 'I'll probably see you again', and somehow he knew she was right.

"Please don't do anything I wouldn't do." - she said.

"I'll try, but since I don't really know you, it's kind of difficult to determine what that means."

Kim looked at him once again, this time with a much more serious intent. "Mr. Riedle, if you ever feel things are getting out of control, or if you sense some kind of immediate danger, please promise you'll call me. I can help."

"Thank you, but I doubt this incident at my office is in any way serious."

"I certainly hope you're right."

Michael stumbled back out of the building onto crowded Dearborn Ave. virtually gasping for fresh air. He stood in the middle of the sidewalk for a good minute or two trying to collect his thoughts. Then he remembered the messages from Alex. The first SMS message just said 'please call me', but then there was a bit of an obvious escalation since the next one read 'damn, where are you?', and the third stated rather tersely – 'fuck, I need to see you NOW!'

Michael got the message and called his friend.

Chapter 17

Alex sounded worried, but he didn't want to tell Michael what it was all about. Instead he insisted they meet somewhere for lunch. They agreed to get together at a place they often visited together, Hackney's On Harms in Glenview, which was close to Alex's work. When Michael got there, Alex was already stuffing his face with fried onion rings and washing them down with a beer. He looked tense and frazzled.

"So what's up?" – asked Michael while sitting down at Alex's table.

"I got this letter at work."

"Let me guess – from Belize."

"No, from Fort Wayne."

"Fort Wayne? Who the hell from?"

"I've no idea. Here it is."

Alex produced a single sheet of paper with a short typewritten paragraph.

If you want to find out about operation Black Eagle, open a new Facebook account under the name 'Kris Semp' with access strictly limited only to friends. I am sure you know how to do it. You will receive an access request from 'Andreas Bulat'. Accept it and wait for further instructions. Do not accept any other requests. Be extremely careful and share this letter only with your friend Michael. Good luck.

Michael read the letter a couple of times and then gave it back to Alex. Its contents immediately reminded him of Kim's parting request to contact her when in danger.

"Don't you think it's time we told someone about all this? Like the FBI."

"Maybe. But if we do that now, we'll probably never find out who this guy in Fort Wayne is and what he knows. The thing that bothers me most is the fact that he or she knows about us and also knows we got somehow entangled in all this crap."

"You're right. It's a bit scary."

"Anyway, I've decided to open this stupid Facebook account later today. Let's see what happens and then we'll decide what to do next."

"OK."

"What happened at the FBI?"

"Nothing much, although special agent Kim Swanson turned out to be the federal version of Raquel Welch. She asked me a few questions and I navigated all around them. But I'm pretty sure she knows something is going on. She almost said as much."

"Listen, I got to get back to work. Let's talk more this evening. Can I come to your place around 7?"

"Sure. See you then... One more thing. I hope you realize that Fort Wayne is one of the places mentioned in the Nazi distribution list."

"Yeah, I do. That was my first thought when I got this thing."

It was very unusual for Alex to slack off at work or not meet deadlines or miss meetings. But this particular afternoon he did all of that. While sitting at his desk, he stared aimlessly at his computer, totally distracted and unable to do anything useful. A few of his colleagues passed by, looked at him, and asked if he was all right. He assured them he was, even though it was probably safe to assume nobody believed him. At one point, when nobody was around, Alex quickly went on Facebook and became 'Kris Semp' by creating an account bearing that name. And once he did that, he started checking for new messages for

Kris almost obsessively, a couple of times an hour. But none came.

At quitting time he quickly gathered his things and went home. It was late afternoon and he got hopelessly stuck in traffic on Milwaukee Avenue. Irritated and anxious, he swerved into a side street, got out of the car and walked into 'Latin Cantina' where he asked the somewhat surprised bartender, servicing a predominantly Mexican crowd, clearly unaccustomed to seeing 'gringos', for a Corona with a twist of lime. He managed to have two of those before he heard his cell phone ring.

"Alex, where the hell are you?" - Michael sounded a bit testy.

"I was trying to get home, but got stuck. Are you at your place?"

"Yes. Get over here now!"

"Are you all right?"

"Yes, just get your ass over here."

"All right, take it easy. I'll be there soon."

It took Alex another 45 minutes to navigate all the traffic and reach Cermak Ave. in Berwyn. When he walked through his friend's front door, he was a bit shocked at what he saw. Michael was sitting on the floor, in the middle of his living room, and was putting all kinds of bits and pieces into a large cardboard box. The entire apartment seemed to have been totally trashed. Books, papers, clothes, and various other items were strewn chaotically all over the place, and some pieces of furniture had been tipped over and cut up. It was a scene of utter devastation and Michael looked almost grotesque, sitting there, in the midst of this monumental mess, patiently sorting things out.

Alex walked up to him and sat down on the floor. He wasn't quite sure what to say. To his utter amazement, Michael put his finger on his lips clearly asking him to keep quiet. Then he got up and led the way out of the apartment into the dimly lit hallway. They both sat down on the stairs leading down to the first floor.

"They were looking for it." - said Michael.

"For what? And who?"

"For the documents we got in Breslau. They trashed the place, but didn't take anything. Alex, I have no idea who these people are and what they're up to, but this is beginning to look too serious for us to handle."

"Did you call the police?"

"Hell no. I'm not going to sit through two hours of useless interrogation. Besides, nothing was stolen. I just need to tidy this place up and repair some furniture."

"Why exactly are we sitting on these moldy stairs?"

"I'll explain in a while."

"OK, so what do we do now?"

"I don't know. I really don't know. Any luck with our Deep Face?"

"What?"

"Did you get the Facebook account going?"

"Yeah, but no contact yet."

Michael was silent for a while which in his case usually preceded some sort of a pronouncement which Alex would not like or outright hate.

"You know" - he finally said - "I feel like there is this invisible noose that is being tightened around us by a bunch of really bad people. Obviously they will do almost anything to get what they want and sooner or later they will succeed unless we do something drastic."

Alex didn't like the sound of this.

"Drastic? What the hell do you mean?"

"We need to disappear."

As Alex's jaw was dropping down below his waistline, he gaped at Michael, shook his head in disbelief, and then recovered enough to be able to speak again.

"I think you've gone mad, my friend. Disappear? Why? And how? This is just crazy."

"Hear me out, please. Just give me a couple of minutes... OK, so I'm convinced that if we don't go to the FBI with all of this shit immediately, they - whoever they may be - will fucking kill us, like they did the Belize guy. And yet if we do tell the spooks about everything, we may never find out what all of that Nazi stuff means, and they can still kill us while executing their plans to send America to hell."

"Beautiful. I really love disjunctive statements with exactly the same stuff on both sides of 'or'. Either they will kill us or they will kill us. I like our chances."

"All I'm saying is that we have to somehow take ourselves out of this situation, even if temporarily, to be able to work things out in some safe, quiet environment. It may be too late. They may be following us everywhere, listening to our phone conversations, bugging our apartments. Who knows?"

"Is that why we're sitting here rather than on your slashed couch?"

"Yes. The only chance we have is to cut ourselves off from all the possible lines of communication, both the ones we know about and the ones we may be unaware of. Like possible bugs installed in my place."

"You're a paranoid nutjob."

"Perhaps. But if we don't do what I'm suggesting, we may end up in no position of suggesting anything at all in the future on account of us being two stiffs."

Alex sighed, rubbed his forehead as if trying to squeeze a bit of additional wisdom out of his skull, and then asked the inevitable.

"So, what is it that you are suggesting?"

"We disappear for a while, almost like on a self-organized witness protection program. And we need to do this immediately, like tomorrow morning."

"You must be shitting me."

"No, Alex, we really need to do this. I've made some preparations..."

"Great, I can't wait to hear all about that."

Instead of continuing the conversation, Michael reached in his pocket and produced two cell phones. He handed one to his friend.

"As of now" - he said - "we only call each other on these two 'throw away' phones. Don't call me at home or at work, don't send me emails, or SMS's or anything else. Tomorrow we go to work normally, but split at lunchtime and never show up again. We get whatever money we can from our bank accounts, meet somewhere, and then leave town."

"You mean we just leave our jobs? Without telling anybody about it?"

"Yes. At least for a few days."

"But they will start looking for us."

"I know. But it doesn't matter. I hope by the time there is any serious effort to find us, we'll know what we need to know."

Alex felt a bit dizzy, but not dizzy enough to forget about his most important question.

"All right, Darth Evader, where are we going?" - he asked.

"What?"

"You said we were leaving town. Where the fuck are we going?"

Michael looked at Alex with a bit of bewilderment.

"Well, that's the part I haven't quite worked out yet."

Alex giggled in a hysterical sort of way, the way people giggle when they feel the situation is funny enough to be tragically dangerous. All of this stuff was way too much for him, and the fact that his friend was seriously proposing disappearing into a non-specified place brought back fond memories of Dick Cheney's permanent stay at a 'secure undisclosed' location. However, Alex also realized that something needed to be done pretty soon, and out of all the possible wacky scenarios presenting themselves to his confused mind disappearing into thin air didn't seem to be such a bad idea. And he even knew where they could disappear to.

"Let's go to Fort Wayne." - he said with a quiet certitude of a man who has just decided to jump off a skyscraper window.

"Why? You want to chase the guy who asked you to open the Facebook account?"

"Not quite. First, we should probably stay away from hotels, and I have good friends there. I'm sure we could stay at their house for a while."

"Well, how well do you know them?"

"I lived in Fort Wayne for a while and they were my neighbors and best friends."

"You lived in Fort Wayne? What the hell for?"

"Doesn't matter. It was in the good all times, before meeting you. The point is I can call them and we might be able to stay at their place. But the second advantage of our being there is that at some point we could be in a position to meet this Deep Face - as you call him - and since he is in Fort Wayne, it would be relatively easy to do."

"Do you think it would be possible to arrange our going there by tomorrow?"

"Maybe. I can try. Let's assume this works out. What's our plan?"

They spent another hour on the stairs in front of Michael's apartment plotting their clandestine exit from the city of Chicago. Finally it was agreed that they would both leave their respective places of work by some side door, like a service gate or delivery entrance, making sure that nobody was following them. Then they would show up at Union Station around noon where they would buy - totally independently of each other - tickets for a train going from Chicago to New York. Michael would also collect the Wrocław papers from the storage locker while Alex was to be in charge of packing his laptop and whatever else he thought was going to be needed. Their get-off point was a station in Waterloo, Indiana, which was about 20 miles north of Fort Wayne. Each of them was supposed to go to the bank in the morning to withdraw as much cash as possible, not using ATM cards.

"Do you think we have a chance? - asked Michael as Alex was leaving.

"Hell, I don't even know what chance is in this case."

"I'll see you tomorrow on the train. Look for me in the restaurant car."

"Where else?"

Chapter 18

By all measures, Union Station in Chicago is a somewhat weird, grandiose building which today seems to be completely out of place. It took twelve years to build and, when it was finally completed in 1925, it was one of the best places in the country to catch a train to almost anywhere in the United States. Although Alex lived in Chicago for decades, he actually never caught any train leaving the city, and he only knew about the so-called Great Hall, the incredibly large, vaulted centerpiece of the station, from a few dramatic scenes in the movie 'The Untouchables'. It therefore seemed a bit odd to him that he was walking down the same stairs - wide, marble, and a bit uninviting - on which the fictitious Eliot Ness was chasing a baby carriage under a hail of bullets shot by Al Capone's thugs.

Oddly, it was also somewhat appropriate that he was walking down these stairs since the entire day promised to be almost as intriguing as Eliot's final showdown with Al. A bit earlier Alex left his work for 'lunch', running down the back stairs out onto a side street and then walking to a bus stop. The bus, which came surprisingly quickly, took him downtown. He stopped by a branch of his bank, withdrew 900 dollars from his account, leaving exactly 6 cents in it, and headed for the railroad station. Once there, he bought his ticket. Every now and then he looked around to see if Michael was anywhere to be seen, but the station was pretty crowded with people who still inexplicably thought Amtrak was actually capable of taking them to their destinations.

Alex headed for the underground platform and boarded the train. He decided he would not make any attempt to find his friend until they actually started moving. So he sat down in a very uncomfortable seat, next to a noisy kid and his totally indifferent mother, and waited. To his surprise, the train squeaked, groaned and jerked to finally move out of the station - right on time.

A day before giving Chicago a surreptitious finger Alex called his old friend back in Fort Wayne. He knew this was going to be an awkward conversation – he last spoke to Jimmy Klonowski a couple of years earlier. They used to be best buddies when Alex was living in Fort Wayne, but - once he left - staying in touch was becoming more and more difficult until they more or less went their separate ways. Back in the years they lived along the same quiet street in what Indiana residents inexplicably call 'additions' and what is known by most of America as 'subdivisions', they went to bars, watched major sports events, and shared moments of frequent hilarity, albeit often tainted by excessive consumption of alcohol and exotic food. Jimmy was Alex's soul mate, a guy he could comfortably talk to about anything in the world, however stupid or intricately wise. Additionally they shared one more important trait – they both ended up in Fort Wayne almost accidentally, as a result of their twisted professional careers and personal lives. Jimmy was a lifetime and devout Chicagoan, with a heavy local accent to boot, who would happily die on the 50-yard line of Soldier Field during a Chicago Bears play-off game. Alex, on the other hand, was not particularly attached to any concrete geographical coordinates, but always felt out of place in Fort Wayne. They were thus comrades-in-banishment to Midwestern oblivion.

Alex dialed Jimmy's cell phone number, using his newly acquired throwaway piece of trash, and waited only briefly for an answer.

"Hello, this is Jimmy Klonowski. How can I help you?"

"Hi, Jimmy. This is Alex."

"Alex? Holy shit! How the heck are you?" – Jimmy seemed to be genuinely pleased to hear from his ex-pal.

"I'm doing great. And you and your family?"

"Everyone's fine. It's been a while since I heard from you."

"Yeah, I know. I've been a bit pre-occupied... Listen, I know this is going to sound weird, but I need to kind of stay away from things for a while. Actually me and my friend here in Chicago... I was wondering if we could hang around your place for a few days..."

"You mean you'd want to stay with us for a while?"

"Yes."

"Sure. You know me – I invite perfect strangers to my house every day. When would you be coming?"

"Well, that's the hard part. We have train tickets for tomorrow."

There was a bit of a silence, which Alex tried desperately not to assign to Jimmy's shock.

"Train? Why the hell are you taking a train? Anyway, that's fine." – said Jimmy a bit hesitantly.

"Are you sure?"

"Yes. But if you are getting off at Waterloo, I can't pick you up, because I'll be at work, and Mairéad is out of town until next week."

"Oh, that's no problem. We'll get a cab or something."

"Well then, I'll expect you tomorrow. I'll be home by about 5 pm."

"Great, we'll see you then."

"Hey, Alex."

"Yeah?"

"When you say you need to stay away from things, does it mean you're in some kind of trouble?"

Alex took a deep breath.

"Well, not really. At least not in a criminal sense."

As soon as he said it, he realized that it sounded incredibly stupid.

"I mean, I've run into some problems, and I need a quiet place to sort everything out. I'll tell you more when I get there."

"All right. Would a few cold beers aid the sorting out process?"

"I forgot how well you know me".

"See you, my friend."

As Alex reminisced about his conversation with Jimmy, the train fought its way through eastern suburbs of Chicago on its tortuous way through some switching stations leading towards Gary and South Bend in Indiana. It then gained some speed, leaving behind all the soot-spewing smoke stacks peppering this part of Lake Michigan coast. Alex got up, picked up his bag, making sure it 'accidently' banged the head of the noisy kid, and went through a few cars to reach the restaurant area. He had no trouble spotting Michael sipping his beer and sitting at a tiny table by the window which was showing a never-ending panorama of Midwestern flatlands dotted with dilapidated industrial crap.

"Hi, Michael" – he said as he was sitting down. "No problems getting out of Chicago?"

"None. And you?"

"Same."

"Did you talk to your friend in Fort Wayne?"

"Yeah, we're good to go."

"Who exactly is this guy?"

"His name is Jimmy. Jimmy Klonowski."

"Another Polack?"

"He's as much a Polack as you're a Kraut. Anyway, he is a good friend of mine. We used to live close by. He's very easy going and relaxed, so it should be a perfect fit for you since you're hopelessly uptight and painfully anal retentive."

"Ha, ha. Very funny."

"Listen, Michael. We do have one problem. We need to decide what we tell him. So far all he knows is that we're in some kind of trouble and we need a place to stay for a few days. But this will not fly. Jimmy has a wife and two fantastic daughters, and I cannot just barge into his life pretending nothing much is happening. We may be putting his family in danger."

"So, what do you propose?"

"I think we should tell him everything."

"Everything?"

"Everything. I trust him enough to know that if he feels he needs to kick our asses out of his house, he will. And if he does, he'll never admit to anyone that he even saw us. On the other hand, he may decide to stick with us to see what the hell this whole thing is about. Either way, we don't lose anything by sharing with him whatever we know."

Michael was clearly not quite convinced. He was particularly worried about the fact that their mysterious Facebook informer insisted nobody else should be in on the entire story. Yet he also felt that their moving into Jimmy's place for a while would provide them with a bit of a breathing space which they certainly needed. And, after all, absolutely no one, other than Jimmy, knew where they were and what they were going to do which was a good thing, because Michael had no idea what they were going to do either.

"So when we get to Fort Wayne, what's our next step?" – asked Michael, almost continuing his train of thought.

"I guess we'll have to sit tight and watch that Facebook account for any news. And remember, although the letter came from Fort Wayne, it doesn't mean this person is actually there."

"Oh, I don't know, Alex. Somehow I feel he is there."

"Or she?"

"I don't think so."

The Waterloo Amtrak station just north of Fort Wayne was one of those rare places which begged for some rational explanation of its existence. It was not much more than a railroad track laid alongside a wooden shack stuck in the middle of nowhere. Whoever first thought of establishing a railroad stop here probably forgot about it just a few minutes later and rode off on horseback heading due west. The actual passenger platform was so short that arriving trains had to first stop with the first set of cars aligned with it so that half of the passengers could disembark, at which time half of the people waiting for their relatives reached a premature conclusion that the people they were waiting for had mysteriously vanished. Only after a couple of minutes the train moved forward a bit to align the remaining cars with the platform.

None of this mattered to Alex and Michael who got off with the first batch of passengers and started looking for a cab. It wasn't difficult to find one – they gave the driver their destination and soon found themselves going south on I-69 towards the city. Michael couldn't help noticing that their driver was an exceedingly despondent character who looked like he hated what he was doing and didn't want to say anything to anybody. "He should take lessons from our Wrocław cabbie" – thought Michael almost nostalgically.

As they were approaching Fort Wayne, they realized it was too early to show up at Jimmy's place. So they asked the driver to change course and drop them off at Jefferson Point, one of the main mall-like hangouts for disgruntled local youth. They had a couple of hours to kill. Alex suggested they go to Panera Bread where they would have free Internet access and something half-decent to stuff their faces with. As soon as they got there, Michael went to get some food while Alex logged into his new Facebook account. He immediately saw a 'friend request' from 'Andreas Bulat' which he quickly accepted. He left his laptop logged in, shoving it to the side of the table to make room for the sandwich Michael was just bringing. They sat there, in the middle of mid-western nowhere, munching away on their sandwiches, not saying anything and not knowing what could happen next. Alex was keeping a keen eye on the laptop screen, which remained totally unchanged for a long time. But then, just at the last bite of the sandwich, a little popup message showed up in the lower right-hand corner of the display. "Where are you?" – it asked with disturbing directness.

"Hey, Michael" – said Alex – "this guy is now my Facebook 'friend' and he wants to know where I am".

"Shit, that's weird. Why does he even care? Just ignore the question and ask him something back."

"Oh yeah? Like what?"

"I don't know. Think of something."

Alex thought of something.

"I'm with my friend, Michael" – typed Alex – "We're ready to proceed. Waiting for instructions."

There was an eon of cyber silence after this initial exchange. They sat at the tiny table staring at the laptop screen and expecting an immediate response, but nothing was happening. Finally, after about 5 minutes, the popup screen showed up again.

"I'm Albert Brunner. I got to go now. Will be in touch."

Chapter 19

"What the hell?" – said Alex, staring at the last message from their mysterious contact.

"Seems like our Deep Face was in a bit of a hurry. But it doesn't matter – he'll be back. Did you recognize the name?"

"Not really. Do you know him?"

"His last name is Brunner. A different Brunner is listed in the Nazi document and he was assigned to Fort Wayne."

"So what are you saying? Brunner number 2? A relative of the original Brunner?"

"I don't know. Anything is possible. Perhaps we can ask him if he ever talks to us for more than 5 seconds. I find it curious though that he asked where I was – as if expecting I'd left Chicago."

They were just about ready to leave Panera when Michael's cell phone rang rather loudly, startling both of them. The only person who knew this number was standing right in front of Michael and he certainly wasn't calling him. They looked at the phone screen with a bit of panic and let it ring a few more times, noting that the caller was shown as 'unknown'. Once the ringing stopped, they sat back down in their chairs.

"Someone could've dialed a wrong number." – said Alex rather cautiously.

"True. I certainly hope that's the case. Let's hang around here for a few minutes more. My voicemail on this thing is not configured, so nobody can leave me a message. But let's see if I get another call."

The phone rang again after a few minutes. It seemed more insistent and urgent than before, even though it was still the same phone playing very much the same ringtone. Michael looked at Alex with trepidation. His friend just mouthed the words 'answer it'.

"Hello." – said Michael.

There was a moment of silence, but it was obvious to him that someone was on the other end of the line.

"Hello." – he repeated.

"Yes, hi." – said a female voice which – to Michael's surprise – sounded somehow familiar.

"Who is this?" – he asked.

"Err... this is Kim. Kim Swanson."

It took Michael quite a while to realize that he was talking to his 'Raquel Welch' FBI agent. It took him even longer to fully understand what that meant.

"Oh no, how the hell do you know this number?" – he asked with a quiet resignation in his voice. He knew what the answer would be.

"I'm with the FBI." – said Kim, fully meeting Michael's expectations.

"So you probably also know where I am."

"No, but I will if we continue this conversation for the next 57 seconds."

"Great. So, what do you want, Kim?"

"You skipped town."

"Yes."

"Why?"

"I had my reasons."

"Listen, Michael... Can I call you Michael?"

"You can call me dumbshit for all I care."

"I want to help you. I know you're in some deep trouble and you're running with your pal. And I also sense all of this could be really important. So let me join you."

"Join us?"

"Yeah, not as an FBI agent, but as a girl who happens to be off duty – you know, like on vacation."

"But why? If you think something big is going down, why not alert your bosses?"

"Alert them about what? I don't have anything. You probably do, and I think we should join forces as soon as possible."

"Kim... I'm sorry, but your 56 seconds are up."

Michael shut off his phone abruptly, thus buying himself some time to think about what just happened. He related his conversation to Alex. They were still sitting at their table, but they could have just as well been almost anywhere else since they were lost in their thoughts about their failed attempt to 'disappear'.

"I think you should stall her." – said Alex.

"What do you mean?"

"When she calls again, let her know that you might be willing to take her offer, but need more time to think about it."

"I doubt she'll buy it."

"Who cares? We need some time to find about the Deep Face dude. Once we know what the heck is going on, perhaps she could help us."

"Do you think she knows where we are?"

"Maybe. If she does, I hope it's only because she used some fancy FBI crap to find out. Otherwise other people might know too."

Alex called Jimmy to ask him if on his way home he could swing by Jefferson Point to pick them up. He said he was going to be there in a few minutes. They were still keeping an eye on the laptop screen, which remained stuck on exactly the same pixels. The late afternoon crowd was beginning to storm Panera in search of coffee and sandwiches, so they left and stood outside waiting for Jimmy to show up. They looked strangely out of place with their bags lying in front of them on the sidewalk.

"Hell, it's really you! And I thought you were just kidding."

122

The loud, cheerful voice belonged to a guy who just stopped in front of Michael and Alex. He was sitting in his red car, which showed some obvious signs of metal fatigue, and waved at them enthusiastically. They grabbed their bags and quickly got in the car. As Jimmy was driving away, he got hurriedly introduced to Michael. Then Alex half-hugged his Fort Wayne friend causing him to swerve dangerously, albeit briefly, to the left.

"Hey, take your dirty paws off me, you pervert!" – said Jimmy with a wicked chuckle.

"So, you really thought I wasn't coming?" – asked Alex.

"Heck, I don't know. You sounded a bit weird, I mean weirder than usual, and somewhat conspiratorial. Not to mention the fact that you ditched your old friend as soon as you moved back to Chicago."

"I didn't ditch you. We kind of mutually ditched each other. It's always this way – it's called drifting apart."

"I thought drifting apart was reserved for marriages. Anyway, you're here and it's great to see you, although I'm not sure it'll still be great to see you once you tell me what it's all about."

"Right..." – said Alex with barely veiled foreboding.

"Oh, no. You really stepped in some serious crap, didn't you? And don't tell me you and crap mutually stepped into each other."

"Well, serious crap was shipped to us, or rather to Michael. From Belize."

"What? Are you talking about that sliver of land hanging somewhere below the *cojones* of Mexico and Guatemala?"

"Yes."

"So what did you get from there? I thought they barely had any ship to shit... I mean shit to ship. Damn, I can't even talk any more. See what you've done."

"Hold on, Jimmy. Let's get to your house, relax a bit, have a few beers, and we'll tell you everything."

"Well, that's the first sensible thing you said so far. I mean that bit about having a few beers."

In just a few minutes they arrived at Jimmy's house where Alex was greeted with justifiably reserved warmth by his two daughters. The visitors moved into their assigned rooms and spent some time washing away all traces of their early morning escape from Chicago. Then they reconvened in Jimmy's basement where beer was already being poured into glasses. Since there was no roundabout way of explaining to Jimmy the events of the last days, Alex simply told him everything straight up, right from the night he met Michael at the Green Mill jazz bar up until their decision to 'disappear'. As the tale progressed, it was easy to see that Jimmy was getting increasingly stunned by what he was hearing. When Alex started to relate the story of Michael's FBI interview and the subsequent break-in into his apartment, Jimmy started waving his hands as though he wanted to scare off some threatening demons.

"Wait, wait... stop for a second." – he said – "This is nuts. Are you playing some kind of a joke on me? You don't seriously expect me to believe all this stuff, do you? It could be a good script for a very bad thriller, but otherwise I have a major problem with imagining both of you flying all the way to Eastern Europe and crawling in some smelly ancient dungeon to retrieve secret Nazi shit. From a sand-filled barrel? Come on, give me a break!"

"Well, I know this sounds crazy, but this is exactly what happened. If you want proof, here it is."

Alex handed Jimmy the envelope brought back from Wrocław. Their host examined it very carefully, then opened it, took out the contents, and stared at the yellow sheets of paper for a good minute.

"Jesus Christ!" – he then said.

"Jesus Christ!" – he repeated his earlier opinion as if to reinforce it.

Given the chance to continue, Alex proceeded to finish the story, including the 'Deep Face' part of it and the 'Raquel Welch' phone call just an hour earlier. Jimmy was incredulous enough to get everyone another beer. He was clearly intrigued.

"Why the hell did you get into all this?" – he asked.

"What do you mean?" – asked Michael and Alex almost in unison.

"Well, most normal people when they get some cryptic message from an anonymous source, they either throw it away or call some jackass at the police department to tell them about it. You did neither. You chased this half-ass story around the world. Why? What the fuck?"

Michael felt he needed to express his fake contrition.

"OK, it was mainly my fault. There was something about this Belize letter that convinced me I had to act on it and I more or less forced Alex to help me. And then things just kind of snowballed."

"They sure did. I think you guys have only one rational option. Get the FBI chick to help you. What do you know about her?"

"Virtually nothing. She has big tits, long legs, and she works for the government".

"Perfect qualifications, I would say. Besides, what else can you do? Live in Fort Wayne until your retirement age kicks in?"

Alex listened to this conversation with growing anxiety, because he thought the discussion was missing one vital point – their safety. And so he decided to speak.

"Jimmy, I'm sure you realize that our staying at your place, for however short a time, could expose you and your family to some risks. After all, we raced out of Chicago precisely because we felt threatened in some way. So, you need to be very honest with us. Are you sure we can stay here?"

Jimmy gave Alex a weird, almost offended look.

"Of course you can stay. And I'm willing to help you any way I can, but remember that I work and – unlike you – I'm not ready to just disappear."

"OK then, so it seems we have two avenues to pursue. One is Kim and her offer to help. I'm sure she's going to call again. Are we in agreement that Michael should cautiously invite her to join us?"

Michael and Jimmy both nodded in approval.

"Good. But remember, Michael, be very careful. She may already know where we are, but if she wants to come here, you probably need to meet her at some agreed place by yourself. So start planning this."

"Yes, sir." – said Michael which gave Alex a pause. He suddenly realized that he had assumed a role of a leader, in almost a military sense, barking orders and instructions at his 'subordinates'. It was not a role that he either wanted or cherished, but he quickly brushed aside his qualms and convinced himself that the tasks at hand demanded extraordinary measures and unusual role-playing arrangements.

"Now, the other avenue is this Deep Face crap. My laptop is running all the time and it's logged into Facebook. If this guy really is the son of one of the Nazis shipped off to the US at the end of the war, he may be the key to the whole thing. It could be a totally fake thing, but I kind of doubt it. So my immediate task is to find out who he is, what he knows and what he wants."

"OK, so what do I do?" – asked Jimmy.

"Well, for starters you can get us another beer" – replied Alex obligingly, with his first totally relaxed smile of the day spread right across his face. "But after that, there **is** something important you can help with.

"Like what?"

"Beer first!"

Once everybody was properly replenished, Alex asked Jimmy to do some research into any neo-Nazi activity in the Fort Wayne vicinity, especially in the last ten years. He was hoping that the authorities, either state or federal, were keeping tabs on such things. If so, there could be some publicly available documents, newspaper articles or police archives detailing such matters.

The remaining hours of the day were spent on idle talk about 'the good old times', Chicago Cubs ill fortunes, politics, random babblings of no immediate import, and whatever else suddenly came to their beer-infused minds. Well past midnight they all went to bed, in expectation of a few intriguing days to come. Alex fell asleep almost immediately, but was soon awakened by a loud cyber 'Bing!'. He opened one eye and looked at the suddenly illuminated laptop screen. "Damn" – he thought – "this guy has strange habits."

Deep Face just surfaced again. At 3 am.

Chapter 20

Alex dragged his reluctant body out of bed, splashed some water on his face from a glass standing on a little table, and slumped into a chair in front of his laptop.

"Are you there? – said the cyber message from his Facebook pal. It took Alex a few minutes to regain enough consciousness to be able to answer.

"Yes, go on." – he typed.

"I don't have much time. I think they're on to me."

"Who?"

"Doesn't matter. I'll tell you all you need to know in a few hours. "

"OK."

There was a sudden lull in this weird, silent conversation and Alex – sensing it might abruptly end – searched frantically for something to ask. He opted for going all the way.

"Are you the son of Karl Brunner?"

"Yes." The answer came immediately, as if the question was actually expected.

"Is operation 'Black Eagle' still in play?"

This time nothing showed up on the screen for a good minute or so, and Alex was beginning to lose hope.

"Yes. You have just days."

"Days for what?"

"For stopping this."

"Come on, you need to be more specific." – typed Alex betraying his growing irritation.

"I will. Not now."

"Can we meet?"

"No."

"Did you know the guy in Belize?"

Long silence again.

"Yes, he was my uncle."

"How can I get in touch with you?"

"Only here."

"Why?"

"Don't get distracted by such things. Black Eagle fires off very soon. You don't have much time."

"What does that mean...? What will happen...? Albert? Damn it, say something."

Deep Face has disappeared again, leaving Alex frustrated and tired. He couldn't sleep and he didn't want to rummage through Jimmy's house at almost 4 am. So he sat in his room waiting for the morning to arrive and for something else to happen. He was also afraid that he would not notice the next Facebook communication if he went back to sleep.

What he just learnt from his infrequent informer didn't make much sense to him, although he thought two pieces of information were crucial. Since Krugman was Albert Brunner's uncle, there must have been some direct connection between the Belize guy and Albert's dad who was on the Nazi list as the 'delegate' to Fort Wayne. Secondly, for the first time there was an approximate time framework for something to happen, something that Albert was asking them to somehow stop. And it was days away. At the same time it seemed to Alex that Deep Face was working under some major constraints and could only communicate briefly from time to time, apparently putting himself in some sort of danger.

At 6 am the house was still totally quiet, but Alex's computer once again came alive.

"You there?" – asked the cyber non-voice.

"Yes, go on." – answered Alex looking desperately for a piece of paper and something to write with.

"I'm afraid I'll be dead soon."

"What? Why? How soon?"

"Almost now... Listen, the center for this operation is in Indiana. They are called National Socialist Brotherhood and they have all kinds of contacts in Europe."

"Where in Europe?"

"Don't interrupt me...All kind of places in Europe. But the main thing is this bunch of fascist nuts in the Czech Republic called 'Krev a Čest'. They were sent to pursue you, but they were idiots and they totally failed."

"Were they supposed to kill us?"

"Never mind that. My dad was initially in charge of the whole thing and great friends with Krugman who married his sister, I mean my aunt. But then they had a big argument and Krugman went to Belize. He thought all this crap was totally crazy and will never happen anyway. Now other people are in charge."

"Who?"

"The Indiana crew."

"OK, Albert. Please – how do we stop it? And what is it that we're stopping?"

There was no response. Alex was still sitting there with his eyes glued to the laptop screen that showed an almost totally empty Facebook page of Mr. Andreas Bulat. Nothing showed up for the next few minutes. Alex was losing hope, but typed once again into the instant messenger field.

"How do we stop it, Albert? Come back and tell me how to stop it?"

Nothing. Flashing cursor and absolutely nothing. About 10 minutes later Albert answered.

"You can only stop it by going to their HQ and unplugging their damn computers."

"What HQ? Where?" – Alex was almost shouting, albeit silently, by frantically punching the keys.

Brief silence.

"Everything is already set in motion. Every day between 5:15 and 5:17 pm on this weird Georgia monument thing..."

"What Georgia monument thing?" – Alex was at the end of his rope.

"And then there is going to a series of .... Shit... OK, it's quits for me... Beware of Linda... Goodbye and good luck."

"Who the fuck is Linda? Albert...? Albert...?

If a cold, pixel-starved flashing cursor could be an effective symbol of death, this was the time.

Alex shut his machine off and went downstairs to the kitchen where he found Jimmy making a batch of pancakes while whistling something merrily. He looked up from over his frying pan.

"Wow, you look like a piece of shit." – he said.

"What happened to 'good morning'?"

"Good morning. You look like a piece of shit."

"Thanks. Where's my Teutonic pal?"

"Still in the arms of the German goddess of slumber, such as she is. Seriously though, you don't look too good. You couldn't sleep or something?"

"I was woken up at 3 am by the Facebook guy."

"Oh yeah? Did he have anything interesting to say?"

"Yes... but I'm afraid he is now dead."

Jimmy froze for a few seconds with one of the pancakes dangling lifelessly from his spatula. He waited for Alex to continue.

"He kept logging on and off and feeding me somewhat disjointed information, but as he went along it was obvious he was hurried and felt threatened. And then he suddenly said goodbye and vanished."

"So you really don't know that he was killed."

"No, I don't. But I have a feeling something really bad happened to him. He more or less told me he was just about to die."

"So what else did he tell you?"

"Let's wait for Michael."

Jimmy finished his pancakes and started serving breakfast. They were soon joined by sleepy looking Michael who slumped into his chair at the kitchen table.

"OK, the Strategic Pancake Command Center is now in session." – said Jimmy, struggling to cheer his guests up.

He failed. Alex, looking somber and dejected, proceeded to relate his intermittent communications with Deep Face who could now possibly be Deceased Face. Jimmy and Michael listened intently. Then everybody was quiet for a while.

"You know, my wife's second name is Linda." – said Jimmy.

Michael looked at him in a puzzled sort of way and smirked.

"So you're suggesting that she's training Nazi salutes somewhere in Indiana?"

"No, she's training drinking wine with her family on the East Coast. Not that she needs any training. But I'm just saying... her second name is Linda. Anyway, what does 'Krev a Čest' mean?"

"I think it means 'Blood and Honor'" – replied Alex – "so, Jimmy, when you search for stuff later today, include this name too, together with this National Socialist Brotherhood stuff. Perhaps you can find something about the connections between these idiots. But can you actually do all this while at work?"

"Sure I can – I'm a viciously effective multitasker."

"If you say so. What are you going to do, Michael?"

"Well, I have a date with Kim."

"What? Really?"

"Yes, she called me on my cell soon after we all split last night. She was kind of insistent and wanted to know where we were and was surprised when I told her we were in Fort Wayne. As we agreed, I treaded cautiously and agreed to meet her today at noon."

"Where?"

"At the Jefferson Point Walmart."

Jimmy and Alex looked at Michael and laughed.

"Why the hell did you choose Walmart?" – asked Jimmy.

"Well, I wanted to talk to her in an open, public place, not in some cozy little café. Besides, while we chat walking around women's lingerie department, it will look like I'm her dad who is helping his grown daughter pick up a pair of sexy, colorful panties... Just kidding..."

"Anybody has any idea about this Georgia thing?" asked Alex.

"Not a clue." – said Michael.

"Same here." – added Jimmy, but then he paused for a while and continued – "But if we're talking about weird monuments in the state of Georgia, and if we exclude general Pulaski's monument in Savannah, there is perhaps only one candidate."

Michael and Alex looked at him with sudden interest and pressured him with their eager eyes to go on.

"Well, there is this thing called The Georgia Guidestones which is a granite monument looking like a modern, remote cousin of Stonehenge in England. I'm not sure about the details, but I think it's located somewhat east of Athens, on some rented farmland."

"Why do you think it's weird?" – asked Alex.

"I'm kind of surprised that you don't know about it. It was erected at the request of this mysterious dude whose real name was never disclosed. In 1979 he approached a stone polishing company in the area and asked them about building a huge monument consisting of four 20-ton vertical slabs of granite, crowned with another slab. And then he wanted all the slabs to be etched with some bizarre 10 commandments in 8 different languages and notched in various spots so that the whole thing could also function as a calendar and sundial, and allow for some strange star gazing crap. Once all of this was completed, he vanished and never showed up again."

"Wait a minute" – interrupted Michael – "How could he have financed something like this while being totally anonymous?"

"That's the thing. Apparently he talked to a local banker and struck a deal with him – he would disclose his real name only to him on the condition that on completion of the project all documentation about it would be destroyed and the banker would never say a word about it. And that's exactly how it went down."

"You mean this thing is still there?" – asked Alex.

"Sure. I don't remember exactly, but I think in 2005 'National Geographic' put it on the list of America's tourist attractions."

Michael and Alex digested all this information with growing puzzlement.

"Come one, guys" – said Jimmy – "I'm not suggesting that any of this has anything to do with whatever this Deep Face character said to Alex. It's just what came to my mind when I heard a Georgia monument mentioned. Anyway, I'm off to work. Let's get back here by about 5 pm and we'll discuss what we know over dinner."

"Wait, what are **you** going to do, Alex?" asked Michael.

"If Jimmy doesn't mind, I'll hang around his house and analyze once again what we already know and what we don't have any clue about. And perhaps I can dig up some more stuff about this granite thing, just in case."

"All right, let's get to work."

Chapter 21

The smell was there, and Michael could immediately sense it. The odor of cheap Chinese stuff pervading the vast expanse of the Jefferson Point 'Walmart Supercenter', where genetically modified carrots were only yards away from 'pure cotton' wonder-bras, was very distinct. But he didn't have time for such trivial musings. He fought his way past a bunch of seriously overweight customers, slumped over their carts in pursuit of low-priced happiness, to emerge into a relatively open space, just in between 'kitchen utensils' and 'men's apparel'. He was looking for Kim, but he couldn't see her anywhere. And then she just showed up.

She emerged from one of the two main entrances and started straight down the middle isle of the store. Contrary to her previous sexy apparition, she was dressed in a much more conservative fashion – pants, and a blouse revealing virtually nothing. She wandered about the store for a while unaware of the fact that Michael was watching her intently from behind a shelf full of extra-large boxer shorts. Eventually he came out of his hideout casually - to feign surprise at seeing her.

"Hello, Michael." – she said in her fake Ingrid Bergman voice.

"Hi."

"I must say – this is a pretty strange place to meet."

"Why? You have something against Walmart?"

"No, not really. But I'm sure Fort Wayne has some more attractive rendezvous places."

"I wouldn't know. Don't know anything about this town".

"So why exactly are you here?"

"It's a long story."

"All right then, let's cut this crap. Just tell me what happened in Poland and why you're running."

Michael was briefly startled by Kim's directness.

"Kim, let me ask you this first – why do you care? Why do you want to help?"

"Oh, come on, I don't even know, because I have no idea what's going on. I just felt – when I talked to you back at the FBI – that you were hiding something and you were scared."

"That's a surprisingly correct diagnosis."

"So, what is it? Why did you suddenly decide to ditch your life and vanish from Chicago?"

Michael realized that he had to tell her more or less everything, because otherwise her offer to help would either be withdrawn or be of absolutely no consequence. So, he dragged her into a Walmart food niche called Subway, sat her at a table, bought her a 6-inch Spicy Italian sandwich, and spilled his guts to her, up until the time of the hasty Chicago departure.

Kim listened to his story very attentively, betraying virtually no emotion. Every now and then she would frown slightly, as if to signal her impatience, but otherwise she remained totally silent. Once Michael was finished, they both sat at their tiny table and said nothing.

"All right" – Kim finally said – "this is a damn weird story, but I don't understand one thing. Why did you come to Fort Wayne?"

"Oh, that's just because of Alex. He has some connections here… And because of Deep Face."

"Who?"

"Well, I forgot to mention that we established contact via Facebook with a guy who claims he is deeply involved in all of this. Or was involved…"

"What? Who is he?"

"Kim, I wish I could tell you more, but all I know is that this guy started talking to Alex and warned him about all kinds of things, but then he suggested he was just about to be killed and – for all we know – he was."

"By whom? What the hell are you saying?"

"I have no clue."

For the first time Kim appeared to be a bit rattled by all the news. She asked Michael what he knew about Alex's last communication with Deep Face and wanted to know if they were certain he had been talking to them from somewhere in Fort Wayne. Michael was not much help.

"So, where are these documents now?" – she finally asked.

"Well, they are safe." – said Michael, straining hopelessly to mask his caution.

"You mean you don't want to tell me."

"OK, I do mean that. But it doesn't matter Kim, they are in a safe place."

"All right, where are you staying in this town?"

"Again, it's not important. We are glad you want to help us and I just told you the whole story, so let's plan on getting together on some neutral territory to discuss what we need to do."

"Fair enough. Do you carry?"

"Carry what?"

"A piece?"

"A piece of what?"

"My god, don't you ever watch TV crime movies? Do you have a gun?

"Listen, Kim. I write pieces for a newspaper. I don't carry them. If I did, my legs would have been full of holes right now. And why are you asking me about guns?"

"Because this doesn't seem to be a fairy tale about two Chicago schmucks stumbling on some faded pieces of paper in a Polish city. It's more about two Chicago schmucks just about to be snuffed for reasons unknown. So, once again, do you have a gun and – if not – would you know how to use one?"

"No, and no."

"And Alex?"

"Same."

"Great."

"Well, shit, what do you want me to say? It's not like I've chased international conspiracies all my life."

"Exactly. So my question is – what in the name of god are you doing here?"

"I had to do it. Perhaps subconsciously I thought it would never come to this, but it did."

Kim stared at the remnants of her Spicy Italian sandwich for a while.

"Are you married?" – asked Michael, surprising not only Kim, but also himself.

"What?"

"Are you married?"

"Why do you want to know?"

The problem was Michael didn't really know why he wanted to know.

"Just curious." – he said.

"OK... I was."

"What happened? You carried to many pieces to bed."

"Very funny... No, he carried his piece to too many beds."

"Ah, sorry to hear that."

"How about you?"

"Divorced a long time ago."

"Hey, I'm all right with all this idle chit-chat, but I guess we have more important things to discuss."

"Right. So now that you know everything, call your Chicago buddies and let them do their jobs. I'm kind of ready to retire from my Indiana Jones duties."

"I can't do that, Michael. No yet."

"Why the hell not?"

"Just think. I practically don't know you and you tell me some half-baked story about Nazi documents in Poland and a 'Deep Face' character whom you've never seen. Do you really think I can come to my boss with all of this and tell him to mobilize his forces to come to, out of all places, Fort Wayne to chase a 65-year old plot?"

"Hm, I guess you're right. So what do you suggest?

"Get back to Alex, discuss the situation once again and then meet me at my hotel with your papers in hand. Perhaps we can formulate some plan or something."

Michael was just about to agree when his cell phone rang. It was Alex.

"Michael, are you still with Kim?" – he said in a strangely tense voice.

"Yes."

"All right. Just listen. Jimmy called and told me that he found at least three Nazi groups present in the vicinity of Fort Wayne. None of them is called NSB, but I asked him to widen his search and he found them in a place called Wakarusa."

"Where the hell is that?"

"About 90 miles from here, a bit south of South Bend. Don't share any of that with Kim yet. We need to discuss this first."

"OK. I'll see you in a while."

Although Kim was a bit intrigued about Michael's phone conversation, he lied blatantly and explained that his friend wanted to meet him in an hour at a bar way across town. They agreed he would call her at some point the next day to set up a meeting at her hotel room.

As soon as Kim marched out of Walmart, Michael sat down on a little bench usually reserved for people trying on shoes whose life expectancy was about two months. He was toying with the idea of breaking his self-imposed rule and calling his not-much-of-a-friend at the 'Chicago Tribune', Rick Weigert, using the throw away cell phone. He knew that if someone was really after him, Rick's phone could easily be monitored. On the other hand, he had this nagging thought that he really needed to do what he was just about to do. And so he did it – he whipped up his cell phone and dialed Rick's phone.

"Hi Rick, this is Michael."

"Michael? Jesus, where the hell are you? People are worried sick about you over here. Are you all right?"

"Listen, Rick, I'll explain all of this soon, but right now I need your help with something."

"What? Michael, you need to show up here immediately. The Chicago finest are investigating, and..."

"Rick, shut up! Just shut the hell up and listen to me for just a few seconds."

"OK..."

"Do you still have your contact at the FBI in the Dearborn office?"

"Yes, but..."

"Can you have him run a little bio inquiry on special agent Kim Swanson."

"What, the chick that interviewed you?"

"Yes."

"I guess, but what's it all about?"

"Never mind. I'm not asking for anything illegal or secret – just a little background information which is most likely generally available. If you can do this for me, get the info and I'll call you tomorrow to give you a fax number to send this to me."

"Fax number? Are you in North Korea or something? Who uses faxes anymore?"

"I will – tomorrow. I promise I'll explain all of this soon."

"I'm no longer sure I want to know."

"One more thing – keep all of this to yourself for the time being. It's very important. I would like you to tell everyone that I called and that I am all right. Tell them that I had to leave immediately on some urgent family business and that I'll be back soon. But not a word about Kim, FBI or any other stuff like that. Stick to what I just told you."

"This is going to be increasingly difficult to accomplish, but I'll do it. I sure hope you're not in some sort of deep shit."

"So do I..."

Chapter 22

Alex spent most of the day traversing cyberspace in search of any possible connection between the documents recovered in Wrocław and some 'nutjob' group in the Fort Wayne area. When Jimmy called him from work with the news that none of the local groups had anything to do with National Socialist Brotherhood, he asked him to expand his search to the whole state of Indiana and Jimmy quickly zeroed in on Wakarusa where NSB had a confirmed presence for a few years.

The problem was that Alex knew absolutely nothing about Wakarusa and all he gathered from the Internet was that it appeared to be a sleepy little town in the middle of nowhere, surrounded by farming communities. He thought it was an extremely unlikely place to host a bunch of fascist fanatics hell-bent on mayhem and destruction. However, he quickly changed his mind when Jimmy came back from work.

Jimmy did his assigned job very well and – when he found out that Wakarusa was a point of interest - he engaged in some major digging and came up with two interesting facts. First, the town was in the news on August 5th, 2009, following the visit of president Barack Obama to announce that Indiana was to receive $400 million dollars in federal stimulus funds to help revive the state economy. A presidential visit in such a small place in a politically hostile state was quite unusual. Second, there were some newspaper reports about a farm outside of town that apparently was 'off limits' to almost anybody except for some shadowy 'social group'.

When Jimmy got home, he discussed his findings with Alex. While waiting for Michael to return, they speculated on what all of this could possibly mean.

"Dou you think we should go to Wakarusa and check it out?" – asked Alex.

"Well, I don't know, but I certainly can't go with you. Also, if this sinister farm outside of town is really 'off limits', what can you possibly check out? There will almost certainly be some well-armed goons patrolling the perimeter. And they will probably tell you to go to hell".

"Right... But perhaps we can ask Kim to do some checking."

"What? You think she can just show off her legs and be let in? Because she certainly can't just show her FBI badge."

"Just on the basis of her legs, I would certainly let her in..."

"I know you would, you horny old bastard."

"Oh, crap, Jimmy, I don't know. Do you think we're well over our heads with all of this?"

"Absolutely. I told you so earlier. Perhaps instead of rushing to some compound in the middle of rural America or sending an off-duty FBI Barbie doll to check it out, you should try to find out what this place is by some safer means. I'm sure someone somewhere in the vast virtual space, in which you mostly live, knows all about it."

"Ok, ok - I guess you're right. My only named, contemporary contact to all this was Albert Brunner, unless of course he was some sort of a fake. I'll search for his name and we'll see what happens."

"You seem to be quite certain of the fact that he 'was', but no longer 'is'."

"I'm not sure how to explain this to you, Jimmy, but I somehow feel that he was either killed or removed from the scene in some other way."

"All right, you do your search and I'll take my daughter to her baseball practice. I'll be back in half an hour."

Jimmy stood up and was ready to leave, but then hesitated for a moment and turned back to Alex. If Alex had been paying more attention, he would have seen an impish twinkle in his host's eye.

"You know, Alex, I think you may have missed a very important fact about Wakarusa which may be of key significance."

"What? What is it? – asked Alex impatiently.

"Well, Wakarusa happens to be the place Gayle Sayers calls home."

"Who the hell is Gayle Sayers?"

"Ah, my dear misguided Polish friend, I weep at your lack of football knowledge. Gayle Sayers used to be a running back for the Chicago Bears, well before you decided to ditch the reds in your country and come over here."

"So what are you saying? Gayle Sayers had something to do with all of this?"

"No, you Slavonic dimwit, I'm quite sure he had jack shit to do with all of this, but it's an interesting fact."

At this point Jimmy started laughing hysterically, betraying the fact that he was just poking fun at Alex's growing obsession with Wakarusa.

"I can see you haven't changed much." – said Alex, trying not to show that he was indeed a little bit amused.

About five minutes later Michael showed up in Jimmy's house. He told Alex all about the meeting he had with Kim. What followed was a rather animated conversation between the two of them about pros and cons of involving Kim in their exploits. Michael expressed his doubts in no uncertain terms.

"There's something weird about Kim's willingness to help us" – he said.

"What do you mean?"

"Well, why would she? What's in in for her?"

"Perhaps she just likes you."

"Yeah, right."

"Ok then, maybe she just thinks this stuff might by pretty important and it's her duty to do something about it."

"Sometimes you're such a sentimental slop that I want to cry and puke all at the same time. Anyway, I decided to check her out."

"What?"

"I asked Rick at the Tribune to get a little bio background on her."

"Michael, you're crazy. You actually talked to Rick?"

"Yes, but relax – I used my trash phone and he will say nothing to anybody. He is an absolute asshole, but I think I can rely on him."

"All right, but I don't understand what you are after. What possible significance could Kim's past have?"

"I have no idea, but I needed to do this. Anyway, I'll get this information tomorrow and then we'll meet her at her hotel."

"Fine."

While they were talking, Alex was constantly staring at his laptop and searching for any cyberspace traces of Albert Brunner. On about a tenth try he got a rather cryptic result on Google, apparently linked to a PDF file:

Field manual for spring exercise, A. Brunner, Wakarusa, Base 1.

The link was dead. But Alex certainly found what he was looking for.

Chapter 23

Police chief Oliver Louis Thompson hated his job. In fact he hated his job so much that he sometimes forgot to hate his life. As the main representative of 'the law' in Wakarusa, a town of utmost, dusty boredom, his duties consisted mainly of sitting in his office in a squeaky rocking chair and picking his nose. Sometimes his office phone rang, about twice a day on average, but the caller was almost always sergeant Willard Atkins who had the habit of dutifully informing his boss about blood curdling crime events such as drunks peeing profusely behind the house of Reverend Jack Whaley or unhinged youths terrorizing the god-fearing populace by jumping over all kinds of things on their bikes.

The last major crime Mr. Thompson had to deal with happened on the occasion of an astonishingly unexpected presidential visit in 2009. On the eve of this event his office was unceremoniously invaded by tall menacing guys wearing dark glasses and speaking constantly to their cuffs, as if there was something down there. They informed him that his authority was being suspended for 24 hours and that he could therefore quietly fuck off and not bother them.

Although Oliver was deeply offended, he never quite relinquished his post and – on his way home – noticed two suspicious characters trying to hang a big sign on the side of one of the houses in the center of Wakarusa. The sign read: 'Find your peace, Obama – go back to Africa or die'. Oliver, who had no particular political affiliations and astutely regarded events in Washington as a never-ending circus, gave chase. This was certainly a daring undertaking as he was a person of enormous girth and of weight commensurate with it. The two suspects were duly apprehended and delivered to the goons in dark glasses who thanked the police chief copiously and told him again to just fuck off.

However, that was all in the past. Now Oliver was sitting in his chair, reminiscing fondly about all kinds of other, more pleasant aspects of his police career. And then his phone rang.

"Atkins?" – he barked, sensing correctly that this was once again a call from his sergeant.

"Yeah, boss, this is Willard."

"I know. Now what?"

"Err... we have another problem with them damn Sunday soldiers at the Hawkins ranch."

"Oh, no – what is it now?"

"Well, apparently they threatened some hunters who accidentally strayed into their area and there was a confrontation involving weapons."

"Shit! Anybody got hurt?"

"No, no shots were fired, but I can't deal with this by myself anymore. Them guys are nuts."

"Which them guys? I mean, which guys?"

"The dumbshits patrolling the Hawkins ranch. I know they play war every second day, but shouldn't we like tell them to back off and stay away from people? Or at least tell them to hide their stupid guns?"

"Well, we don't want Charlton Heston types down here."

"Who the fuck is Charlton Heston?"

"Doesn't matter. Is everything all right now?"

"Yeah, but there's something else."

"What?"

"I'm not sure how to say it, but I think there's something special going on at that ranch."

"What do you mean?"

"Well, for one thing there are many more guards than usual. Also I saw a bunch of out of state cars driving into the compound - almost like a procession of them."

"From what states?"

"I didn't see all of them, but I caught a glimpse of some Colorado, Georgia, Illinois and Delaware plates."

"Well, Willard, as long as these guys don't shoot anybody or don't commit crimes, we need to leave them alone. Maybe they're having a party of some sort. But it's their land and they can do whatever they want."

"Ok, chief, but you need to know that their patrols are becoming more and more aggressive. The confrontation with the hunters is the third dust-up like this in only two weeks. And sooner or later someone will get hurt."

"So, what do you want me to do? Arrest them?"

"I dunno. Just saying..."

Oliver L. Thompson was pretty familiar with the Hawkins ranch and a bunch of weirdos running around it. Back in the 80's, after poor old Gregory Hawkins had died childless, the ranch was bought by some outsiders who quickly turned it into a secluded "exercise area". Oliver never quite understood what that meant, but since the new owners never caused any major trouble and kept largely to themselves, he stayed out of their way. At one point he got a call from an FBI agent who asked him a lot of questions about the ranch and people living there, but since he knew very little, the conversation didn't last long.

He was just about to hoist his enormous body frame off the chair to make a valiant attempt at standing up when the phone rang again. "Damn" – he thought, fully expecting Willard to strike again. It was indeed his sergeant, but this time he sounded hurried and anxious.

"Hey chief, this is Willard again."

"Thanks. I wouldn't have guessed."

"I just got a call from Sarah Goral - you know, the retired professor who lives out in the boonies."

148

"Yeah, I know who you mean. What did she want?"

"She found a dead body."

Oliver paused for a while trying to decide whether his subordinate was drunk or crazy.

"A dead body? In Wakarusa?"

"Yes. She told me she was walking across the field at the back of her house when she saw this guy just lying there."

"Who is it?"

"Well, that may be difficult to figure out. She says the body is all messed up and bloody and the face is just completely bashed in. Plus she is a bit hysterical, so it's difficult to understand what exactly is going on."

The chief was briefly lost for words. He couldn't even remember the last time he had to deal with a murder case, so he was trying to hastily assemble his rusty thoughts into some kind of police strategy that would make sense.

"All right, Willard" – he finally said – "I'll meet you at Goral's house in 15 minutes. Wait for me there and don't touch anything."

"All right, chief."

While what he said to his sergeant sounded very decisive and professional, the reality of the situation was decidedly different. The truth was Oliver had no idea what to do and was probably as panicked as Sarah. To begin with, he had no tools to investigate a murder, no forensic help of any sort within the radius of a hundred miles, and no personnel other than Willard and his part-time secretary Maggie who was an old cantankerous witch ignorant of any police work other than typing up parking tickets. As Oliver started driving out of town towards the Goral house, he also realized that he didn't have a single body bag, so he started calculating in his mind how many black garbage bags he would need to fashion a do-it-yourself body container.

Willard was waiting for him in the field, standing over the dead guy. Sarah was nowhere to be seen and the sergeant motioned towards the house when asked where she was. Oliver wasn't quite prepared for what he saw. He was looking at a person who was savagely beaten and did not have a recognizable face any more. His hands were tied behind his back, and one of his legs was grotesquely twisted away from the rest of the body, almost completely torn off. But strangely there were no other traces of anything around the victim – no tire tracks, no footprints, no nothing. It looked almost as if someone just dropped this cadaver straight from the sky.

"Did you see any papers on this poor bastard?" – asked Oliver.

"Well, no" – answered Willard who seemed somewhat taken aback - "You asked me not to touch anything, so I didn't. And looking at this mess, I don't think we'll find any ID on him."

"Yeah, you're probably right. And Sarah didn't see anybody around here, right? She just discovered the body lying in the field?"

"That's right. She didn't hear any noises, cars or anything else."

"Damn..." – said Chief Thompson philosophically while scratching his balding head.

With a heavy sigh he grabbed his cell phone out of his pocket and called his old school buddy in South Bend, Charlie Anderson, who worked as a coroner. He asked him to come to Wakarusa as soon as he possibly could. Charlie was surprised and wanted to know why, so Oliver told him everything and asked him for help in properly dealing with the body. Charlie was briefly incredulous, but then promised he would drive to Wakarusa immediately.

"All right, Willard, we need to cover this guy with something. I brought some plastic bags and duct tape. You do it and stay here until I come back with Charlie."

"Where are you going?

"First I'll go and talk to Sarah. Then back to the station – I need to make some calls and figure out what to do next."

Chief Thompson's interview with Sarah wasn't very long. She was obviously distraught and visibly trembled when answering questions.

"Ms. Goral, I know it's difficult for you, but I need to ask you about a few things." – he said cautiously – "Is that all right with you?"

She nodded.

"OK, so please first tell me at what time you discovered the corpse...err, I mean the body."

"I usually go for a morning walk across the field, and I did the same today. Must have been shortly after 9."

"All right then. Prior to that time did you see anybody around your house or out in the fields?"

"No."

"Were you inside the house until the moment you started your walk?"

"Yes."

"Hm... Did you hear any noises?"

"What do you mean?"

"Well... like voices, strange sounds..."

"No, just the freight train in the distance..."

"That's it?"

"Yes... Oh, and the crop duster?"

Chief Thompson suddenly got interested.

"Crop duster?"

"Yes, you know, the little planes. They fly low over the fields quite often around here."

"Right, except it's November so there are no crops to dust."

"I never even thought about that. Anyway, I heard a plane about half an hour before I left the house."

"But you didn't see it?"

"No."

"And did it sound like the plane was coming and going, or just flew past one time."

"It just flew over once, I think."

"Great. Thank you, Ms. Goral, you've been very helpful."

"Chief Thompson?" – said Sarah meekly.

"Yes."

"Do you know who this poor man was?"

"No, I don't. And please don't worry - I don't think you are in any danger out here."

Chapter 24

While Chief Thompson was bravely trying to do something about the first murder on his hands in years, Michael got up relatively early and drove to a nearby FedEx store where he got their fax number and immediately called his revolting friend Rick.

"Hey, it's Michael. Did you get the info I asked you for?"

There was a moment of silence suggesting that Rick was either seriously hyperventilating or unconscious.

"Rick?"

"Yeah, I'm here. Listen, I got the stuff for you, but I have serious doubts about all that. People around here are beginning to speculate that you got involved in something heavy or that you are dead."

"Which of these options would you prefer?"

"Oh, stop it. Everyone seems to have some theory about what happened to you."

"You didn't tell them anything, did you?"

"No, no. But there are all kinds of rumors circling around."

"Never mind that, Rick, everything we'll be over in a few days."

"Over? What do you mean?"

"I'll come back and tell you all about it. Or I won't, in which case it'll really be over."

"What?"

"Sorry. Just scratch all of that. Right now I'm going to give you a fax number and you go ahead and fax me what you got."

"All right. But it's just one paragraph."

"That's OK."

In a minute or so Michael was reading the single paragraph from Rick:

Federal Bureau of Investigation
Chicago Office
Special agent Kim Swanson
Status: on active duty
Basic background information:

Kim Swanson, born Kimberley Linda Brunner in Huntington, Indiana, May 5, 1973. Married Trent Swanson 2000, divorced 2004. Graduate of Indiana University. Joined FBI in Chicago 2007.

If the store clerk could see Michael's face staring through the front windows of the FedEx facility, he would probably think someone had just faxed him a death certificate of a close family member. The note was very terse, but obviously contained a bombshell piece of information. Michael read the paragraph over and over again as if trying to make sure that it wouldn't change into something a bit more positive on a third or fourth reading. Then he carefully folded the sheet of paper in two, put it in his pocket and went outside to meet a cold day that started throwing sleet at him.

He didn't exactly remember how he drove back to Jimmy's house, but once he got there he saw his host and Alex just finishing breakfast. He didn't have to say anything – they knew something was wrong. Therefore Michael just took the paper out of his pocket and placed it right in the middle of the table, between a plate of half-eaten scrambled eggs and a piece of toast, jagged by Alex's teeth. Then he slumped into a chair and waited for their friends' reaction.

"Where did you get this?" – asked Jimmy after a while.

"I had a friend of mine at the 'Tribune' contact an FBI insider."

"Is this reliable?"

"Absolutely... I am sorry to say."

Another long period of silence. Then Alex decided to throw a hail Mary.

"Well, it's still possible that Kim... or Linda... or whatever her name is... really chases the same people we are after and therefore is trying to help us..."

There was no point in continuing his thought, because he saw that his friends' faces were more or less telling him, in a wordless sort of way, 'shut the hell up!'.

"You can't be serious, Alex." – said Michael, this time using real spoken words – "After all, Albert the Dead's last words were 'beware of Linda', and it so happens that her birth name is the same as his – Brunner."

"It all makes sense." – said Jimmy with a surprising air of certainty.

"What does?" – asked Michael.

"Well, I think it would be fair to assume that Linda is the daughter of Albert Brunner and therefore the granddaughter of Karl Brunner, the original Nazi plug in Fort Wayne. Since I never attended their family dinners, I am in no position to say what happened to their cozy little nest in Midwest, but it's quite possible that at some point Albert came to the conclusion that he is surrounded by dangerous, extremist nitwits, and started working against them. He said as much in his role of Deep Face. At the same time, his long-legged daughter continued working with the crazies, under the cover of the FBI, probably not realizing that her dad had a change of heart."

"Wait a second" – said Michael – "that would explain why she was so rattled when I told her during our conversation in Walmart that we'd been talking to some guy 'on the inside' of the plot, whatever the plot may be. I doubt she suspected her father, but she may have known there was a mole within their organization".

Alex was beginning to understand the scale of the problem they were facing.

"So, what you're saying is that she is a rogue FBI agent who is after us at the behest of her real bosses who are planning to do something really bad."

"Right" – added Jimmy with shamelessly dishonest cheerfulness – "and one of these bad things, outside of blowing up America, might be a prior act of getting rid of us. Permanently."

"But why would they want to kill us?" – asked Alex while looking at Jimmy and probably hoping for some rational refutation of any murderous designs against them – "All we have is the Wrocław papers, and we still have no idea what is going to happen, how, and exactly when."

"True, but they must feel we are getting dangerously close. In fact, they probably thought so much earlier, at the time you two were skipping Chicago. Why else would they send the sex bomb after you?"

"You are certainly right about that." – said Michael almost wistfully – "No one has sent a sex bomb after me ever before. However, I am planning to send myself after her."

Both Alex and Jimmy looked at him dejectedly, almost pleading with him not to say what he was just about to say. It didn't help.

"Tomorrow morning I'm going to see her in her hotel room and I will confront her with all we know."

"Are you out of your mind?" – said his friend Alex.

"Why not? What's she going to do – shoot me in the head? I just want to see what happens once she realizes we know what we know".

"And then what?"

"No idea. We'll see what her reaction is. You can come with me if you want."

Alex turned away from his friends and started pacing along one of the edges of the room. Then he faced them again and made a startling announcement.

"I'm flying to Atlanta in a couple of hours."

"What?" – exclaimed Jimmy and Michael almost simultaneously.

"I'm going to check out this Georgia monument and I'll be back tomorrow morning."

It was becoming apparent that Jimmy was seriously considering throwing both of his guests out onto the street.

"Can I be honest with you?" – he asked.

"Sure." – said Alex.

"Good. You're both fucking idiots. One of you is going to meet some Nazi bitch, probably plotting to end the world as we know it, and ready to do whatever fascists are ready to do whenever they run out of options. And you, Alex, are planning to go and see a collection of stinking rocks in the middle of nowhere with the hope of finding a connection between the alignment of stars, the alignment of dog shit northeast of Athens, and the Wakarusa plot to abolish America. Now, if this isn't a recipe for success, I don't know what is."

"OK, tell us how you really feel" – said Alex after a moment of nervous silence. "Look" – he continued – "I don't expect to find anything in Georgia, but what other options do we have? Albert said something was going to happen or someone was going to be there at a specific time, so why not check it out? I realize this may not be the monument Deep Face meant, but we'll never know unless I go. I'm flying direct from here to Atlanta and I'll be back at around 9 am tomorrow".

"By which time I'll be going to see Linda."

Michael and Alex looked at Jimmy almost imploringly, waiting for any signal which might suggest that he would continue to work with them, their being 'fucking idiots' notwithstanding. Jimmy sat motionlessly in his favorite armchair and said nothing. Then he stood up, walked up to them, and offered them a truce.

"OK. Go and do your crazy shit, and then let's decide how to proceed. My wife is coming home on Thanksgiving morning, and I'd really like her to come back to the same reality she left."

"Thanks, Jimmy." – said Michael.

"Nothing to thank me for. Anyway, I need to go to work. Tomorrow I'm taking a day off, so I'll be here when you get back, Alex. Perhaps when Michael returns, assuming we will ever see him again, we can sit down over lunch and plan how to finish Hitler off for the second time in less than a hundred years."

"It's a deal." – said Alex who was already busy stuffing random pieces of garments into a duffel bag and searching for his electronic ticket printout – "And Michael, since you have the rest of the day to yourself, perhaps you could zero in on Wakarusa. You know, like where is this damn compound, what shows on Google Earth, any history behind it, etc."

"OK, will do. Have a nice trip and try not to cause a world war."

"I'll do my very best."

Chapter 25

Alex had no problem with finding the Georgia Guidestones monument. As he was driving north on Hartwell Highway, away from the town of Elberton, he suddenly found himself in northern Georgia hilly country – a wide expanse of land peppered with undulating forests and interrupted here and there with open fields and ploughed plots waiting for spring. And then to his right he suddenly saw an intriguing structure which rose above the horizon in an awkward kind of way, as if it didn't really belong there.

Many years earlier Alex had visited Stonehenge in England during a short European trip. Back then the mysterious circle of rocks made a big impression on him, primarily because of the fact that scientists never really figured out what this whole thing was and why it had been built on that spot. On top of that, it was a mystery that was perhaps 5 thousand years old.

The minute Alex saw the Georgia Guidestones, he came to the conclusion that this was no Stonehenge. There was something almost pathetic about four big, vertical slabs of granite shooting up from a barren field just an hour's drive from Atlanta. And, as Alex very well remembered, it had been constructed a few decades earlier by some secretive guy whose motives remained unknown.

Undeterred, Alex drove up to the entrance gate where he encountered an incredibly fat Georgian guy who was manning, or rather filling, a small booth. He turned out to be a very pleasant introduction to the monument area.

"Hello there!" – he roared cheerfully.

"Hi. Is there an entrance fee for this?"

"Nope, just go on right ahead."

"Thanks. Hey, if I wanted to learn a few things about this place, who should I talk to you."

"Not me, for sure. But look down there, a bit to your left. Do you see a ranger's hat attached to a very small person?"

"Yes."

"This is Karolina Obalek. She is a delightful kid. A student in Athens, but she works as our part-time park ranger. She knows more or less everything about the monument."

"Great. Thanks."

As Alex started driving away, his newly minted friend in the booth flashed a big smile at him which suggested that either dentists were in extremely short supply in this part of the world or that they were all murderous heathens, universally despised by the toothless population. Alex drove into a small, gravel covered parking lot, got out of the car and started walking slowly around the monument. He realized very quickly that his first impressions of the monument were a bit premature. The vertical granite slabs, crowned with a rectangular rock, were pretty imposing when viewed from up close. It was about 4:30 pm and the Georgia sun, almost ready to retire for the night, was shooting beams of golden light at the structure at very acute angles, resulting in extremely intricate shadows sprawling all over the area. He marveled at the incomprehensible inscriptions on each of the slabs and stared aimlessly upward to see if any of this stuff aligned with the sun or – for that matter – with anything else. And he was constantly watching Karolina. Although there were only a few visitors at the monument, a small group of them gathered around her and listened attentively to what she was saying. Alex was too far away to hear anything, so he waited for his chance to approach the park ranger. His chance came a few minutes later when most visitors left.

"Excuse me" – he said – "are you Karolina?"

The young woman turned abruptly towards him and eyed him with a bit of suspicion. Alex couldn't help noticing that she looked a bit out of place in her ranger's uniform which seemed to be about two sizes too large, probably because nobody makes park ranger's uniforms in kid sizes.

"Yes, I am Karolina, and I congratulate you on pronouncing my first name correctly."

"You mean most people butcher it?"

"Yes, they certainly do. It's Polish, you know."

"I do. I'm Polish."

"Ah, that would explain your surprising acumen. I'm also sort of Polish. But anyway, what can I do for you?"

"Well, the guy at the entrance told me that you more or less know everything about this place."

"What, Joel? He is such a big liar."

"You mean you really don't know that much."

"Well no, I don't mean that. Just kidding. I know a great deal. What would you like to know?"

"Well, for a start, what are all these languages on the slabs and what do these writings mean?"

"Oh, good. I was afraid you were going to ask me more complicated questions."

"You mean I've just disappointed you with my primitivism."

Karolina looked at him with a little playful twinkle in her eye.

"Tell me, sir, what are you really after?"

"OK, I'll come straight to the point. Is this place in any way fascist?"

"What? I'm not sure what you mean."

"Well, can this monument be interpreted by some misguided individuals as being a symbol for the far right."

Karolina thought for a brief moment.

"I guess it depends on the level of misguidance. But I would say someone would have to be a complete nut to interpret this place in such a way."

"Why?"

"The message on these slabs, which has been inscribed in English, Spanish, Swahili, Hindi, Hebrew, Arabic, Chinese and Russian, is this wishy-washy liberal manifesto advocating world peace, closeness to nature, and effective population control. Somehow I don't think this could be a part of 'Mein Kampf'. And, by the way, there is no German version – Hitler would have been mortified.

Alex was becoming acutely aware of the fact that in some abstruse way Karolina was making fun of him, although she was doing it very diplomatically. The problem facing him was that his next round of questions could show him to be a complete idiot.

"So what happens here at 5:15 pm?" – he asked, feeling like a man who has just jumped off a plane without a parachute.

Karolina was noticeably puzzled. She looked at this middle-aged man with growing anxiety, and probably thought he was not feeling very well or just lost track of reality. An obvious alternative was that he was just crazy.

"I'm not sure I understand what you mean." – she said very cautiously.

"I know it sounds strange, but isn't this place supposed to be, among other things, some sort of a sundial which might display information depending on the time of day, light angle, etc.?"

"Well, I hate to disappoint you, but not really. It is a sundial of sorts, but a pretty lame one. Otherwise, the sun shows up, with its usual Georgian inevitability, and then it goes down. There are shadows, reflections and all that, but nothing happens beyond that. So, going back to your question, at 5:15 pm absolutely nothing happens, very much like nothing happens at 5:14, or – for that matter – at 4:59. Oh, and the most shocking thing is that nothing is going to happen at 5:16 either."

Alex couldn't help laughing at Karolina's dry wit.

"OK, I get it, you think I am not quite 'there'."

"If by 'there' you mean 'among other sane people', you may have a point."

"Do you get all this derision from your park ranger training?"

"No, it's all self-taught."

"OK, let me ask you a different question. Do you see organized gatherings of people around here, like demonstrations, protests, or something like that."

"No, I've never seen any such thing. Just a steady, if weak, stream of visitors."

"Acts of vandalism?"

"I think there was one incident of defacing these stones, but it was a long time ago."

"OK, finally then, is it true that no one really knows to this day who financed this monument and what its purpose might be?"

"That's right. The guy who wanted this to be built is known as Robert Christian, but it wasn't his real name. There have been all kinds of theories about what these slabs might mean, but it's all sheer speculation. My personal feeling is that the Georgia Guidestones are here so that people like you can come to see them and ask weird questions of part-time park rangers."

Alex smiled and nodded his head in acknowledgment of being chastised by well-deserved sarcasm.

"Are you studying to become a lawyer, by any chance?"

"On no, I am way too intelligent for that."

"I would have to agree with that... Anyway, Karolina, thank you very much for your help. It was great to meet you. I'll hang around here until 5:15 to see for myself that nothing happens."

"Go ahead. Unfortunately I won't be a witness to your non-discovery, because I'm off duty in exactly two minutes. However, if you see something earth shattering, I'm counting on you to let me know. Have a good evening... Oh, wait, before I go, can I ask **you** a question for a change?"

"Sure."

"Why are you here? What is it that you're looking for?"

"Oh, it's a long and convoluted story, and I'm not even sure I'm in the right place."

"Somehow I have a feeling you are."

Alex gave her a weird, puzzled look.

"Really? How could you possibly know?"

Karolina smiled faintly, waved to him, and walked slowly away. He was left with a very strange feeling of having just talked to a daughter he never had.

The monument was basked in the orange light of the fast approaching sunset. There were only a few people left around the slabs – some standing and reading the inscriptions, some sitting on benches and just gazing at the strange structure. Alex started walking slowly around the monument, looking closely at every possible detail. Then he stood in front of the English version of the 'commandments' and read laboriously through them. He silently agreed with Karolina's term 'wishy-washy liberal manifesto'. It seemed to him that whoever put these words together must have been light years away from any right-wing radicalism. "So what the hell am I doing here?" – Alex asked himself.

"What are you doing here? – asked Joel, the friendly, oversized gatekeeper of the monument grounds.

Alex was briefly startled.

"Err, I was just hoping to spend a few minutes more so that I can finish reading this."

"Technically we close at 5 pm, but I can give you about a quarter of an hour before I really need to send everyone home."

"You close? How's that possible? There are no fences around here and after you leave and have dinner in the evening anybody can just walk in."

"You're a Yank, aren't you?"

"What?"

"Well, you know, you are from up there... the north."

Alex suddenly felt like general Sherman's troops might be attacking any minute on their way to Savannah.

"Depends what you mean by the north" – he said slyly – "I'm more of a mid-western Polish Yank type."

164

This time it was Joel's time to be stumped. Alex quickly came to the rescue of his perplexed buddy.

"Never mind that, it doesn't matter. Why is my being a Yank so obvious to you?"

"Well, first, you speak funny. But that's not really it. You said there were no fences around here, which is true. But there is a sign at my booth that says this place closes at 5 pm. And there is the official booth. It means to the locals that there is a fence, except it's not visible, and that after 5 pm this place is off limits. So after 5 nobody hangs around here except for Yanks and foreigners who don't know any better."

"I see. So how often is this invisible fence being violated by fools like me?"

"Oh, don't be so hard on yourself" – said Joel almost jovially – "People come here from all kinds of places and they don't pay any attention to anything. And I must tell you that I'm really fed up with some of these jerks, especially the recent wave of smartly dressed idiots who just stand there and stare at this pile of shit, err... I mean rocks, as if they expected something to suddenly spring up from there."

"What do you mean?" – asked Alex, trying to mask his suddenly awakened curiosity.

"Well, I don't know what it is, but for the past few months there's been a steady stream of visitors who are all well-dressed, middle-aged gentlemen, looking at the monument at around this time of the afternoon, very much like you - except you're not well-dressed."

"Thank you. But what do they do here?"

"That's the thing. I have no clue. They circle around the monument, lean over some crap, circle some more, and leave. And they all look a bit out of place, if you know what I mean.

"I'm not sure I do."

"It's difficult to explain, but they don't look like tourists and they behave strangely."

"Do they ever cause any trouble?"

165

"Hell, no. But that's another thing – they almost never say anything to anybody."

"Well, that's shocking... Do you see any of these guys here right now?"

"No, not today."

"OK, listen Joel, can I hang around for a few minutes?"

"Sure. But remember that we're technically closed. And don't trip over our fence on your way out."

"OK, thanks. I promise I'll be very careful."

Joel gave him a chuckle worthy of John Cleese and his Python crew.

Alex glanced at his watch – it was 5:13. He completed another circle around the monument, looked up towards the top of the four vertical slabs and then down on the little flat surface at the bottom. Nothing. Just the bright sunlight and very long shadows. At 5:15 he backed away from the monument to have a wider view. According to Albert, if such a person ever existed, he had exactly two minutes to see something, although he had absolutely no idea what. He approached the monument once again and, batting his eyes because of the bright light, took another look. And then he saw it.

At one of the corners of the bottom flat slab he noticed a bright spot which looked almost like an area illuminated by a concentrated and well-directed beam. He took a few steps forward and looked down. The bright spot was obviously a projection of some sort, but he couldn't figure out its source, nor did he see anything on any of the slabs that might be in some way connected to the projected image. And the image was a very simple message:

It's time – Nov. 25th, 2010, 11 am.

At exactly 5:17 the message disappeared.

Chapter 26

After his brief talk with Mrs. Goral, Chief Thompson became convinced, admittedly on rather flimsy grounds, that the mangled body of an unknown person was unceremoniously dumped from a passing plane onto an empty field under his police jurisdiction. He shared his suspicions with Charlie who had just come back to Wakarusa with preliminary autopsy report. They were having lunch at Raymond's Restaurant & Lounge, one of the few culinary establishments catering to the local populace.

"So this poor guy was just beaten to death?" – asked the chief.

"It seems so. There are no knife or bullet wounds – just lots of broken bones. And his head was hit repeatedly with some blunt object... One more thing – he had his hands tied behind his back as he was being beaten."

"Oh, that's just great. And we still have no idea who this is?"

"Nope. No papers on the body, and his fingerprints don't match any criminals. I sent some DNA stuff to a crime lab in Chicago, but we won't get results for days."

"And you can't confirm that he was dumped on the field from some height, right?"

"Right. Given the fact that the soil is pretty soft right now, and that the drop would have probably occurred from a low altitude, you can't pinpoint any fall damage to a completely messed up body.

Chief Thompson looked somewhat despondent despite the fact that a large steak, topped with all kinds of cardiovascular dangers, was just placed in front of him by their waitress.

"So, what do you think about my airplane theory?" – he asked.

"Well, if you're sure that there were no tracks or footprints around the body, and if Ms. Goral's story about the plane is true, you may have a point. However, if this guy was dropped from a plane, your situation gets even more complicated in two ways."

"I'm not sure I want to hear that."

"First, we have to assume that it had to be a small plane, like a Cessna, or something similar. That means the body could have been flown in from as far away as 500 miles, from some other state. I don't know the exact time of death yet, but it looks like we're dealing here with – if you pardon me this unappealing term over lunch – a fresh corpse. So it seems the guy was killed and then almost immediately put on a plane bound for some random dumping ground. Who the hell knows where this murder occurred?"

"And second?"

"If at some point it turns out that the body was transported over state lines, we are then dealing with a federal crime, and that means sooner or later some FBI types will show up here and start breathing down your neck."

"Shit. That's all I need... So what do you think I should do?"

"I've no idea. For the time being you should probably wait for the full autopsy stuff and the DNA test results."

Chief Thompson's cell phone rang with Willard-like urgency.

"What?" – barked the chief, sensing the usual phone futility.

"Nothing, chief." – said Willard - "Just letting you know I scoured Mrs. Goral's field and I found no trace of anybody or anything out there - except our tracks, of course."

"OK, good job... Hey, Willard, can I ask you a question?"

"Sure, chief."

"Do you know of anybody around here that owns a small plane, like a Cessna or something?"

"What? You're flying somewhere?"

"No, goddamn it, just answer the stinking question."

"All right, calm down... Let's see... I know there's a small airstrip in Mishawaka and another one in Goshen. There must have a few small airplanes at both of these places".

"Anybody closer than that?"

"No, nobody in Wakarusa or close to it... unless you believe in gossip."

"What the hell do you mean?"

"Boy, you seem to be very edgy today, chief?"

"Shit, Willard, we've just had a guy butchered in this town, and this will most likely result in a lot of unwelcome crap for both of us, so don't be too fucking concerned about my state of mind. I'm ordering you to shut up and to tell me what you mean by gossip."

"How can I first shut up and then tell you anything?"

Chief Thompson briefly entertained the idea of terminating his trusted sergeant with extreme prejudice by impaling him on the broken lamppost which had stood uselessly for the past ten years in the town center. But then he collected his rattled wits around the task at hand and continued the conversation.

"OK, let's get back to what you said about believing in gossip. What did you mean by that?"

"Well, from time to time people claim that there is some kind of a plane at the Hawkins ranch."

"What? How do they know?"

"They don't know. Nobody knows."

"Has anybody ever seen anything flying out of there?"

"Not to my knowledge."

"That's just fantastic... Listen, go back to the station and stay there until I come back."

"OK, chief. And try to get some rest or something."

Charlie listened to his lunch companion's conversation with varying degrees of intensity, but continued to eat his hamburger and minding his own business. He was sure Chief Thompson would share some of his thoughts as soon as he finished the call or as soon as he threw his cell phone through the restaurant's window. He was not disappointed.

"I hate this shit." – the chief said, leaving a lot of room for semantic interpretation.

"You hate what shit?" – asked Charlie.

"Well, it's possible that this group of total jackasses, living a bit out of town on an old farm ranch, might have a small plane."

"So?"

"So, I will have to go there and ask them about this. That's what I hate."

"Why?"

"Because they're rude, gun-toting idiots who think they will one day save the state of Indiana from UN communist takeover by shooting everyone in sight. Every single time I went to that place in the past, for whatever reason, I got this 'we don't recognize any of your authority' bullshit from them."

"Do you think they had anything to do with this dead guy?"

"I doubt it. But I still need to check it out."

"OK, Oliver, I have to start on my way back. I'll let you know as soon as I have more info from the full autopsy."

"Great, thanks Charlie."

Having said goodbye to his friend, Chief Thompson got into his car, stopped by his office to pick up half-asleep Willard, and then drove to the Hawkins ranch, expecting the worst. As he veered off the main road onto a dusty unpaved dirt path leading towards the main gate of the complex, he suddenly remembered the old days, back when old Gregory Hawkins was still on his ranch. He was a very gregarious fellow who would invite people, a much younger Oliver included, to his house to sample the products of his land – fresh tomatoes, cabbages, lettuce, melons, and apples. Each Halloween he would also invite local kids to his pumpkin patch. But then he died and everything changed dramatically.

"Here we are." – said Willard, yanking his boss brusquely out of his daydreaming.

They were indeed there. Their car stopped in front of a weirdly constructed barricade that looked like a cross between railroad gates and an abandoned East German border post. Guarding this twisted monstrosity were too oversized goons, dressed in paramilitary uniforms, who had small semi-automatic guns and who both wore dark glasses, even though it was a murky, damp November day. One of them stepped right in front of the car and raised his hand, signaling that further progress was not going to be possible.

"Here goes nothing." – muttered the chief to himself, as he struggled fearlessly to lift his XXL body out of the vehicle.

"Stay in the car, Willard. I'll handle this." – he said to his sergeant who seemed to be greatly relieved that he actually didn't have to do anything.

Chief Thompson walked towards one of the guards, keeping a keen eye on the other one, who was staying at the back and 'manning' the barricade.

"Hello there. How are you doing today, sir?" – he said with phony cheeriness.

"Everything is fine here." – said the guard, sounding terribly goonish and strangely defensive.

"Well, I didn't say anything was wrong, did I? Anyway, I need to talk to someone in charge here. Like your boss or something."

"Why?"

"Because I need to ask him or her a few simple questions about an investigation I'm conducting."

"What investigation?"

The chief was already getting quite irritated.

"I'd say that's none of your business, son." – he said, almost exploding with anger.

"I don't think he is available right now."

"Is that right? I'll tell you what. Either you get his ass over here right now or I'm going to ram through this wooden pile of crap you're guarding and show up at his doorstep. You can of

171

course shoot me, but I think a few people in Wakarusa might actually notice that their police chief is missing."

The goon looked at the chief with sheer disdain.

"Wait here." – he said.

He abruptly turned around, walked over to the other guy, and whispered something to him. Chief Thompson could see that one of them took a walkie-talkie out of his pocket and was having some sort of an argument with whoever was on the other side of the conversation. This went on for a few minutes, which lulled Willard, still stuck in the police cruiser, back to sleep.

Finally the guard returned to Chief Thompson.

"OK, a commanding officer will be here shortly." – he said.

Sure enough after a few minutes a Humvee emerged from some deep recesses of the compound and screeched to a halt just on the other side of the mock Berlin Wall. Out came a tall, balding man in his early fifties, dressed in a rather incongruous looking uniform, adorned with all kinds of insignia, emblems and stars. To some degree he looked like a totally white version of Idi Amin Dada, the long deceased ruler of Uganda. He had a semi-automatic weapon of some sort slung over his shoulder. The man stood by his car for a while and talked to his driver. Then he walked briskly to Chief Thompson and greeted him with a military salute.

"Hello, sir. I'm Major Travis Prescott Jr." – he said pompously. "What can I do for you?"

If his intention was to impress the guest, he failed miserably.

"Hi, I'm Lieutenant General Oliver Thompson Sr. of the Wakarusa Police Light Brigade." – answered the chief, his voice seething with undisguised scorn. "I hate to drag you away from your everyday duties, which – I'm sure – are of utmost importance, but I need to ask you a few questions about an investigation I'm conducting."

Major Prescott seemed to be a bit baffled.

"Investigation? Whatever it is you are investigating, how can I have anything to do with it?"

"I didn't say you had anything to do with it. However, it would be helpful if you could tell me if you guys have a small plane on these premises."

There was a moment of rather tense silence during which Major Prescott seemed to have been weighing hurriedly all kinds of elocutionary options.

"Yes, we do." – he then said rather unexpectedly.

"What kind of a plane?"

"Oh, it's just an old Cessna which we got a bunch of years ago. But what's the point of these questions, if I may ask?"

"Never mind that. Has this plane been used in recent days – I mean, was it flown anywhere?"

It was obvious to Chief Thompson that Prescott was getting increasingly nervous.

"Oh no, we never use this thing anymore." – he said.

"I'd like to see it."

"Why?"

"I'm sorry, but this is an active investigation, and I'm not at liberty to say."

"Look, unless you tell me what it's all about, you're not looking at anything inside this compound."

"Really? OK, then. I'm investigating a murder and I have reason to believe that the body of the victim was transported on board of a small plane. So, once again, I need to have a look at your plane."

"That's not going to happen." – blurted out Prescott while suddenly glancing furtively at the two guards, loitering around his Humvee, as if trying to summon their help.

"Why not?"

"We are conducting some important business here and we're not going to be distracted by this stuff."

"What important business? A communal squirrel shoot? Beer can target practice? Or is it a hotdog eating competition?"

"That's none of your business. If you want to see the plane, come back with a court order. I'm sure you can get it."

Chief Thompson gave Major Prescott a very long, hard look. He saw a man who was doing his best to get rid of him without provoking a major incident. He also saw someone strangely stressed out, almost panicky, although not in a way that would be immediately obvious to a casual observer.

"Well, thanks for your non-cooperation" – said the chief – "I'll be back with the court papers, so you'd better get that plane ready."

Chief Thompson got back in his car, thumped Willard on his head to wake him up, and told him to drive back to town. Although he didn't get to see the plane, he was almost certain that the body in Ms. Goral's field came from the Hawkins ranch.

Chapter 27

When Alex got back from Georgia and showed up at Jimmy's place shortly after 9 am, Michael was already gone. Their host was sitting in the kitchen, munching on the remnants of his breakfast and watching the news.

"Hi, Alex." – he said cheerfully.

"Hi. I need a beer."

"At nine in the morning?"

"It's 3 pm in Europe – they're already drinking."

"Excellent point. Pour me one too. I assume you need a beer, because you wasted a day rummaging through some below-the-bible-belt territory to find zilch."

"Wrong. I found the exact date and time of whatever it is that's going to happen."

Jimmy was surprised enough to briefly arrest the movement of a piece of homemade sausage traveling to his mouth on a fork.

"Really? How did you manage to do that? How much time do we have?"

"Wait, wait. I don't want to have to tell the same story twice. Wasn't Michael supposed to be back by now?"

"I don't know. He left before I got up. Maybe he's making out with the feminazi James Bond."

"Yeah, right. It wouldn't take him that long... Here's your beer."

Alex joined Jimmy at the kitchen table and they both relaxed a bit while talking about the ever so distant prospects of the Cubs winning the World Series at some point in the 21st century. As

Jimmy was just about to launch a major statistical analysis disproving the curse of Billy the Goat, Michael stormed through the front door, veered towards the kitchen in a rather violent manner, and stood in front of them trembling with excitement.

"Hey, what's wrong, Michael?" – asked Alex.

"Nothing. Listen, we have very little time."

"Little time for what? Michael, please sit down and try to relax. Tell us what happened with Linda."

"Never mind that. I'll tell you later. I think she'll be here any minute."

"What? Linda? What the hell for?"

"Listen, guys. Listen very carefully. She'll show up here very soon. I don't have time to explain, but I need to ask you not to panic no matter what happens."

Alex and Jimmy looked at each other with obvious bewilderment.

"What's supposed to happen?" – asked Jimmy.

"I don't know. Maybe nothing will happen. But stay calm no matter what and let me handle this."

Both Jimmy and Alex had a little bit of a problem with letting Michael handle whatever it was he was going to handle, because both of them noticed that his hands trembled a bit and he was obviously distraught about something. But there was no time for further deliberations. The doorbell rang. Michael stepped out of the kitchen and soon came back with Linda who proceeded to introduce herself to Alex and Jimmy. They were all standing awkwardly around a small table as if waiting for something to happen.

"It's great to finally meet all of you." – Linda said with a faint smile on her face.

"So, do you want to be called Linda or Kim?" – asked Alex.

She looked at them intently for a few seconds while backing away from the table towards the kitchen door.

"It doesn't matter what you call me. I'm afraid our acquaintanceship will not last long."

While uttering these ominous words, she suddenly reached into her handbag and produced a gun with a grey silencer attached to it. All three men turned ashen white and instinctively moved away from the weapon which was already pointed at them.

"Did you come here to kill us?" – asked Michael. His friends noticed with surprise that his voice sounded strong, almost defiant, which was inexplicable, given the dire position they found themselves in.

"Probably. I'm still waiting for the proper order." – she said calmly.

"From the fuehrer, no doubt." – said Michael.

"Very funny. Come on, boys, let's go down to the basement."

She followed them down the stairs and told them to sit on the floor by the back wall.

"Would this be a good moment not to panic?" – muttered Alex to Michael.

"We'll see." – Michael replied.

Linda paced around the room, obviously waiting for something. Michael once again surprised his friends.

"Hey, Linda, since we're still waiting for your orders to put bullets in our heads, why don't you tell us what exactly happened in Belize and why."

Linda seemed to consider the pros and cons of satisfying this request, but eventually came to the conclusion that there was no harm in spilling some beans to the condemned.

"I think you already know most of it." – she said – "Krugman betrayed us and was going to screw everything up, so we sent a team over there to take care of him. Unfortunately for you, in his apartment we found a copy of the letter he sent to Chicago and very shortly afterwards we discovered that you and Alex went to Poland in search of the damn papers."

"So why didn't you go after us?"

"Well, we did, in a way. We contacted our Czech brothers and asked them to deal with this problem, but the idiots they sent screwed it up completely. First you beat them to the papers underground, and then they missed completely your escape to Dresden. They also tried to scare you off by calling the Breslau police and branding you as smugglers, but obviously it didn't work. The only thing these jerks did right was to get to the Pohradniček place before you."

"So why kill us?"

"That's not something I decide. You had your chance to live. If we'd managed to get the papers before you left Chicago, you would've possibly been just beaten up or perhaps crippled. But once you got to Fort Wayne and started getting too close to the center of our operation, my bosses got pretty worried. Anyway, it doesn't matter anymore. You're too late".

"So what exactly is going to happen on Thanksgiving?" – asked Alex.

Linda was at pains to hide her surprise.

"So you also know the date. Hmm, just as well you won't be able to disclose it to anybody. As to what's going to happen, unfortunately you won't live long enough to see."

"Neither did your father." – said Michael.

"What?"

"Your father Albert. I think your Nazi buddies murdered him."

Linda abruptly stopped her pacing and went up to Michael, leaning over him and pointing her gun straight at his head.

"You stupid jerk, do you really think you can get me rattled by such idiotic tricks? My father is very much alive and waiting for the coming days of glory."

"Sure. Except he may be waiting for his days of glory in his grave. He was Alex's Facebook informer and in his last communication with him he said he was just about to be killed."

"You're lying, you damn faggot!" – screamed Linda.

"Faggot? You obviously know more about my sexual life than I do."

"Shut the fuck up. Just keep your mouth shut."

Alex and Jimmy realized that their friend was playing some sort of a desperate game, but had no idea where all of this was going and whether any of this bravado could possibly prevent them from lying in a pool of blood in just a few minutes. But Jimmy decided to join in, just to test the waters. He also wanted to drag Linda and her gun away from Michael's head.

"Hey, Linda."

"What?" – she snapped, backing away from Michael.

"I'm just curious. Do you have a swastika embossed on your Nazi ass?"

Linda looked at him and smiled in a weird sort of way. It was the kind of smile people produce when they know they are in absolute control and can do whatever they want. And she certainly was in control.

"Come over here and find out for yourself." – she said mockingly.

"No, thank you. Once you see one Nazi ass, you've seen them all. I want the first Nazi ass I ever see to be of much better quality than yours. But anyway, are you really an FBI agent?"

Linda eyed him briefly with evident hatred, but - for reasons known only to her – she didn't take the bait and stayed away from further discussing her rear bodily parts.

"Sure. I'm totally legit" – she said – "We are everywhere. But don't worry – come December FBI will be known as Bureau of National Security."

"I'm sure it will. Why not something like Kim's Gulag Bureau? At least your abbreviation will be instantly recognizable."

"You're all so dumb. You can't even begin to understand our mission and its importance for this country."

"How many people do you need to kill to accomplish your glorious mission? I'm sure it's not going to be just us, but thousands."

"It doesn't matter."

"Of course it doesn't. It didn't matter to your patron Adolf, did it?"

"No it didn't, and that's why he was a great man. He knew what needed to be done and he tried to do it. And now we'll finally finish the job."

"I doubt it." – said Michael with baffling conviction in his voice.

Linda looked at him with disdain, but didn't have time to react – the cell phone in her handbag started ringing. She backed away from them and stood in the remote corner of the basement room. They could hear her whispering something in German to someone who could possibly be a remote henchman.

"Listen, guys" – said Michael quietly – "stay calm, I think we're going to be OK".

"You think we're going to be OK?" – asked Alex, sounding incredulous and panicked.

"I'm always very calm before dying." – said Jimmy.

Linda finished her phone conversation. She once again approached them and told them to stand up and face her. She was still brandishing her gun.

"Sorry, boys. Our National Executive Council has decided that all three of you constitute a threat to our security and therefore need to be eliminated. I'm afraid I'm going to have to shoot you. Please stand with your backs tight against the wall. Oh, and Jimmy, for that nasty comment about my ass, you're going to die first."

"Wait" – said Michael – "don't we get a last wish... you know, like in that movie with Richard Pryor, 'See No Evil, Hear No Evil' or something, when he asks 'would a fuck be out of the question?' and the woman with the gun says 'no'".

Jimmy and Alex were noticeably shocked. Faced with imminent death, they did not have the luxury of dissecting analytically Michael's madness, but they were pretty sure it would feature prominently in their post mortems. On the other hand, Linda was unforgiving.

"Sorry" – she said – "a last-wish fuck is out of the question."

With these terse words she aimed the gun at Jimmy's skull and pulled the trigger. There was a very loud click after which

Jimmy was still alive and did not appear to have a large hole between his eyes. Linda tried three more times, but her gun produced nothing but harmless noises. Bewildered, she looked down at her weapon and jiggled something on it, but her time was up. All three men quickly lunged towards her as if acting on some precisely timed order. In no time at all Linda was on the floor, face down, with Alex literally sitting on her and Michael holding both of her hands behind her back. Strangely enough, she put up no struggle and all of these events evolved in almost total silence. Until Michael spoke.

"Hey, Jimmy, we need to restrain her somehow."

Jimmy was standing over both of them and seemed to be a bit lost for words.

"Come on, man, don't you have any experience in tying up women?"

"Well, not in this context." – said Jimmy sheepishly.

"Oh, for Christ's sake, go and get some duct tape."

Eventually they managed to tape together her legs and hands. Then they sat her on the couch. She was quiet, if somewhat surprised, but they could see in her eyes that she thought she still held all the cards in her hands. In fact, she watched them with an air of utmost contempt painted all over her face.

"So you think you're winning, right?" – she said almost laughing.

"Shut up." – said Alex.

"No, I won't. Come on, face it. You have no chance. We are on the verge of our greatest triumph, and there's nothing you can do to stop it. Very shortly you'll be begging us for mercy."

"Do you have some more of that duct tape?" – asked Alex looking at Jimmy.

"Yeah."

"Tape her fucking mouth and let's go upstairs."

Chapter 28

By all accounts, this particular morning at the Klonowski house had not gone according to the usual daily routine which included such non-dramatic events as taking the dogs for a walk, watching squirrels steal bird feed, and observing neighbors doing all kinds of weird things. Normally young women, be it FBI agents or otherwise, were not accosted in Jimmy's basement and they were certainly not duct-taped in order to shut them up. It was therefore not surprising that Jimmy, having emerged from the basement with his two friends, was clearly distraught. He headed straight for the refrigerator, grabbed a bottle of beer, and motioned to the other two guys to follow him outside onto the back porch.

Although it was pretty cold, they all slumped into patio armchairs and remained silent for a while, panting and clearly waiting for their host to speak. And he certainly did.

"So, can either of you explain to me, preferably in simple terms, which even an Italian Polack can understand, what has just happened? In particular, Michael, what sort of a stupid game were you playing when you kept saying that we would somehow not die? Did you have a hunch that the gun wouldn't fire? Did god showed up in your shower to tell you we were going to be OK? Or perhaps you took some stinking scientology classes with Tom Cruise and learned that at some weird junctures of the history of this universe weapons just failed for no apparent reason?"

"Well, not exactly." – said Michael.

"Not exactly? So how did you know that her gun was busted?"

"Err, I kind of broke it."

"What?"

"I bent the firing pin so it couldn't have fired."

Jimmy and Alex looked at each other and then looked at Michael. Then they looked at each other again, trying very hard to establish who in this entire trio had totally flipped.

"Last time I checked" – said Alex – "you didn't know anything about guns. Heck, I would venture to say you didn't even know where the damn firing pin was or what it was. I certainly don't."

"True... but I watched a YouTube video about disabling guns by bending their firing pins".

"Oh my god!" – said Jimmy.

"Jesus Christ!" – added Alex.

Jimmy continued.

"You mean to tell me that when this Nazi bitch pointed a gun at my head and pulled the trigger, the only thing that separated me from being irreversibly dead was your YouTube-based gun manipulation effort?"

"Yes, that's what I'm saying. And by the way, I don't know if you've noticed, but we're all alive."

"Holy shit!" – said Jimmy, clearly resigning himself to the fact that his continued existence was purely accidental - "I just can't believe you've put us through all this on the basis of your 'expertise' in gun disabling."

"I had no other choice..."

"Wait, wait" – exclaimed Alex – "but how did you manage to do that?"

"OK, let's backtrack a bit. I went to see Linda, or whatever the hell her name is, at her hotel. When I knocked on her door, she said she was just about to take a shower and asked me to sit down and wait for her. So I did. And then I noticed her gun lying on the table, although it didn't have the silencer on it yet. It took me just a minute to screw the firing pin up. And the reason I did that was simple - it seemed obvious to me that if she'd been working for these fascist nuts, one way or the other she'll have to 'deal' with us. I needed an insurance policy of some sort. So I went to see her a bit prepared."

"Really? And what if she had four other guns with pins sadly unbent? Or four Ukrainian giants with Kalashnikovs at her disposal?" – asked Jimmy sarcastically.

"Well, I guess we would've been dead by now." – answered Michael calmly.

This last comment seemed to have killed the conversation for a while. They all went back into the house and milled aimlessly around the kitchen, not knowing what to do or say.

"All right" – said Jimmy finally – "Michael, you go downstairs and check on that murderous tramp. Maybe she needs a slap across her face or something."

"What?"

"Nothing, just check if she's securely tied up and come back here."

When Michael returned, they went to the front room and sat down around a coffee table.

"So did you confront her with what we've discovered?" – asked Alex looking at Michael.

"Sure I did. And she reacted very professionally. Seemed to be very calm, told me I knew too little to make any judgments, implied that all of this was some sort of a super secret FBI operation, and that she would explain everything once we got all together. But it was obvious she was lying, not to mention the fact that when talking to me she answered a call on her cell phone and spent a few minutes back in her bathroom whispering most of the time. Then she insisted on meeting all of us immediately and I knew she probably just got the order to get rid of us. So at that point I was ready to get her in here. I gave her Jimmy's address and she said she would be joining us in a few minutes."

"She didn't admit to anything?"

"Absolutely not."

Jimmy was sitting in one of the corners of the room, slightly away from the table, and he was playing intently with his almost empty beer glass while seemingly listening to what was going on. It was pretty obvious his thoughts were elsewhere. It took him a few good minutes to address their situation from a decidedly different angle.

"OK, we almost died, but somehow managed not to, which is a stinking miracle. However, in a sense what happened prior to just moments ago doesn't mean a damn thing anymore. So, let's deal with certain painful realities."

"What do you mean?" – asked Alex.

"What do I mean?" – Jimmy almost pounced.

"I'll tell you what I mean. In a few hours my daughters are coming back from school, and they will be followed by my wife coming back from her East Coast trip. But it so happens that in my basement there is a relatively attractive woman, a federal agent no less, bound and gagged. So what, in your infinite wisdom, do you propose I say when greeting my better half? How about 'Hi, honey, welcome back, and oh, by the way, don't be alarmed by this slightly tied up sex object downstairs – I only use her sparingly and with caution'. Or perhaps I should cram the Mein Kampf Linda behind the furnace, hoping she'll remain perfectly quiet?"

Both Michael and Alex wisely decided to remain silent for a while.

"OK, do you guys think that there is any more useful information we can get from her, preferably without waterboarding?" – Jimmy continued.

"I doubt it" – said Alex – "she's useless, because I'm sure she'll not saying anything – she knows perfectly well we're almost out of time. Also, I really don't want to talk to her anymore."

"Well, then, we have to get rid of her." – said Michael almost philosophically.

Jimmy looked at him with puzzled horror.

"Get rid of her? What, do you want to whack her with a hammer, cut up her body, and take the pieces to the garbage dump?"

"No, no. We have to stash her somewhere until after Thanksgiving, so that she is isolated from her pals."

"Great. It's just that I'm fresh out of ideas about stashing FBI babes, or any humans for that matter".

"Come on. Think... We have to move her somewhere so that she's not in your house and yet we continue having full control over her. Today is Monday, so we're talking about just two days before this whole Thanksgiving plot is supposed to kick in. Jimmy, don't you know of any empty houses, people leaving for the holidays, or perhaps even a forsaken or repossessed house."

Jimmy gave Michael a somewhat bizarre look, but didn't say anything. Then he got up, went to one of the windows and stared down his street.

"It's a long shot, but what the fuck..." – he muttered.

"What was that?" – asked Alex.

"I have an idea, but it's so crazy I shouldn't even mention it".

"Why don't you try us?"

"Fine... I'm friends with a married couple living just a few houses down the street – Janice and Archibald. As far as I know they are just about to leave to visit some family and won't be back until Saturday at which time we should all be safely tucked away in concentration camps."

"So, what are you saying? We wait until they leave and then get Linda into their house."

"Hell no. I'm not breaking into their house. I would have to go and ask Janice to do me a big favor. She's very nice, but..."

"But what?"

"Well, almost nobody is as nice as to host kidnapped federal agents. And her husband is a lawyer."

"Damn." – said Alex.

Jimmy was quickly and rather chaotically considering his options which did not seem to be particularly appetizing. He knew he had to remove Linda from his house almost immediately, but the only way he could think of doing that would require him to convince his neighbors that their having a bound, homicidal sex bomb down in the basement was not so bad after all. He didn't regret getting entangled in the mess he found himself in, but was worried it was just about to explode in his face. He decided to do what was almost impossible to imagine.

"I guess I have no other option." – he said – "If I go over there now, she'll be by herself, so at least the risk of Archibald kicking my ass isn't going to be high. Can you offer some ingenious opening lines for me? You know, like 'hey, Janice, can I briefly stash something in your house?' or 'wanna have a woman ready for S&M in your basement?'"

„What's S&M?" – asked Michael.

Jimmy and Alex looked at him with the astonished air of people who know better and don't understand why others don't.

"Oh, never mind" – said Michael hastily – "I get it."

"Jimmy, before you go, let's assume that you'll be successful and discuss what happens next." – said Alex.

"That's a big assumption. But anyway, I guess no matter what you want to do, I'll have to stay here, not only because otherwise my kids will hate me and my wife will divorce me, or the other way round, but also because we can't just leave this woman tied up and alone for two days. However much I dread this, I'll have to give her something to eat every now and then and also take her to the bathroom, although I'm warning you right up front – I'm not wiping her hitlerite ass."

"How are you going to pull all of it off?"

"Well, that's actually much easier then convincing my neighbors about the wisdom of using their house as a hostage hideout. Janice and Archibald have three yappy little dogs, so I can go over there a few times a day to take care of them. I've done that before, except this time around there will be an additional bitch to feed."

"Great. So if we manage to transfer Linda to their house, I suggest Michael and I go immediately to Wakarusa. I have no idea what we're going to do once there, but obviously we can't do anything here."

"I agree. Just stay in touch with me, so that I know what the hell is going on. Also, come Thanksgiving afternoon, what do I do with lovely Ms. Linda?"

"Let her go." – said Michael with surprising authority in his voice.

"Are you nuts?"

"All right, first kick her, and then let her out. Come on, by that time either this entire gang will be shut down and on its way to jail or she wins and becomes Chief Thug of Indiana or something. One way or the other, we can't keep her and I'm assuming none of us wants to unbend the firing pin to put a bullet in her head."

"OK, just let me know when to let her go... Or they'll come for me, I'll be dead, and she'll be free anyway... All right, I'm off to Janice's place."

"Good luck."

"Yeah, right. See you."

Chapter 29

Janice was not a woman to be taken lightly. Short, tenacious, and opinionated, she was the kind of person who would complain to a member of Best Buy personnel about not being paid enough attention to when shopping for another useless electronic gadget. Or she would be first to periodically complain to Comcast about their cable TV service being too damn expensive.

Having dispatched Archibald to work, she gently settled into her morning routine that consisted of sipping the morning coffee, watching the news, and talking to her dogs who followed her faithfully everywhere she went. She almost never got any visitors at this time of the day, so she was a bit surprised to hear a knock on her door followed by a cacophony of all her dogs yelping in defense of their sacred home territory.

She opened the door and saw her neighbor Jimmy. This was indeed a surprise. Although he was a good friend, normally at this hour he was at work, not to mention the fact that he almost never stopped by Janice's house outside of the context of various wild parties organized by a small circle of liberally minded locals stuck in the middle of very conservative Indiana.

"Hi, Janice." – said Jimmy.

Janice knew almost immediately that something was wrong. Jimmy was strangely uptight, even though he struggled to be his usual cheerful self.

"Hey, what's up?" – she said.

"Not much. Sorry to bother you, but I wonder if I can discuss something with you briefly."

"Sure. Come in. Let's go into the kitchen. Are you off work today?"

"Yeah. Mairéad is coming back, so I need to clean the house a bit."

"Well, sure you do. Can I offer you a glass of wine?"

"You know what, why the hell not."

"OK, coming up."

Soon they both settled into high stools surrounding a kitchen island. Janice treaded carefully and waited for Jimmy to speak his mind. She didn't have to wait long.

"Janice, I am here to ask you to do me a big favor."

"Really? For a while I thought you came to tell me that someone had died or something."

"Was it really that obvious? Well, someone almost did."

"What?"

"Sorry, that's probably not the best introduction to what I'm going to say. The reason I'm here is that I need to ask your permission to stash something in your house for a couple of days."

"Stash something in my house? Sure you can. But why? Are you trying to hide something?"

"Yes... And here's the thing. It's not something. It's someone."

Janice stared at him for a while, then took a precariously large gulp of her wine.

"Jimmy, you're beginning to worry me. What the hell do you mean?"

Jimmy took a deep breath and plunged forward all the way, painfully aware of the fact that there was no going back.

"OK, right now in my house there is a young, female FBI agent who just an hour ago tried to shoot both me and two friends of mine. She is bound and gagged in my basement, and I can't leave her there, because Mairéad and the kids are going to be back soon. So I need to put her somewhere until Thursday and I

190

thought your house would be a good place since you won't be here anyway."

As Janice listened to this short monologue, her face showed a steadily increasing level of anxiety and concern. The silence that ensued was chilling and very disturbing to Jimmy who expected the worst.

"How many drinks have you had today, Jimmy?" – asked Janice.

"None, I swear. Come on, Janice, I'm not drunk. Let me explain."

"Explain? You mean what you've just told me needs an explanation? Oh, please, don't worry about it. Things like this happen in this neighborhood every day. You know, like people being shot at, bondage sessions in basements, FBI agents trying to kill you... Just our everyday stinking existence, isn't it?"

"I know, I know. I deserve all this. But it's all true. Listen, I can't explain everything, but let me just say this – the woman in my basement is very dangerous and she is a part of a plan to attack America in a couple of days."

Janice, understandably, was neither impressed nor convinced.

"Oh, give me a fucking break, Jimmy! Who the hell are you? James Bond? And how come you, of all people, end up involved in saving this country from whatever threats it's supposed to be facing? Is this some elaborate joke designed to get me prematurely out of my jammies? Because if it is, I'm sticking to my coffee and my attire."

Jimmy spent the next few minutes telling Janice the story of how his two friends from Chicago got him involved in a bizarre story full of the ghosts of World War II and contemporary fascist maniacs. He didn't tell her everything, but he did describe in graphic detail the dramatic scenes that had occurred in his house just a couple of hours earlier.

"Janice, just this once I'm asking you to trust me" – he finally said – "I would never even be here if this whole thing wasn't serious."

"Did she really try to shoot you in the head?" – asked Janice with some hesitation as if she didn't really believe she was actually posing such a question.

"Yes."

"And did you really say her ass was not up to snuff?"

"Yes, Janice. Come on. This is not something we have time to discuss right now."

"All right, all right... Let's just assume for a second that you're not nuts, which is damn difficult, and that you're telling me the truth. What exactly is it that you want me to do?"

"When are you leaving for Thanksgiving?"

"This evening."

"And coming back?"

"Saturday afternoon."

"OK, then. All that would happen is this – we bring this woman over here in a few minutes and put her in your basement. Then you leave and I take care of your dogs and of her. By the time you come back she is gone and your dogs are fed and happy. It's as simple as that."

"No, it ain't."

"Why?"

"Archibald."

"Shit, you don't even have to tell him."

"Oh, be serious. Do you think he's going to miss a tied up babe in the basement?"

"So what if you tell him all about it?"

"He's going to shit in his pants and have two martinis".

"Can you make him have four martinis?"

"Come on, Jimmy, he needs to know what the hell is going on."

"Fine. But we're kind of running out of time. I need to hide this bitch... errr... woman almost immediately. So what do you say?"

Janice sat down again and looked at Jimmy sternly as if she was just about to admonish him about something. But she didn't.

192

Instead she abruptly stood up and went up to Jimmy, confronting him face to face.

"OK" – she said – "bring her over here, and I'll call Archibald in a while to tell him about it. But I don't want to see her, do you understand? Just put her in the basement and do whatever you need to do – I don't want to know."

"Fine."

"And, by the way, all of this is illegal, isn't it?"

"Yes, it is. But so is trying to shoot three people in cold blood."

"Right... Anyway, go and get her."

"OK."

"Hey, Jimmy."

"Yes?"

"Is she really a fanatic killer?"

"Yes, she is."

"All right then. Maybe before I leave for my turkey day I can kick her once in the shins."

"Be my guest. Kick her in whatever part of her anatomy you want. But what happened to your not wanting to see her."

"I'll make an exception."

"Spoken like the Janice I know and admire."

The transfer of Linda to Janice's house went off without a hitch. She was led to Jimmy's garage, loaded into the back of his car and driven down the street where she was quickly unloaded and brought down to Janice's basement. The hostess wisely refrained from kicking her in the shins and stayed away from the whole scene, earnestly pretending to be busy in the kitchen.

As soon as Jimmy led his prisoner into the basement, he immediately taped her legs together again and placed her on a couch. He was a bit puzzled by the fact that Linda was perfectly calm and didn't resist in any way. In fact it was possible to see a little ironic smirk struggling to show up from behind the duct tape covering her mouth.

"Do you need to go to the bathroom?" – he asked her.

She gestured that she didn't.

"Are you hungry or thirsty?"

Same response.

"OK, suit yourself then. I'll be back in a couple of hours."

She looked straight at him and grunted something. Jimmy hesitated, but then decided to temporarily ungag her. He came to the conclusion that even if Linda screamed briefly, she would only make the dogs upstairs mad and Janice even more nervous than she already was. He went up to her and yanked the tape off in one swift motion.

Linda took a couple of deep breaths, gasping for air, and for a brief moment looked like a large FBI fish unexpectedly removed from water. But before she could say a word, Jimmy launched a pre-emptive strike.

"Listen, I'm not really interested in any more discussion about how we'll soon all die or get jailed, and how you and your totally fucked-up brethren will march on to glory. Here is what's going to happen – you'll stay in this basement until Thursday. A few times a day I'll come by to feed the dogs and unfortunately also you. All I need you to do is to sit tight and keep quiet."

Linda for a brief moment seemed lost for words.

"What happens after Thursday?" – she finally asked.

"That's none of your business" – he said.

"Right, you simply don't know".

"I warned you." – said Jimmy and immediately put the duct tape back on her mouth. Then he checked all the other 'tapings' on her body and went upstairs.

While all of this was going on, back at Jimmy's house Michael and Alex were plotting their next move. Their progress was excruciatingly slow. A bit earlier they rented a car by phone since they knew they were definitely driving to Wakarusa, but they argued about what to do once there. Finally, Alex suggested that they would go to the town of Elkhart, just round the corner from Wakarusa, and check into a motel. Then the plan was to show up at the local police station.

194

"And then what? – asked Michael.

"I don't know. Perhaps we can introduce ourselves as Chicago journalists writing an article about radical supremacy groups in the Midwest. After all, you are a journalist, and since you were a fake plumber in Poland, I can certainly be a fake journalist in Wakarusa."

"All right, but what does it get us?"

"Well, we can ask the cops about the compound. I'm sure they at least know of its existence. I guess we have to start somewhere."

"OK, call Jimmy, ask him if everything is OK on his end, and tell him we're getting the hell out of here."

Chapter 30

Sergeant Willard Atkins briefly felt extremely full of himself, and – on top of that – not in any gastric sort of way. Chief Thompson told him to man the front office of the police station while he was talking to various people on the phone in the back room. Willard had absolutely no idea what was going on, and very little interest in whatever it was, but correctly assumed that the chief was trying to figure out what to do about the mangled body found in Mrs. Goral's field. "Things ain't going good" – he thought while listening to the frantic, undulating speech of his superior.

The undulation in Chief Thompson's voice was understandable. He was trying to find out who the victim of the gruesome murder was, because without a positive ID absolutely nothing further could be done. And he was getting increasingly anxious, because he sensed that his tiny town could soon once again be invaded by federal agents who would yet one more time tell him to quietly fuck off and not bother them. Unfortunately, despite his best efforts, he didn't find anything out. His friend in South Bend promised however that he would call him the minute he gets any news.

Willard wasn't burdened with the mundane trivialities of criminal pursuits. He was enjoying his time in chief's chair, and was busy trying to imagine how it would feel to be in charge and to order various unimportant underlings about. After a spell of daydreaming, he squashed a fat fly sitting on his cheese sandwich, shook it off, and started to eat his sanitized early lunch. Very shortly afterwards a car pulled up to the front of the station. Willard immediately put his sandwich down and stared at two middle-aged men who got out of the vehicle and started walking towards the front door. Here was his chance to play boss.

"Hi." – said one of the men cheerfully after they got inside and stood in front of Willard – "Are you the police chief?"

The sergeant briefly entertained the idea of pretending that he was, but decided against it, which probably saved his life.

"No, I'm a ...err ... deputy" – he said guardedly – "What can I do for you, gentlemen?"

"My name is Michael Riedle and this is my colleague Alex Malak. We're Chicago-based journalists and we're looking for some information."

Willard blinked three times in rapid succession as if someone just pointed a search light straight at his face.

"Oh, crap – how did you find out so quickly?" – he said after a few seconds.

This time it was Michael's turn to blink and look silly.

"Find out about what?"

"About the stinking murder?"

"What murder?"

Willard's face showed an alarming level of confusion. He stood up, looked at both of them briefly and decided to seek help.

"Just... just wait here, ok? I'll go and get the chief".

He rushed into the back room and found Chief Thompson sitting at a small dilapidated desk with the phone handset pressed to his ear.

"Are you on hold, chief?" – asked Willard in a timid kind of voice.

"Damn right I am. What do you want?"

"Well, there are these two guys in the front office. They say they are reporters from Chicago".

Chief Thompson's massive body visibly shuddered.

"What? Oh, that's just great, that's all we need. How the hell did they get the whiff of all of this so quickly?"

"I don't know, chief, but..."

"Just go back there and kick their asses out... No, wait, I'll do it myself."

"But chief, the thing is..."

"Just shut up, Willard. I'll deal with this."

Chief Thompson burst into the front office, waved at his two guests perfunctorily, and went on to accomplish the task of kicking their asses out of the police station.

"Listen guys, I'm sorry, but this is just the beginning of the investigation and I'm in no position to comment in any way about this whole mess. I really appreciate your interest, but I'm going to have to ask you to leave. If you give me your names and numbers, I'll call you whenever I have something I can share with you."

Chief Thompson was standing right in front of them, leaning slightly forward which, given his voluminous frame and lack of a well-defined center of gravity, bordered on keeling over and falling face down. It was very obvious he wanted desperately to get rid of them.

Alex cleared his throat.

"Excuse me, chief, ... by the way, what's your name sir?"

"Thompson. I'm Chief Thompson."

"Great" – continued Alex – "so, Chief Thompson, we have no idea what you're talking about and we know nothing about any murder investigation."

"You don't?"

"No, we don't."

"So what the hell do you want?"

"Well, as we were trying to explain to your assistant, we're reporters from Chicago and we're working on a piece about extremist right-wing hate groups in the Midwest."

Chief Thompson's jaw dropped about an inch closer to the floor.

"What? I don't even know what that means. And even if I did, what does any of this have to with me and my town?"

"Chief, we have reason to believe that one of these groups operates right outside of Wakarusa and we were hoping you might provide us with whatever information you have on their activities."

At this point Chief Thompson glanced surreptitiously at Willard, presumably trying to stop him from saying anything, but he was too late.

"Oh, you mean them idiots at the Hawkins ranch." – Willard blurted out.

"Willard, keep you stinking mouth shut. Please don't listen to him. There are these guys who play Sunday soldiers at a ranch a bit out of town, and I actually hate them, because they are a snotty bunch, but they don't bother anybody".

"But, chief, how about the murder..."

Chief Thompson turned to his sergeant abruptly and it seemed he was ready to strangle him with his bare hands.

"Get back to your work." – hissed the chief angrily through his clenched teeth.

"Sorry about that. He tends to be too eager at times." – he said turning back to Michael and Alex.

"Wait a second" – said Alex – "did we hear correctly that there was a murder around here and that it was tied to this group at the ranch?"

"You heard incorrectly. Yes, there was a murder a couple of days ago, but nobody knows who the victim is and there are certainly no suspects, and even if there were, I wouldn't be able to tell you anything about it, because right now it's an open investigation."

"You mean you don't know who was killed."

"No, I don't. The poor guy was beaten beyond recognition and had no papers on him. Anything else...? OK then, I need to go back to work."

"Chief, I'm sorry, but could you give us 5 minutes more?" – pleaded Alex – "We came here all the way from Chicago and all we need is to ask you just a few simple questions".

Chief Thompson looked at them in a somewhat unfriendly way. He really couldn't care less about big city reporters writing about whomever it was they were writing about. He was also a bit ashamed of himself for hiding from them the possible connection between the murder and the Hawkins crowd. Perhaps out of this quiet embarrassment arose a very reluctant acquiescence.

"Oh, all right, I'll talk to you briefly. Please sit down... What do you want to know?"

"So who are these people at the ranch?" – asked Michael.

"Difficult to say. They bought this place a number of years ago and they mostly keep to themselves."

"Do they cause any trouble?"

"Just minor things. They have armed guards around the perimeter, so sometimes there are run-ins between them and people straying into their territory."

"What do they do in that compound?"

"No clue. Playing soldiers, I guess. They are real shitizens."

"Shitizens?"

"Yes, citizens full of shit."

"Have you ever been inside the compound?"

"No, never. I sometimes speak to their people, but only on the outside? They tend to be real jerks."

"In what sense?"

"Oh, they all think they're very important and no authority can ever touch them."

"So where exactly is this Hawkins ranch?"

"A couple of miles south of town... Wait a second, you're not thinking about going there, are you?"

Michael and Alex hesitated briefly.

"Well, yeah, we might take a look." – said Alex.

Chief Thompson stood up, walked up to the window and sighed. He stared for a while down the almost totally deserted main street and then turned to his guests again.

"Listen, guys, I've got to tell you something. These people might be dangerous. You'd better stay away from them".

"Dangerous?" – asked Alex feigning total ignorance.

"Yes... I should've told you this to begin with. I suspect they might have something to do with this murder. I can't go into any details, but I personally think they clobbered this guy to death for some reason and then dumped his body on a nearby field out of a Cessna plane."

Michael and Alex looked a bit dumbfounded as they sat glued to their chairs mulling the significance of what they had just heard. Their confused ponderings were interrupted by a sharp ring of chief's cell phone.

"Excuse me, I'm going to take this in the back office." said Chief Thompson and walked out.

"Are you thinking what I'm thinking? – whispered Alex to Michael.

"Yes. The dead dude is probably Albert."

"Right. Do we say anything to the chief?"

"I don't know. Better not, I guess. Let's just stick to what we need to do."

"Great, except all we know is that there is a guarded compound two miles from here and the crew in there is obnoxious."

They kept quiet for a few moments. Chief Thompson returned and seemed somehow relieved, which was a bit puzzling.

"OK, your time is up" – he said almost cheerfully – "I really need to get going."

Michael and Alex stood up and started walking out of the office, but before they reached the door, Chief Thompson had one more thing to say.

"By the way, I think I got it wrong about this murder. It probably didn't have anything to do with the guys at the ranch."

"Why do you say that?" – asked Alex.

"Well, I just got off the phone with my buddy in South Bend, who is a coroner. He finally got news from Chicago about the identity of the victim. It seems the dead guy is a foreign national."

"Really? Who is he?"

"I'm not supposed to tell you that, but it'll be in the papers tomorrow anyway. He was from Poland."

"What...? I mean... what would a guy from Poland be doing here?" – asked Alex desperately trying to cover up his shock and dismay.

"Beats me, but I doubt the yokels at the Hawkins ranch have international contacts."

"What's his name?"

"Whose?"

"The dead guy's name."

"Oh, here, I wrote it down, but there's no freaking way I can pronounce this." – said the chief and handed Alex a small piece of paper.

Alex looked down at the note and stood in the middle of the office in absolute stillness. Then he put the paper down on the desk.

"Thank you, chief. You were very helpful. Let's go Michael."

Without waiting for any reaction from either Michael or Chief Thompson, Alex staggered quickly out into the street, walked briskly about twenty paces, sat down on the curb, and put his face in his hands. Michael instinctively knew something terrible had happened, but decided to give his friend time to react in any way he wanted. So he sat down beside him and waited. However, nothing ensued for a few minutes, so he finally broke the silence.

"Alex, what was the name on that piece of paper?" – he asked quietly.

"Kazimierz Bielecki".

"Who's that?"

"Kazik... However, it's still 'pan Kazik' to you." – said Alex, trying to cover up his tears.

Chapter 31

Janice's house was quiet and peaceful, despite the fact that a woman of FBI repute was lounging down in her basement in a slightly immobilized fashion. Since she and Archibald were supposed to leave for their Thanksgiving trip later in the day, Janice was busy packing a few things and tiding up the house. Jimmy was supposed to come back any minute to make sure that her 'guest' was comfortable, fed, and physiologically relieved. She felt somewhat weird since she was acutely aware of the fact that a human being, such as she was, was being forcibly held in her house.

Jimmy was right on time. He checked on Linda once again and then sat with Janice in her kitchen, waiting somewhat apprehensively for Archibald to come home. He knew him pretty well and was acutely aware of the fact that he was the kind of man whose face invariably suggested he was never quite happy with the state of things for more than 30 seconds at a time. On the other hand, Archibald was well known around the neighborhood for his sarcastic sense of humor and Jimmy quietly hoped that he would find something to laugh about, even under these most unusual circumstances. He wasn't totally wrong.

"Hey, Jimmy!" - bellowed Archibald as soon as he stepped inside the house - "I hear your new line of work is hostage taking. Aren't you too old for that?".

"Hi." - said Jimmy, not really knowing how to respond.

His host immediately poured himself a vodka martini, consisting of a glass of Absolut and two drops of vermouth, and sat on a high chair facing Jimmy. As always, he didn't look very pleased.

"So where the hell is she?"

"In the basement... Tied... Listen, I..."

"Never mind. Never mind. Tell me, Jimmy, how is it possible for an old fart like you to get involved with this kind of shit? Wouldn't it be a bit safer to just sit at home, sip beer, and watch the Cubs lose?"

"It's a long story, and I'll tell you everything later, but..."

"I need to know one thing. Did she really try to shoot you and your friends in the head?"

"Yes, she lined us up in my basement, pointed her gun at my head, and pulled the trigger."

"I'll be damned... You know, sometimes you are an obnoxious guy, but so far I've never even once considered shooting you, although that's rapidly changing. Anyway, I hear she is sexy."

"In a way."

"Can I see her?"

"No, you can't." - said Janice tartly.

"Listen, Archibald" - continued Jimmy - "I'm really sorry to intrude like this, but I didn't know what else I could do. All I ask is for a couple of days. By the time you guys get back, she won't be here. In fact, you will both have some plausible deniability since she didn't see any of you."

"Wow, the last time I heard the term 'plausible deniability' was just before Nixon flew out of the White House in his stinking helicopter, not to be seen again."

"Sorry. All I mean is that you are just about to leave, and you'll never see this woman again."

"Unless you fail in whatever the fuck you're trying to do, they win, and she'll be back, lining Janice and myself against the wall in my basement."

"Archibald, if they succeed, we'll all be screwed anyway, although I can't predict in exactly what way."

Archibald took a long, hard look at Jimmy.

"Tell me something" - he said - "if you stop these guys, is that going to be something to be proud of?"

"I'm not sure I know what you mean."

"Well, obviously what you're doing now is totally illegal, and what you are asking us to do has more or less the same status. So, at the end of the day, will there be some redeeming factors which will allow us to reminisce affectionately about all this crap in the future?"

"Yes, I assure you. I think this is very important for all of us."

"All right, then. She can stay and we're getting the hell out of here. And I never saw you today. In fact, I hardly even know you."

"Fair enough. I don't know how to thank you."

"Don't. Just make sure she's not here in two days. Oh, and no hanky-panky in my basement."

"You don't even know how unlikely that is".

Further conversation was interrupted by Jimmy's cell phone which rang with what seemed to be a lot of urgency.

"Excuse me." - Jimmy said, and then stood up, went to the living room, and answered the call. There was something about Michael's voice on the other end of the line that immediately convinced him there was a problem. He wasn't prepared for its magnitude.

Jimmy listened to the news from Wakarusa with growing anxiety, partly because he knew about 'pan Kazik' only in a very fragmentary way, and partly because he immediately sensed that the very presence of this person in the US, and in the immediate context of what was happening around them, complicated the situation in a bunch of scary ways.

"Michael, I don't even know what the hell you're telling me" - said Jimmy.

"Well, join the club, because I have no idea what's going on either. Alex is totally distraught about this and he is into all kinds of conspiracy theories."

"Conspiracy theories?"

"Hell, yes. Come on. Think about it. What was this Polish guy who helped us in Wrocław doing here? And if he was killed by the idiots we're chasing, why? And most importantly, if back in Poland he was playing some kind of a double role, what was it? This is all totally crazy. I think Alex is trying to handle both the shock of his friend's death and the mystery surrounding his being here in the first place. On top of that, he seems to think he's in some strange way partially responsible for Kazik's demise, and that doesn't make any sense to me.".

"All right. So what are you both going to do?"

"Shit, I don't know. Alex is out of it, at least for a while, and I really need him, because Kazik's death doesn't change a damn thing. We are still running out of time".

"Right. Listen, perhaps you should go back to your motel and kind of re-group for tomorrow."

"You may be right, Jimmy."

"Did you actually make any progress today? I mean prior to the news about Kazik."

"Not really."

"OK, hope you have better news tomorrow".

By the time Jimmy finished his conversation, Janice and Archibald were almost packed and ready to go.

"Will I ever see you again?" - asked Archibald almost wistfully.

Jimmy was stumped for a while, not knowing how to respond. He suspected Archibald was not quite serious and was testing his guts. On the other hand, he was painfully aware of the fact that his host might have a scary point. It was quite possible that all of their normal reality, the one consisting of daily comings and goings and of futile fights about absolutely nothing, would suddenly dissolve and give way to some sinister new world.

"Relax, Jimmy" - said Archibald reassuringly - "I'm sure I'll see you in hell."

"No doubt about that. You guys have a great trip and I will see you when you get back."

207

"And no sex toys in the basement, right?" - asked Archibald.

"None."

Chapter 32

Most Elkhart motels are probably not places to write glorious reports about. Neither was the one Michael and Alex reconvened at after their traumatic trip to Wakarusa. It was a shabby establishment, the kind travelers choose whenever there is absolutely no other choice. The reception was dirty and smelly, and the rooms contained a bed, a very noisy in-wall ac/heater unit, and a whiff of desolation. Which was a good thing, because that's exactly how Alex and Michael felt.

For a few hours there was no point in even trying to talk to Alex, because he was just sitting there, in one corner of the room, staring at the crooked picture of Indiana cornfields, which for some reason was adorning one of the walls. And then, late at night, he suddenly spoke.

"I'm done" - he said.

"What?

"I'm done. I can't do this anymore. I don't even know what it would mean to go on".

"Alex, wait. You can't do this. Not after all the shit we went through. We need to finish this one way or the other".

Alex looked at Michael with a bit of sad, dejected disdain.

"Finish it? What do you mean? I go with you to Europe, we discover a weird document, and then we are being chased by a fake FBI agent, which results, by some inexplicable twist of fate, in the horrid death of my friend. And, as a side effect, I lose my normal life. You know, the one in which I go to work every morning, I hate everyone and everything, but then I go and have

209

a few relaxing drinks with my best friend Michael. I need to go back to that".

Michael was desperately searching for something sensible to say, but was having a very tough time. But then he had a brilliant idea.

"So, you don't really care?" - he asked.

"About what?"

"Well, no matter what happened so far, wouldn't you want to know why your friend was murdered and who he really was? And most importantly, who did it?"

Alex looked stumped and Michael decided to press on.

"Obviously Kazik wasn't just a plumber or a disenchanted philosopher, was he?"

"Looks that way..." - Michael grunted reluctantly, and then he continued.

"I'm totally at a loss. He never gave me any indication that he was involved in some spy crap."

"Well, we don't really know he was. On the other hand, is it remotely possible that he was working with this 'consonantal cluster' policeman who accosted us in Wrocław?"

"What? You mean Trzepizór? Anything is possible, I guess. But if he was sent over here by Polish spooks and ended up beaten to a pulp in Wakarusa, obviously they were on to something and might have been actually working together with the Americans."

"Right, but his death would then mean that he was somehow unmasked which spelt his doom."

"Wait, wait... let's assume Kazik was a Polish agent. If so, then we were simply used to recover the documents."

"Yes, I know. The question then is why they didn't confiscate them back in Wrocław?"

"Who the hell knows. But perhaps they counted on the fact that two jerks like us stood a better chance of getting all this to the point at which the authorities could intervene."

Michael thought quietly, and not without satisfaction, that his mission was accomplished. Alex was back on board. It was time to convince him they needed to act, and act swiftly.

"So, are we going back to Wakarusa tomorrow morning?" - he asked, looking Alex straight in the face.

Alex hesitated. Then he hesitated for a while longer.

"Well, we probably should." - he said finally. "But the thing is I have no idea what to do when we get there. Do you?"

Michael didn't. While Alex was going through his trauma, Michael kept considering all kinds of weird options and invariably rejected them as being just too damn weird, too damn dangerous or both. One thought however was coming back to him all the time - he remembered that Albert, just before his departure for hell, managed to tell Alex that the key to stopping whatever it was they were supposed to stop was to cut power to the computers in the compound. And that thought always led Michael to the same person: Chief Oliver Thompson.

"I think we need to ask Chief Thompson for assistance." - he said boldly while sensing impending ridicule.

"What? You must be out of your mind." - said predictably Alex.

"Wait a minute. Just hear me out. He is the only person in this little town who actually can help us, because he is the local authority. Also, he is burdened with a troubling murder case which - I'm sure - he would like either to quickly solve or somehow get rid of. In other words, he might have a vested interest in helping us if we convince him that he is going to come out of all this as a local hero."

"Perhaps. But what are we going to tell him?"

"Everything."

"As my dear grandmother used to say, you've got bats in your belfry. Thompson will first laugh and then kick us out of town."

"Maybe, maybe not. But why not try? What other options do we have?"

Alex ran out of arguments. He instinctively knew that they had to go on and that going on meant both of them returning to

Wakarusa. So first thing in the morning, having feasted on stale bagels smeared with suspiciously runny cream cheese, they set out on their way back to Chief Thompson's kingdom.

They could not have known that the kingdom was in a rotten shape as early as 6 am. At exactly that time the phone right by chief's ear rang loudly, in a Willard sort of way. Except it wasn't Willard.

"What in the name of god do you want now?" - groaned Oliver.

"Is this Chief Oliver Thompson of the Wakarusa police department?" - said a relatively pleasant female voice.

"Err... yes. I'm sorry. Who is this?"

"Sir, I'm sorry to disturb you at this early hour. My name is Susan Griffin and I work for special agent George Mattison in the Washington DC FBI headquarters.

"Holy fucking shit!" - thought Thompson. However, he knew he had to respond in a radically different way.

"Well, yes... It's no problem. What can I do for you?"

"I understand that you are investigating a murder committed in your area. Is that right?"

Chief Thompson was fast approaching an early morning state of panic.

"Yes, that's right. But why would FBI be interested in this?"

"Well, as I understand the victim was a foreign national. I am not at liberty to tell you too much, but we have reason to believe that he was involved in espionage."

"Espionage? Excuse me my disbelief, but what espionage activities would any sane person be conducting in Wakarusa, Indiana?"

"Exactly. We are puzzled by that too. So, I am calling to let you know that we may be sending an agent your way to have a look at this case. I promise he won't bother you too much."

If Mr. Thompson's heart could sink even more than it just did, it would have ended up on the floor.

"Could you tell me when I should expect the agent?"

"Oh, nothing has been decided yet. We don't even know for sure that we will send someone. But I'll give you another call in a couple of days one way or the other."

"OK, thanks."

Chief Thompson dragged himself out of bed to start his day. It was a difficult task, not only because horizontal-to-vertical transitions were physically exerting for him, but also because he already hated his day with a passion, even though it barely started. As was his custom in the face of impending crises, he grabbed the phone and called Willard to spread some of the doom on him. His deeply mistrusted assistant was surprised, because he knew Chief Thompson was not an early riser.

"Boy, chief, I hope you're calling me about something really important."

"You bet your sweet ass I am" - growled his boss.

"OK, what can I do for you?"

"Not much. I need to see your face at the office in about 30 minutes."

"Anything I did?"

"No, but you probably will. Just be there."

Willard did as he was told. He showed up at the office promptly and saw immediately that his boss was not in a good mood. Chief Thompson was trying to extract a cup of coffee out of a wobbly coffee maker while issuing all kinds of expletives under his nose. Then he turned to his sergeant and said rather inexplicably: "What the hell do you want?".

"Well, nothing, chief." - responded Willard guardedly - "You told me to be here, so here I am."

"Oh yeah, right. Listen, there may be an FBI agent visiting us in a few days."

"Why?"

"Why? It doesn't fucking matter why. It's none of your business anyway. Just be ready."

"Err... ready in what sense?"

Chief Thompson looked just about as puzzled as his underling.

213

"I... you know... we need to, you know... get ready."

"OK, chief, whatever. But why are we here at 7 am in the morning if the agent is coming in a few days?"

Oliver seemed to have been caught off guard by this simple question and was clearly struggling to produce a sensible answer. On the other hand, Willard, who saw that his boss was under so much stress that there was not much point in talking to him, was desperately trying to decide on his next move, and his options seemed to be fairly limited. But then he caught a glimpse of two guys who were just about to enter the office.

"Hallelujah - the Chicago jerks!" - he thought, while praising silently the Holy Spirit with whom he had been having a haphazard relationship throughout his life.

"Chief, we have guests." - he said almost joyously.

Chief Thompson swung around just in time to see Alex and Michael walking in through the front door. It wasn't the sight that he cherished. In fact, it was the sight that was just adding to his morning misery.

"Oh, come on guys, what are you still doing here? I told you I couldn't tell you anything else about this murder." - he said.

"Yes, chief, you did tell us that" - said Alex - "but we are here to have a serious talk with you about not only the murder, about which we happen to know something, but also about some very important stuff, so I suggest we grab some coffee, sit down, and get to it before it's too late."

"Too late? Too late for what? Listen, I don't really have time for..."

"You really need to have time" - interrupted Michael rather sternly - "we are not kidding."

It was obvious that Chief Thompson was torn between two options: throwing the intruders out of his office or listening to what they had to say. He weighed these options for about 30 seconds, and then decided that he had nothing to lose and plenty to gain by talking to his uninvited guests who intrigued him by claiming to have some knowledge about the murder.

"Willard, go and milk a cow or something" - he said to his sergeant.

"Right, chief." - said Willard cheerfully, sensing a clear possibility of going back to bed. He disappeared almost immediately.

"All right. Let's go and sit in my office." - said Chief Thompson with thinly disguised reluctance.

On their way from Elkhart to Wakarusa Alex and Michael discussed all kinds of possible strategies and rhetorical maneuvers which could possibly facilitate telling Chief Thompson their story in such a way that they would not look like two totally confused Martians who had just landed in alien territory. However, eventually they both agreed that there was no such strategy and that they simply needed to tell him their story straight up. And they did just that, beginning with the letter from Belize and ending with Kazik's death and their suspicions about it. Additionally Alex confessed that he wasn't really a journalist, but a computer geek at a rubber factory in Morton Grove.

Chief Thompson wasn't an attentive and sympathetic listener, which was to be expected. In fact, he started getting clearly restless right about the time the story went into a detailed account of the way the Nazi papers were recovered from below a Polish supermarket. He was then frequently trying to interrupt, waving his hands wildly and grunting significant phrases such as 'but...', 'wait a minute', and 'you can't be serious'. Michael and Alex were successful only in one sense - they finished the story by squashing forcefully any attempts at interruptions. Now they waited for Chief Thompson's reaction.

Oliver didn't react immediately. He sat at his desk speechless, staring at his half-empty cup of coffee and playing nervously with a stack of papers lying in front of him. Alex and Michael expected some emotional outbursts, but to their surprise none came. Chief Thompson seemed to be mulling something in his mind, but he was obviously not ready to share his thoughts.

"Well, gentlemen" - he finally said - "I've just about had it with you."

"Chief, please, we need..."

"Right, I'm sure you need all kinds of things, including a psychiatrist, but my question is this - assuming for just one second that all this stuff you told me is true, however distant that possibility might be, what the hell do you want from me? You show up in my town, string together a bunch of wacko theories, and then tell me all this weird crap. For what purpose? If you know something concrete about the murder, then please let me know and I'll act on it. Otherwise you can go back to Chicago and pursue your craziness over there."

Alex decided to plunge further into the abyss they both just created.

"Chief, I know it all sounds crazy, but the story we told you is totally true and we are now all sitting in a small town of Wakarusa, Indiana, which will almost certainly play a major role in something really bad coming down in just hours. Come on, you told us yourself that you always had doubts about these guys at the compound. They are really bad people. And whatever happens next is going to be pretty bad for all of us unless we do something. So, please, help us."

"Help you? What exactly do you mean by that? If what you're saying is true, the only rational thing we can do is to call the feds, and since they already called me this morning, I'll return the favor."

Alex and Michael stopped in their tracks.

"Who called you?" - asked Michael.

"What does it matter? Some woman at the FBI in DC. They are probably going to send an agent down here to look into this murder."

"What did you tell her?"

"What sort of a stupid question is that? I didn't tell her anything, because I know nothing. Listen, guys, I've been very patient with you, and I understand you have some sort of a hang-up about these 'Nazis' in the compound, but I seriously doubt they are in any position to blow up anything. Hell, I would be surprised if they could effectively pull up their pants after they are done pooping. So why don't you just pack your bags and get the hell out of here, because if you don't, I'll have to tell this FBI guest of mine that you were here and that you were asking suspicious questions. And another thing..."

Chief Thompson could have probably continued his tirade for much longer were it not for the fact that suddenly the door to his office swung wide open and in staggered a man who was clearly in serious distress. His clothes were filthy and tattered, he had cuts and bruises all over his face, and there were a few blood stains on his pants. He stood motionless for a few seconds, took two wobbly steps forward, raised his hand as if to address someone or something, and then fell face down on the floor.

Michael reacted first, rushing to the fallen man's side and turning his lifeless body face up. He could see that the unexpected guest was not unconscious - his eyes were open and blinking and he was moving his hands uncontrollably in a haphazard sort of way. He was also clearly trying to say something, moving his mouth listlessly without being able to produce any sounds.

Michael knelt by his side and leaned over him so that his ear was very close to the man's lips.

"What is it?" - he said very softly - "what are you trying to say?"

"I... am..." - he heard a raspy, faint whisper - "I'm..."

"Yes?" - prodded him Michael.

"I'm Albert. Albert... Brunner".

Michael abruptly stood up and looked at Alex.

"Please call 911." - he said - "we need to save Deep Face".

Chapter 33

Alex didn't call 911. Or more accurately, he tried, but was stopped by Chief Thompson who suddenly seemed to be much more interested in what was going on than ever before.

"Wait, don't call anybody" - he said.

"Why not?" - asked Alex.

"The closest ER is about 30 miles away. But more importantly, I think we should take a quick look at this guy to see if he's seriously injured or just exhausted".

"What difference does it make?"

Oliver looked at Alex with a bit of incredulity.

"What difference does it make? Just a moment ago you told me a story which to most sane people is total lunacy, and then you asked for my help on the assumption that I might possibly believe all this shit. I didn't, but now here is this mangled dude who seems to confirm that at least some parts of what you told me may be true, even though - according to you - Albert should have been dead a long time ago".

"Well, that's what we thought".

"Whatever... My point is very simple. If you want my help, let's not ship this guy to some hospital, which will waste a bunch of time. How about taking care of him right here. I have a small room at the back with a cot. Let's put him there, give him some food and drink, and ask him about whatever he knows. In my mind this is the quickest way of finding out who is really nuts - you or me."

"It's you." - said a very feeble voice attached to a person lying on the floor. He was pointing at Chief Thompson.

"All right, that's it" - roared Oliver - "grab him and put him in the back room.

Alex and Michael meekly complied. Once Albert was in bed, they gave him some hot tea and a few biscuits. Chief Thompson had a look at his body. While there were no gaping, bleeding wounds, it was pretty obvious that Albert suffered some trauma, and it was the kind of trauma that unsettled Oliver a bit. He was a Vietnam War veteran, although he never talked about it, and he knew exactly how people got to look like Albert. They were 'professionally' beaten and tortured.

The three men returned to chief's front office, slumped into chairs, and just sat there for a few minutes.

"So now what?" – asked Alex finally.

"I guess we have to wait for this guy to recover well enough to tell us something." – replied Chief Thompson.

Michael was definitely not in the waiting mood.

"Chief, we can't wait. We have about 28 hours to play with. 28 hours and counting."

"And then what?"

"I have no idea, and that's why we need to talk to Albert now."

Unfortunately all they could do for the next 30 minutes was more waiting.

"Hell, what if this dude dies on us? – asked Alex.

"I won't. I'm OK" – said Albert who was standing in the back door, still staggering a bit, unsure of his step, but clearly ready to rejoin the living. He tried valiantly to reach Chief Thompson's armchair, but almost collapsed half way over and had to be hoisted into it by Michael and Alex.

Chief Thompson was clearly worried that his unexpected guest was going to harm himself by pretending that he was well enough to live a little bit longer, despite obvious odds against it.

"Listen, Albert..." – he said.

"Stop, please stop. First things first. Do you know when this plot is supposed to fire off?" – he asked, looking squarely at Michael and Alex.

"Yes, tomorrow at 11 am. You mean you don't know that?" – said Alex, somewhat perplexed.

"No, I don't... Shit.... shit..."

"Shit what?"

"It's probably too late. Do you have the documents you retrieved in Breslau?"

"Breslau?" – asked Michael.

"Wrocław, you moron." – said Alex – "Yes, we do, but they're back in Fort Wayne."

"Crap! Why...? Why didn't you bring them with you? Doesn't matter, doesn't matter.... Are you in touch with anybody who has access to them?"

"Yeah, we have a friend over there. The documents are in his house."

"Call him right now. And let me know when you have him on the line".

Albert's head slumped a bit toward one of his shoulders and it was obvious that he was struggling to stay awake and conscious. Alex called Jimmy's number and prayed to his non-existent god that he would answer. He did.

"Hi, Jimmy, this is Alex" – he said hurriedly – "I can't explain what's going on right now, but I need you to get the papers we brought from Poland. Just go and get them."

"OK, Alex, I'll be right back."

Alex turned towards Albert.

"My friend is getting the documents. So now what?"

"Ask him if he has any vodka in his house." – said Albert almost in a whisper.

"What?"

"Just ask him."

Alex knew Jimmy long enough to assume that total absence of this particular beverage in his house was a very remote possibility. However, as soon as his friend came back, he fulfilled Albert's wish.

"All right, Jimmy, one more thing. Do you have any vodka in your house?"

There was a pregnant and telling pause which clearly suggested that Jimmy just concluded his friend Alex was no longer among the part of the population customarily referred to as sane.

"Yes, I do, Alex" – he said – "Shall I pour it into my cell phone or would you perhaps prefer to get it yourself?"

"Jimmy, just bear with me for a minute. I know it sounds crazy, but stay there and I'll explain."

Once again he turned to Albert and almost barked at him.

"Albert, please, go on. This is getting crazy."

"All right. Tell your friend to put the Breslau paper, the one with coded stuff, on some flat surface. Then he needs to pour a shot of vodka over the lower left-hand corner of the document where there shouldn't be any text right now."

"Did you get this, Jimmy?" asked Alex.

"Yes, but who the hell is this guy? Is this **the** Albert? What's going on?"

"Never mind that. Just get the damn vodka and do what he says."

Jimmy did, his growing trepidation notwithstanding.

"All right, Alex, I'm back with a bottle of Absolut and a shot glass. In fact, do you think I should first do a couple of shots to forget about what's happening right now and about how stupid it might turn out to be?"

"Oh, come on. Shut the hell up. I'm as much in the dark as you are. Do what the man says. I'm putting you on speaker phone."

"Great. Live transmissions of vodka pouring ceremonies have always been my thing. All right, everybody, I'm now in the process of dumping the vodka on the lower left-hand corner of the document."

"And?"

"And what?"

"What do you see?"

"Well, I don't quite know how to break this news to you, but I see a piece of paper soaked in booze."

"Shit, Jimmy, try to be a bit more cooperative."

"What? I'm not sure what you mean. Shall I suck on the lower left-hand corner of this thing to get a drink and extract some information from it, or would you want me to just stare at it to scare it into submission?"

"All right, I know this is all weird, but..."

"Tell him to look at it against a light source." – mumbled weakly Albert.

"Pick it up, Jimmy, and place it against some light source, like a lamp or something."

"Yeah, I got it. I'm looking at it. But all I see is paper appetizingly stained with ethanol."

Alex was beginning to be irritated with his role as a relay station between half-conscious Albert and increasingly sardonic Jimmy.

"Listen, Albert, where are we going with this? I mean..."

"Wait!" - shouted Jimmy - "I'll be damned - I can see some faded writing. It's slowly becoming more visible."

People in chief's office held their collective breath.

"All right, it's a short list. Hold on..."

"List of what?" - asked Michael impatiently.

"American cities. Here it is: Chicago, Denver, Washington, Seattle, Miami, Philadelphia, St. Louis, Houston".

"Targets..." - said Albert - "It's a list of targets."

"Oh my god. It all makes sense now." - said Michael.

"It does?" - asked Alex.

"Sure. Remember all the places to which the German agents were supposed to be sent? They were all relatively small towns and they all happen to be in some proximity to the cities on Jimmy's list."

"Hey, it's Hitler's list, not mine." - interjected Jimmy - "Listen, guys, I'd love to chat, but I need to attend to the needs of a certain basement bimbo. Is there anything else you need from me?"

"No, Jimmy. Thanks. By the way, are you doing all right? And how is the bimbo doing?"

"Yeah, all is cool. It's a bit tough, but I'll survive one more day. Stay in touch, no matter what happens. Or, see you in some Alaska concentration camp."

"Right. We'll reserve a cot for you next to Sarah Palin."

"Well, in that case I'll volunteer for Siberia. Talk to you later."

Chapter 34

When Jimmy assured his friends that all was quiet on the Fort Wayne front, he wasn't entirely truthful. Soon after their departure Mairéad came back home from her trip to the East Coast and the family was quickly drawn into hectic Thanksgiving preparations. It involved a lot of cooking and cleaning, which made Jimmy's job of keeping a watchful eye over his FBI 'prisoner' much more complicated. He thought there was no serious risk of his wife directly finding out about the woman tied up in Janice's basement, but his constant trips to 'take care of Janice's dogs' earned him a few impatient comments from Mairéad. The problem for Jimmy was that some of these comments spelled trouble. "You dumbshit" - Mairéad would lovingly say - "why don't you send one of our daughters to feed the dogs and let them out." Jimmy wasn't sure how long he would be able to find reasonable excuses to take care of the dogs himself.

And there was another problem. After lunch Mairéad suddenly expressed a concern about a car parked in the street, about a hundred feet away from their house.

"You know, Jimmy, this car has been in the same spot since the morning." - she said.

"So? - said Jimmy while furiously trying to look totally unconcerned.

"Well, it would be totally normal for someone to park there, but the driver is at the wheel - just sitting there. For hours. Don't you find it a bit strange?"

"Do you want me to go and check him out?"

Jimmy knew that he would have to do it regardless of his wife's response. He hectically entertained all kinds of dark thoughts about the possible identity of the driver and his mission.

"Well, I have to feed Janice's dogs soon anyway, so I'll take a closer look and perhaps ask this guy if he needs some help or something."

"OK. Just don't invite him to dinner."

"Ha, ha, very funny."

Jimmy waited a few agonizing minutes, just to reassure his wife that he was not very concerned about the parked car. Then he put his coat on and went out of the house through the garage door. As he started walking towards the car, he could clearly see that the driver was still inside. He also noticed the vehicle had Illinois license plates. Unfortunately he could not make any further astute discoveries, because suddenly he heard the car's engine, and a few seconds later the driver sped off.

"Crap!" – thought Jimmy. He felt a little helpless, standing by the curb in a little plume of car exhaust. Then he continued on his way to Janice's house. He was getting really tired of the entire situation and wished it was all over soon, one way or the other.

Once inside Janice's house, he grabbed two sandwiches he had prepared earlier and headed downstairs. He found Linda in her usual spot – lying all tied up on the basement couch. And, as usual, he untied her legs, removed her gag, and guided her to the bathroom door. On all the previous occasions she was almost totally silent, answering only "yes" or "no" to Jimmy's questions about her needs. This time around, just before entering the bathroom, she turned around and faced Jimmy.

"I need to ask you what you are going to do tomorrow." – she said quietly.

Jimmy was a bit startled, but recovered quickly.

"Don't worry. I'm not going to blow your brains out. It's not my style and it's not my line of work."

"So what's going to happen?"

"Regardless of what happens tomorrow, you'll go free – either as a fugitive from justice or as a grand wizard of Nazi bullshit. And in the latter case you will have another chance of blowing **my** brains out, because apparently that is **your** line of work."

"If our plan works, there'll be no reason to kill you, although you'll be punished."

"Ah, yes, the punishment. I almost forgot about that part. I hear Auschwitz is beautiful on snowy winter days."

"God, you're such a clueless jerk. People like you will never function in the new America."

"I'm sure you're right. The new America will be functioning thanks to the tireless efforts of zealots, bigots, racists, thugs, and killers, which means that my qualifications for further functioning are none. However, before I stop functioning, please do me a favor – stop talking, get in there, place your flaccid rump on the crapper, and empty your damn totalitarian bladder before you spring a leak."

Jimmy untied Linda's hands, pushed her into the bathroom, closed the door, and sat down on the couch. His patience with the temporary incarceration duties was beginning to wear very thin. He was fatigued, angry and apprehensive, and on top of that he had no way of knowing whether Alex and Michael were making any real progress. To make matters worse, he felt increasingly uncomfortable about playing the cloak-and-dagger game with his wife and wished he could just sit down and tell her everything, even if it meant serious injury administered with a kitchen utensil of her choice. His only consolation was that in less than 24 hours he would sit down with his family to Thanksgiving dinner, and he was determined to do it no matter what.

His further thoughts were brutally interrupted by events which he clearly did not expect. Linda emerged from the bathroom and immediately rushed towards the stairs, taking advantage of the fact that Jimmy was sitting at a certain distance from her. He lunged forward and chased after her, managing to grab one of her ankles half way up the stairs. Both of them first fell, and then rolled back down. Jimmy felt a hard knock on the

226

front of his head. As he landed on the floor, he got entangled with Linda who was nearly on top of him. They scuffled for a minute or so in almost total silence, interrupted only by occasional groans and grunts. Finally Jimmy managed to twist one of Linda's arms behind her back and to push her to the floor face down. While sitting on top of her, he reached in his pocket and took out a small roll of duct tape. He then reached for her second arm and started taping her hands together. Although she was still struggling, he was back in control – he taped her legs at the ankles and started dragging her on the floor towards the couch. He looked briefly up.

Mairéad was standing at the top of the stairs. "Fuck, there goes my Thanksgiving." – thought Jimmy.

Chapter 35

The J. Edgar Hoover building in Washington DC was almost empty. Its vast corridors, usually full of hustle and bustle produced by serious looking individuals taking care of matters of national security, reverberated with nothing more than the sound of vacuum cleaners. After all it was the last afternoon before Thanksgiving and a lot of FBI personnel went home early, presumably assuming that criminals, spies and other bad guys of various description would also need to eat some fat turkey instead of engaging in illicit activities.

However, in one of the offices on the top floor work continued. Special agent George Mattison was having an urgent meeting with one of his top coworkers – Susan Griffin. The subject of the meeting was a mysterious murder in Indiana which Susan thought needed FBI's attention, because the victim was not only a foreign national, but also an officer of a foreign intelligence service.

"So what do we know about this, Sue?" – asked Mattison.

"Well, not a lot. Earlier this month two Chicago guys left for a trip to Poland. Our office in Chicago alerted us..."

"Wait, who exactly alerted us?"

"Special agent Kim Swanson. She said that they might be after some weird war-related plot and that they needed to be stopped before 'something happens', so we got Kazik and his people in ABW to take a look."

"How did she know about these Chicago guys?"

"I have no idea. I tried to get in touch with her to find out more, but she's nowhere to be found."

"What do you mean?"

"Well, a few days ago she requested some time off and went somewhere, but I don't know where. Her cell phone has been switched off since then."

"That's weird... Anyway, go on."

"OK, the ABW people in Poland reported that the Americans had retrieved some documents which were in German, so Kazik translated this stuff for them, because he was friends with one of them. He later told us that all of this probably amounted to nothing and promised to investigate further. Then he suddenly turned up dead in Wakarusa, Indiana".

"Did we ask him to come here?"

"Absolutely not. I have no idea why he showed up in Indiana. And neither do his colleagues back in Poland."

"I don't understand. He came here as a private citizen to investigate something?"

"Apparently."

"Do we know what kind of a war-related plot we're talking about?"

"No, not a clue. Kazik obviously knew, but he can't tell us anything anymore. And he never shared any of this with people in his office either."

"What's in Wakarusa?"

"To put it bluntly, zilch."

"All right, so what do we have on these two Chicago guys?"

"One is a 'Chicago Tribune' journalist, and the other - a naturalized citizen of Polish origin. He works as an IT guy for some company in Morton Grove."

"Criminal records?"

"None."

"Where are these people now?"

"That's the strange part. Both of them kind of vanished from their respective places of work more or less at the same time as Kim Swanson went on vacation. Nobody seems to know where they are. However, one of the reporter's coworkers says he got a call from him, and sent him a fax to a number which is in Fort Wayne, Indiana. The requested fax was a copy of a short background bio of Kim Swanson. Neither of the two guys stayed in any hotels in Fort Wayne."

Mattison got up and started walking nervously around the room.

"You know, Sue, I don't like any of this. There seems to be something fishy going on."

"I agree. I called the police chief in Wakarusa and told him that we might be sending some people over to investigate."

"Do you want to go?"

"Yeah, I'll probably go right after Thanksgiving".

The phone on Mattison's desk suddenly rang which surprised him since everybody was already in 'holiday mode', and either at home or on the way home. As he picked up the receiver, Susan got up and started walking towards the door. Mattison motioned for her to stay while listening attentively to whoever was on the line.

"I understand" – he said – "please send this to me via email immediately. Thanks."

He turned to Susan.

"Well, there is a development. Our guys in Chicago identified the hotel room where Kazik apparently had stayed before he was killed. They searched it and retrieved a bunch of documents which I'll get in a few minutes. Unfortunately most of this stuff is in Polish. How is your Polish these days?"

"Blissfully non-existent. But there is this woman down in the personnel office - Lucy, I think. As far as I know, she is bi-lingual and speaks fluent Polish".

"Great, except she's probably gone by now. What's her last name?"

"Jacak."

"All right, please go and find out if she is still around, and if you find her, bring her over here."

"Sure... But, sorry for asking, what's the emergency, George?"

"I don't know. It's just that I have a bad feeling about this."

Mattison got his email from Chicago a few minutes later. He printed out all the attachments, about a dozen pages in total, stacked them on the desk, and started shuffling through them, looking for any bits and pieces in English. It wasn't long before he caught a glimpse of an intriguing handwritten note:

Swanson is really Brunner. Other moles in FBI?

A bit further down there was a title in English, apparently cut out of some newspaper and pasted onto the page:

Indiana Authorities Discover Neo-Nazi Network

All the rest of the material was in Polish, some of it handwritten, and some typed. However Mattison could clearly see references to various places in the US – mostly Chicago and Wakarusa, but also Philadelphia and Miami. He waited patiently to see if Lucy would materialize. After about half an hour she did. She walked into his office, accompanied by Susan who immediately told her superior that she had explained everything to Ms. Jacak on the way over.

Lucy sat down in one of the armchairs and was handed the stack of papers. She seemed a bit tense, which was understandable, because never before in her career at the Bureau had she been summoned to the office of a high-ranking agent.

"Ms. Jacak" – said Mattison – "there is quite a lot of this, so I don't want you to translate these pages word for word. Please read the whole thing and tell us in your own words what the documents say."

"I understand."

Mattison and Griffin spent the next 10 minutes twitching their fingers and watching their impromptu translator waddling slowly through the pages. She finished reading and put the papers aside.

"Well, this whole thing is a bit chaotic. It's a long series of disjointed notes, comments, thoughts, or what not. But it seems to convey two main things." – she said.

"Yes? Please go on."

"OK, first of all, whoever wrote this was convinced that a Chicago-based FBI agent was working with some radical groups against this country and that there were more rogue agents involved in this."

"Does he give a name?"

"Yes, the agent in question is Kim Swanson."

Mattison looked at Griffin in a thunderstruck sort of way, as if he wanted to convey to her that he was as baffled about all this as she and possibly the rest of the universe.

"OK, what else?"

Lucy hesitated.

"Sir, as I'm sure you know, I'm just an administrative employee and I have absolutely no security clearance of any sort. The other part of this text talks about a terrorist plot, so I need to ask you if you think it's even legal for me to have this conversation with you."

"Well, if it's illegal, I'll make it legal – you have my word. This could be a pretty important matter, so please don't be afraid and tell us about what you've just read."

"All right. Obviously I have no idea who wrote all this, but whoever it was, he was working under some sort of duress. There are frequent references to dangerous meetings, people seemingly following him, etc. But the gist of the story is simple – he thinks there is some shady group camped out somewhere outside of a little place in Indiana..."

"Wakarusa?"

"Yes, Wakarusa. And that group is supposedly on the verge of launching a massive terrorist attack against a bunch of American cities."

"On the verge? What does that mean? Are there any dates?"

"No, no dates. And one more thing – the last thing this person writes is that he is going to stop it and that 'the day of retribution is here'. Those are his exact words."

Mattison sat down and stared briefly into empty FBI space.

"Ms. Jacak" – he said after a while – "thank you very much for your help. I would ask you to keep this entire conversation to yourself until further notice. And I have one more favor to ask. I know it's almost Thanksgiving, but could you spend an hour or so on fully translating all these pages into English? You can go into the adjacent office where you can use whatever equipment you need and nobody will be in your way."

"Certainly, sir. I'll get right on it."

Susan got up, grabbed all the pages and departed, leaving Mattison and Griffin looking at each other with a touch of puzzlement. Both of them realized that there was something sinister going on, but the information they had was too fragmentary and centered almost exclusively around a single individual, Kazik, who apparently came to the US with some sort of a personal mission. Mattison thought it was entirely possible that the Polish visitor was chasing shadows or that he was some sort of a conspiracy freak. The only problem was that conspiracy freaks usually don't get gruesomely murdered in the middle of nowhere. Additionally Mattison was seriously worried about special agent Kim Swanson and a clear reference to 'other moles in FBI', which seemed to suggest some plot to infiltrate the Bureau.

"So what do you think?" – asked Susan.

"What do I think? I think we need to go all the way on this."

"What?"

"Sue, I need you to call whoever you need to call and get at least two attack helicopters and a tactical unit ready to show up in Wakarusa tomorrow."

Susan could not quite hide her shock.

"Tomorrow? On Thanksgiving?"

"Yes. And if any of our people grumble about this, tell them to pack some turkey sandwiches and eat them on the way to Indiana. They can even wear pilgrim hats for all I care. We need to be there by noon at the latest. And don't call anybody in Wakarusa – right now I have no idea who is doing what and for whom over there."

"Aren't you taking this a bit too seriously?"

"Well, that's quite possible. But think about it. We have a potential terrorist plot on our hands, a dead guy who was chasing it, a possible traitor in our ranks, and two nuts from Chicago who disappeared and then asked for info on Kim. And all of this somehow centers on this little town in Indiana where something is 'on the verge' of happening. Don't you think we need to check this out immediately?"

"I guess. The thing I don't quite understand is this - how can you launch a massive terrorist attack from some dusty compound in the boonies?"

"I don't know, Sue... But we have a few hours to spare, so let's at least find out where exactly this secretive group of would-be terrorists might be located so that we can zero in on them tomorrow."

"OK, let's do it. You stay here, and I'll be right back with turkey sandwiches and some coffee. It's almost Thanksgiving, you know."

"Yeah, I know. Just don't bring any pilgrim hats."

Chapter 36

It took Albert a two-hour nap, followed by a meal consisting of a Big Mac and fries, to regain some of his strength. Earlier Chief Thompson took his unexpected guest to his house, let him have a shower, and put a couple of bandages on his face and neck. On their way back to the police station they made a quick stop at a local nutritional recovery station called McDonald's. Michael and Alex impatiently waited for Albert's return and then they watched him slowly eat while Chief Thompson sat in his armchair working on some long overdue paperwork. Albert polished off his food, took a precariously large gulp of Diet Coke and seemed ready to start talking.

"Albert" – started Michael – "I don't want to rush you, but as you know we have very little time. So tell us what happened to you and what we can do to help you."

"Well, let me start by saying you really can't help me and, conversely, there is very little I can do for you. I know bits and pieces, but I was never in the 'inner circle' of this whole thing. But let's start from the beginning. My father, Karl Brunner, came to the US with some weird mission to organize a 'cell' of ex-Nazis and their sympathizers. They were supposed to be 'ready' for some sort of action, but for many years absolutely nothing happened and their activities consisted of utterly silly drills in the woods."

"Were you born in the US?" – asked Alex.

"Yes. And I was raised within this stupid cell. All the children of its members were being constantly indoctrinated and they were supposed to 'carry on the fight'. Initially the group was based in Fort Wayne, but then Krugman, who back then was very much one of the big shots, decided that we needed to be closer to Chicago, and that's why we ended up here. Anyway, as I was growing up, I was learning more and more about the ideology of this whole crap and I was beginning to have serious doubts. And then one day, when I was about 20, Krugman told me about the 'conditions' which had to be satisfied in order for the whole system of cells to be activated. He was a bit of a loner, but I liked him, because he seemed to be much more rational than the rest of this bunch. It was he who told me that there was nothing to be worried about, because these conditions would probably be never satisfied and the 'secret army' would simply die shooting cans and playing soldiers."

"Did he tell you what the conditions were?"

"No, I never knew that. Krugman started having frequent and heated arguments with my father – I could see he was drifting away from the whole group. When my dad died, I wanted to leave, but some new people came, probably from other cells, and they forced everyone to stay. Let me tell you – these people were ruthless killers and they would stop at nothing. Krugman was scared of them and started planning his exit. One day he simply disappeared. Some of us thought he was murdered, but a few weeks ago, after many years of silence, he suddenly called me and told me in great secrecy that the conditions for action had been met and he feared the worst. And then he told me about you and your mission in Poland. He seemed to think that if you got to some war-time documents in time, you would be in a position to alert the authorities, and he asked me to somehow get in touch with you to offer any help possible."

"Well, that didn't work out very well, did it?" – said Alex somewhat awkwardly.

"So when you got in touch with us, you thought that they were just about to nail you in some way for betraying them? – asked Michael who clearly didn't want to dwell on their past strategies of dealing with the whole matter.

"Right, they somehow discovered that I'd talked to Krugman and that he was trying to stop their idiotic plot. Very shortly

236

after that they threw me into a dark cell and beat the shit out of me for three days straight, using all kinds of choice instruments like baseball bats wrapped in wet towels, aluminum pipes, leather belts etc. Really professional work, I would say, although I was in no mood to compliment them. In fact, I knew I was as good as dead."

"Then how come you are not dead?" – asked Alex.

"Well, one day they threw another guy into the same cell. He was in really bad shape – they must have tortured him or something, because for hours he was only half conscious and sometimes screamed in pain. But then he kind off came back and started talking, except I couldn't understand him, because he couldn't speak any English. I had no idea what language he spoke, but during one of his screaming sessions I thought I heard some German words, so I tried that and it worked, although my German is pathetic, so it was tough for me to have a conversation with him. "

As Albert was saying all of this Alex's face was turning pale.

"Was his name Kazik?" – he asked quietly.

"Yes, how did you know?" – asked Albert, clearly surprised.

"He was a good friend of mine."

"What happened to him?"

"You mean you don't know?"

"No. One day they dragged him out of the cell and I never saw him again."

"He turned up mangled and dead in the field out of town."

Albert paused for a moment and seemed genuinely shaken by the news.

"I'm terribly sorry" – he said – "he was a very nice guy."

"Do you know why he was there?"

Albert reacted to this question with a bizarre, scared expression on his face. It became immediately clear to Alex and Michael that he knew something, but was uncomfortable talking about it. He finally looked them straight in the eye and continued.

237

"Well, he came to the US to kill my daughter and me."

Chief Thompson, until now minding his own bureaucratic business, dropped the papers, and all three of them gaped at Albert in disbelief, totally at a loss as to how to react. Alex was first to collect his wits.

"Albert, I know you've been through a lot, but..."

"Wait, wait. I know this sounds very improbable, but he told me as much himself. He came to kill us, and – if possible – disrupt the plot.

Alex was having none of this.

"But this is insane. Kazik would never hurt anyone. And what possible reason would he have to do away with you and your daughter?"

"Well, he had a pretty good reason, I'm afraid. You see, back during... shit, it's a bit difficult for me.... Back in 1943 my father worked in the Gross Rosen concentration camp in Lower Silesia. He never told me about it, but Kazik did. Back then he... he... shot and killed Kazik's mother and his little sister... She was only 3."

"What? Why would he do that?" – asked Michael.

"No German officer or guard in any concentration camp needed any reason to kill someone." – replied Albert coldly – "And he shot them both in the head, point blank. Perhaps he was bothered by the fact that Kazik's mother's maiden name was Rosenzweig. But what does it matter..."

Chief Thompson's office was suddenly shrouded in a thick layer of somber silence. Nobody had any idea what to say, and nobody was volunteering any comments.

"I need some fresh air." – said the chief and steamed out through the front door.

"Albert, I'm sorry, but I must know what Kazik told you." – said Alex.

"When it became obvious to both of us that we were in no position to kill anybody, or even live, and that in a way we were on the same side of the barricade, he told me he'd seen my father's name in the document you had found and that he had decided to track down my family to avenge his. Apparently he was trying to find my father for years and even signed up for intelligence work, so that he could have access to more information.

"What intelligence work?" – asked Alex who didn't even try to mask his shock and disbelief.

"I don't exactly know. He kept mentioning some organization back in Poland."

"ABW?"

"Maybe. I can't really say."

"Did he tell you how he got into the compound?"

"No, he just said he managed to get inside, but was caught prowling just inside the perimeter by the goons who patrol this place."

"So how did you escape?"

"Partly thanks to him. For whatever reason they thought he was a much more important 'catch' than me. I was just an insider, and he was an intruder from outside, and a foreigner on top of that. When they took him out of the cell for the last time, the idiot who was guarding me didn't latch the door properly, so I slipped out at night and managed to reach the road leading to town. I'm sure they are looking for me."

"OK, I hate to be a spoiler, guys, but enough of this." - hollered a familiar voice. Chief Thompson was back.

"Whatever happened, happened, but I think we need to move on and start talking about the immediate future. Albert, as you know, these Chicago dudes here claim that they know the attack, or whatever you want to call it, is set for 11 am tomorrow. Do you actually know what's supposed to happen?"

"I know the general plan. A computer at the compound will trigger a series of very powerful explosions in the cities on that list we recovered. No idea where the explosives are exactly placed or how powerful they are. I also don't know the actual triggering mechanism. It might be totally automatic or it may have to be set in motion by a human operator sitting at the machine."

"All right, so we go 'kaboom' on Thanksgiving day and plenty of half-cooked turkeys land on kitchen floors. But then what?"

"Again, sorry, but I don't know any further details. I was always on the fringe of things, barely trusted by the others. But I did hear various bits and pieces of conversations which always seemed to suggest the same scenario: total chaos, aided by additional acts of sabotage, panic in the streets, tanking markets, and then a campaign to blame foreigners, Muslims, blacks, illegal immigrants, etc. Finally street violence, anarchy, and a possible power grab. Moles in the FBI could actually engineer 'martial law' or something similar."

"I was going to ask about that, Albert" – said Michael – "or more particularly about your daughter Linda".

"Did you meet her?"

"Up close and personal."

"What?"

"She showed up in Fort Wayne and tried to shoot us all."

"Oh my god. I'm so terribly sorry. She turned out to be a spitting image of my dad, mentally and otherwise. But she has no idea I turned against them."

"Yeah, we know."

"She is no longer my daughter, really. She became a totally different person – hateful and cruel."

"We know that too."

"So where is she? Is she alive?"

Michael decided to tread cautiously.

"She is alive, but we can talk about her whereabouts later."

"Couldn't agree more" – said Chief Thompson loudly – "come on, let's get on with it! We don't have time for damn family recriminations."

"You know, chief, for someone who only recently thought we were raving lunatics, you suddenly are very eager to act."

"You could still be lunatics, but I can't take the risk of assuming that anymore."

At this point Willard sauntered lazily into the office, looked around, saw battered Albert, and decided to take part in the proceedings.

"What's up with this guy?" – he asked.

Chief Thompson's soul groaned silently inside his massive body, but he managed to be relatively polite towards his subordinate.

"Sit down and don't say anything, Willard. You might turn out to be useful later on, however unlikely this may seem."

"Fine, chief." said Willard.

Michael turned towards Albert.

"So why are you saying that the key to defeating all this is to somehow cut their computers off?"

"Not the computers, but electric power. I am convinced that if their equipment is down tomorrow at 11, they are dead in the water, because they would have to reprogram the whole thing, which could take weeks or even months."

"Wait a second" – said Alex – "first of all we don't know what computers they have and how many, and which of the machines is the 'trigger guy'. And even if we did know that, it's quite possible these guys have a generator and backup batteries. The batteries would only last for about 15 minutes, but a generator can go forever. How about cutting their Internet access?"

"That won't work – they use some weird satellite hookup, and I don't think we are in a position to shoot down a satellite. My guess is that our only chance is taking away their juice. As for the computers, I really can't tell you anything – they are all kept in this 'command center' and I never had access to that."

"Alex, what do you think?" – asked Michael, looking at him almost imploringly, as if to say 'do something you damn geek'".

"My feeling is that setting off such a massive operation will most likely not be done on some dinky laptop or tablet, or whatever. They must have some central, relatively powerful machine and – if they do have a generator – it's that machine that will be powered in case of an outage. Albert, are you sure you don't know anything about a generator within the compound?"

"Sorry, most of the technical equipment is kept within an inner fence and only a few people can enter."

"I did once." – said someone confidently.

Everybody turned abruptly to look at Willard who was sitting in a chair and scratching his belly with disconcerting abandon. The sergeant returned everybody's stare.

"What? What did I do now?" – he asked with convincing innocence.

"You were within that inner fence?" – snapped at him his boss.

"Yeah, once. They had some weird problems with electrical switches and I went there with that crazy, giant electrician – you know, the one who tests wires for voltage by touching them with his bare hands."

"Jake Sylvester?"

"Yep."

"And?"

"And what?"

"What did you see?"

"I saw their generator. It's a medium-sized gas thing sitting by the side wall."

"Why the fuck didn't you say that earlier?"

"Well, here you go again, chief. Just a moment ago you told me to sit down and not say anything, and now you're complaining that I didn't say anything."

"Shut up!"

"Yes, sir."

It was almost noon. Chief Thompson asked Michael and Alex to join him at a small table to 'discuss options'. He also told Willard to go to the back room with Albert. "Willard" – he said – "take care of him – he's still pretty weak. And make sure that the back door is locked". It was obvious that the chief came to the conclusion that Albert, in his current condition, could not offer them any more help, other than perhaps drawing a simple

242

topographical layout of some of the installations within the compound.

Once Willard and Albert left, the trio sat around a small table by the window, which afforded them a clear view of the street. Alex seemed to be contemplating something in his head and wasn't paying too much attention to what the other two were saying. Then he took out a sheet of paper from his laptop bag and started scribbling something on it.

"What the hell are you doing?" – asked Michael.

"We need a plan of some sort, so I'm trying to put one together."

"Well, thanks for including us in the discussion."

"Sorry, guys, I needed to make some things clear to myself before sharing them with you. So, here is how I see it from the computer perspective. Somehow I need to get within 300 feet or less of their network router and it needs to happen today."

"You're kidding, right?"

"No, unfortunately I'm not."

"So what happens if by force of some unforeseen miracle we accomplish that?"

"If I am that close and have my laptop with me, I can probably break into their network and discover what devices they have, how many, etc. This will tell me whether I can do a zero-day code attack on some of these devices."

"I think it's time for you to start speaking English again."

"All right. I can probably infect most of their machines with a brand new virus which has never been used yet, and therefore will be undetectable for some time to come. This might allow me to later remotely shut all their machines down, although probably not their main computer which is most likely well-protected by some sophisticated firewall."

"Well, great. So all we need is a miracle and that damn virus."

"I have the virus."

Chief Thompson started showing telltale signs of getting uncomfortable.

"Where did you get it? – he asked.

"Well... I have my sources, so to speak."

"Did you actually create it?"

"Hell no, I wouldn't know how."

"So you're telling me that someone else created it, it has never been used before, and you are in possession of it?"

"That's right."

"Great. I think the problem is that what you are proposing amounts to committing at least two different crimes, if not more. Perhaps you forgot, but I work in law enforcement"

Alex looked at the chief with a bit of amazement.

"Yes, I think before this is all over we will be breaking the law in a number of ways. But don't you think that blowing up American cities on a massive scale is a bit more unlawful than a Chicago Polack breaking into someone's network?"

"I can't chase or not chase crimes based on their seriousness." – said Chief Thompson defensively – "But OK, just continue."

"So, if I manage to shut everything down other than the main PC, and their electricity goes down, all we have to do is to disable the generator before 11 am tomorrow."

If derision could be a liquid, it would probably start flowing from Chief Thompson's ears.

"Fantastic. No problem. This ought to be a piece of cake. You just walk into the compound with your laptop in hand, infect their electronics, and then stroll slowly up to the generator to flip the switch to the 'off' position. On your way out you might even shake some hands with the totally demoralized and dejected enemy who by that time will be engaging in giving up all their machine guns and hand grenades."

"Chief, before you blow a gasket or two, I need you to answer a simple question – is it in your power to order an electricity blackout in this area. Like in a couple of hours or so"?

"Right now out of all the possible powers I have, the one to arrest your ass seems to be the most appealing."

"Please..."

"Yes, damn it – I can shut the power down, although I'll have to deal with Betsy."

"Who's Betsy?"

"Betsy Cook works at the local power substation and has her middle-aged, well-manicured paws hovering over all kinds of important switches. She's not exactly happy with her station in life, and has spells of being a really obnoxious hag."

"Where are you going with this, Alex?" – asked Michael.

"Basically I think we need to have two power outages, each about 2-hour long. One later today, and the other one tomorrow shortly after 10 am. We would cut electricity just to the compound and adjacent areas, and..."

"No, no" – objected the chief – "if you cut it just to the compound, they will find out and feel targeted in some way, which will raise suspicions. If you really think this is needed, we have to turn out the lights for the entire town. Of course after it's all over people around here will bake me in their ovens instead of turkeys, but what the hell..."

"That's a good point, chief. I mean, about the entire town blackout, not the ovens... Anyway, I'll explain about the second shutoff soon. Today we need to cut the power later on, let's say around 3 pm. My hope is that their generator will kick in automatically and that they will be sufficiently worried about this, on the eve of their 'big day', to call to find out what's going on. And here's when Jake and myself come in."

"What?" – asked panicked Michael, correctly sensing that his friend was once again into his 'pretend' games.

"When they call, we ask Betsy to tell them that she is sending out a repair crew consisting of Sylvester and me as his newly employed assistant."

"Oh shit, not again." – moaned Michael while sinking his face into his hands.

"Relax, Michael. They already know him, and they certainly don't know me. I'll be there with my laptop and some 'electrical' measuring stuff – fake or real, doesn't matter. If everything goes well, we'll get pretty close to the main building and the generator."

"And if it doesn't?"

"We'll retreat and prepare for long periods of solitary confinement. What do you think, chief?"

"The idea that you are both insane is still my main sentiment. However, I'm willing to go along with this craziness, because I see no other immediate options. Also, Jake the Electric Giant is just the right kind of a crazy idiot to send on such a hopeless mission. How much time do you need, Alex?"

"For what?"

"Well, once you are in, how long will it take you to do your electronic epidemic magic?"

"Difficult to gauge. I would say at least 10 minutes. 15 would be much better."

"I hope Jake can hold their interest for that long with his usual exotic song-and-dance. I'm off to call Betsy. Wish me luck."

Chapter 37

Contrary to what Jimmy expected, his wife never said anything when she saw him dragging a tied-up woman across Janice's floor. For a few seconds she stood at the top of the stairs motionless and silent. And then she just turned around and disappeared – Jimmy didn't even have time to react in any way, and Linda never realized that there was a third person in the room, because she was still lying face down on the floor.

Jimmy put his 'hostage' back on the couch and taped her mouth as quickly as he could. He certainly wasn't in the mood for any further conversations with her. Looking straight at Linda he said through tightly clenched teeth: "If you pull anything like this again, I swear I'll break both your legs in five places." Having delivered this rather straightforward message, he got up, ran upstairs, and went outside. There he sat down on the curb and tried frantically to collect his rattled thoughts. He quickly came to the conclusion that his only option was to tell Mairéad absolutely everything, but he also realized that he was working on a flimsy assumption that his suitcase hadn't been already packed and placed for him conveniently in front of his house.

Jimmy's wife was usually a very understanding person, even though she often complained about his idiosyncrasies and – given a good reason – never missed a chance of calling him all kinds of colorful names. Yet in this particular case Jimmy sensed that her understanding might not stretch far enough to cover what must have looked like a secretive session of bondage frolicking with a young woman in someone else's basement.

Faced with the absence of any other options, Jimmy started walking slowly down the street, dreading almost every step he was taking. He found his house to be calm - way too calm. Mairéad was sitting on the couch in the living room. Jimmy sat down directly opposite her.

"Listen, I know what you're thinking, but I can explain." – he said in a hopeless, pleading sort of way.

"Really? Hey, your head is bleeding. Maybe you should ease off on all of that rough sex. And by the way, no, you don't know what the fuck I'm thinking."

"Mairéad, please allow me to explain."

"Whatever."

"The woman you saw is an FBI agent who tried to kill me."

Jimmy's wife grinned scornfully in a way that probably precedes a lot of beheadings by disgruntled Saudi executioners.

"Oh my god, Jimmy, if you really need to lie to me, have the decency of constructing something slightly more plausible. You know, something like 'Vladimir Putin delivered this KGB babe to me to test her stamina under conditions of extreme American sex slavery', or 'Janice gave her to me as a Thanksgiving present', or 'this is the latest model of a blow-up sex toy I was trying out for Toys-R-Us'... Please, just go away."

"No, I won't. We need to talk. I admit I was hiding some things from you, but I had a very good reason for it, and this woman really tried to shoot me in the head. Just give me 5 minutes to explain and then pass your judgment – I'll accept it, whatever it is... Please."

"All right, I'm listening, but use your time well, because my patience is hanging well below your balls right now."

As soon as Jimmy starting telling the story of how he had been contacted by Alex and how things had developed from that point on, he became aware of the sheer silliness and implausibility of his story, but he persevered and finished his narrative by saying that if Mairéad wanted some confirmation of what he had just said, she could talk to either Janice or Archibald when they were back in town.

"One more thing" – he added – "if you wish, we could go back to Janice's house together and you can ask Linda any questions you want. I have to go back there anyway, because in the midst of all this I forgot to feed the dogs."

Mairéad had a strange expression on her face which could suggest a broad range of things: from 'I'm going to kill this bastard' to 'I'm going to kill that bitch'." But for what seemed to Jimmy like eternity she remained silent. And her first words weren't exactly what Jimmy expected.

"You're such a titanic dickhead, Jimmy."

"Why?"

"I'll tell you why. If any of this crap is true, then you risked not only your life, but also the lives of our kids. Did it ever occur to you that I might've come back from the East Coast to find three dead bodies in my house?"

"Well, it's not like I had plenty of time for such considerations."

"Damn it, next time you decide to save the world by getting killed, please let me know in advance, so that I can pack up and leave. And another thing – are we safe now? Who was that guy in the car out in the street? Can I go shopping as usual or should I first buy a shotgun to take with me to the mall?"

"I don't know about that guy, because he took off before I had a chance to talk to him. But I think we are safe for now."

"For now? Well, that's very reassuring. At the very least I'd like to survive until tomorrow's dinner, because otherwise all this cooking and cleaning is a total waste of time."

"But what would you have done in my place? Would you have told these two guys to go away, because you were busy, scared or unwilling to risk your family's safety? If the idiots in Wakarusa win, our lives will change forever. Heck, this country will probably change forever. I'd like to believe that you would have made the same choices as I did."

"I said you were a dickhead, not a coward or someone who would refuse to help his friends. If all of this is true, I'm actually somewhat proud of what you've done, and I'm willing to temporarily suspend my initial urge to beat the crap out of you and file for a divorce – not necessarily in that order."

Jimmy saw a trace of a tiny, feeble smile on his wife's face, which to him was the first sign that his suitcase might remain unpacked in the closet.

"Listen, Mairéad, let's have a drink, and then let's go and see our lovely prisoner. I'd like you to see for yourself who we're dealing with."

"Do you think it's wise?"

"I don't see any problem with that."

"All right then."

When they both showed up in Janice's basement, Linda seemed to be pretty surprised to see someone else other than Jimmy. As soon as Jimmy ripped off her mouth gag, she turned to Mairéad and said: "Who the hell are you?"

"It's none of your business, but if you must know, this is my wife. She's never seen evil incarnate before, so I thought it might be a good opportunity for her to catch up." – said Jimmy.

"Aaah, what a lovely couple. So, Jimmy, did you tell her about all that steamy sex we have been having for the last couple of days?"

"Yes, in graphic detail. She especially liked that one sex position where you point a gun at my head to arouse me. Pity it didn't work."

"Maybe you are simply too old for me and nothing excites you anymore."

"Not true. There's one thing that excites me, and that's the prospect of kicking your ass out of here tomorrow."

Jimmy was ready to tape Linda's mouth again, but she signaled that she had something else to say.

"Have you said goodbye to your two moronic friends?" – she asked.

"What's that supposed to mean?"

"You didn't expect them to come back from their exploit alive, did you?"

"They'll be back."

"Sadly, they won't. We are only hours away from victory, so I can tell you that if for whatever reason our operation will not fire off at 11 tomorrow, about two minutes later your friends will be blown to bits, together with our base, and selected parts of that stupid dump called Wakarusa. Yes, that's right – the whole place is rigged with explosives, and there is nothing anybody can do to disarm them. So, I certainly hope Alex and Michael fail, because then they will trade certain death for a comfortable, lifetime stay in one of our correctional camps."

"Nice bluff. Lame, but nice."

"We'll see tomorrow."

Jimmy taped Linda's mouth and turned to Mairéad.

"Let's get the hell out of here, before I puke." – she said.

Chapter 38

Chief Thompson always dreaded having to talk to Betsy Cook regardless of reasons. Thankfully their conversations were pretty rare events, usually generated by electrical outages due to lightning strikes. Whenever something like that happened, he would call Betsy to find about the status of any repairs conducted by Mr. Sylvester and his crew or – more precisely – by Mr. Sylvester and his crew of 0, since he was the only electrician in town and frequent efforts to hire some sort of an assistant invariably failed. The chief had always suspected that because all candidates for this job had to be interviewed by Betsy, none of them could have ever possibly decided in favor of working for the 'high-voltage witch', which was Chief Thompson's favorite term of endearment for her.

"This is Betsy Cook, how can I help you?" – said Betsy with totally fake friendliness in her voice."

"Hello, Betsy, this is Chief Thompson."

"What's wrong? We don't have any outages."

In just a second Betsy's tone transformed from warmth to dry ice.

"Nothing is wrong."

"So what do you want? I'm kind of busy."

"Well, if you could possibly drag yourself away from all your blinking fuses, I would appreciate it very much."

"OK, what is it that you want?"

Chief Thompson took a deep breath as if he was just about to go for a world record in diving without oxygen equipment.

252

"I need you to switch off electricity for our entire grid at 3 pm this afternoon."

Betsy was either speechless or unconscious, because she didn't say anything for a long time. And when she finally spoke, it was obvious she was not a happy person.

"Mr. Thompson, I have no idea what you're smoking, but don't let it cloud your judgment. I can't just darken the entire town on a whim."

"Well, I'm afraid you'll have to and it's not a whim, but a part of a police investigation. As police chief I'm ordering you to shut down electricity at 3 pm, just for two hours."

"Have you announced this to people?"

"No, and – what's more – you're not allowed to announce it to anybody either."

"But..."

"And if you do, I'll arrest you."

"I beg your pardon?"

"There is no time for begging, Betsy. Please cooperate and everything is going to be all right. I need to mention two other things. First, if citizens start to call you after the shutdown, just tell them their power will be back shortly. However, if you get a call from the compound outside town – you know, the one with all these Sunday soldiers at the old Hawkins ranch – tell them that there are some problems with switches and that you need to send Mr. Sylvester and his assistant to fix it."

"What? He doesn't have any assistants."

"He will have one. Don't worry. That's not all. Tomorrow at exactly 10:15 am we are cutting power again."

"Oh my god, you must be crazy. Tomorrow is Thanksgiving."

"I'm glad you remember. We'll switch everything back on by about 11:30, so no dinner plans will be ruined."

"What about all those people with electric ovens?"

"They should have switched to gas a long time ago."

"This is all crazy. I must protest."

"If you must, go ahead and do it, but switch the lights off anyway, and – most importantly – keep all of this to yourself. You're now a part of this investigation, and therefore you have new responsibilities."

"This is highly irregular. I'll do it, but I will not accept any blame for whatever happens."

"No problem. I'll gladly take whatever comes my way. Once we hang up, please have Jake come to my office immediately, but don't tell him anything about this conversation. He needs to come in his service van, with all his tools. Are we clear about everything?"

"Clear as mud, Chief Thompson."

"That'll have to do for now."

Chief Thompson was greatly relieved to have this part of the overall plan done. He returned from the back room to his front office where Alex and Michael were still discussing the details of the operation. Michael was worried that - despite the outage – nobody from the compound would ever call, in which case Alex would not be able to get close to the router.

"There is no point speculating about it" – said the chief – "we'll find out pretty soon – the electrician should be here shortly, and in slightly over an hour all the lights will go out".

Jake Sylvester arrived a few minutes later. It was impossible to be unimpressed by his height. He looked like a retired basketball player who devoted his post-career years to consuming vast quantities of beer. He was wearing dark overalls, adorned with a professional looking logo. His attire stretched dangerously over an impressive beer gut that made him look like a very lanky pregnant man.

"Hello there, Mr. Policeman." – he yelled cheerfully, extending his hand to the chief.

"Glad to see you Jake."

"So where's the problem?"

"What?"

"What you'all want me to fix around here?"

"Nothing. Please sit down – I have a bit of an unusual job for you."

"As long as it's all about shorts, wires, and electric sparks, I'm damn ready."

"First of all, meet my guests – this is Michael, and this is Alex." – said the chief pointing to each of the men in turn.

"Pleasure to be sure, gentlemen!"

"There is no easy way to explain what I'm going to ask you to do, but I'll try. At 3 pm Betsy the Hag will cut all power in our grid for 2 hours. We think that a bit later the people at the old Hawkins ranch will call to find out what's going on. At that point she will tell them that she needs to send you and your assistant to fix some circuits over there."

"I ain't got no assistant, chief."

"Yes, you do. It's going to be Alex. He has no clue about electricity, but he's good with computers."

"I'm sorry, chief, but this don't make no sense to me."

"It's simple. We need to get Alex inside the compound, because he has to do something important in there without any of these guys knowing about it. So I'd like you to pretend that you're actually fixing something while he does his thing. All we need is about 15 minutes."

Jake blinked rapidly for a while.

"But I actually won't be fixin' a damn thing, right?"

"Right. Just go to some electric panel or something and fiddle with some shit, and if they get restless or suspicious, throw some of your jargon at them."

"Some of my what?"

"You know, electricians' speak, the crap that nobody understands except for you."

"Oh, I get it. And then I leave and the juice comes back on, like I actually fixed it."

"Exactly."

Jake grinned like an electric Cheshire cat.

"I like that! I ain't gonna ask no stinkin' questions – I'm sure you'all know what you're doin'".

"Great. Two things though. Do you have any piece of small equipment which we can somehow attach to Alex's laptop so that it looks like some kind of sensor or measuring device?"

"I got just the right thing for you. I'll go and get it."

"Wait, how about overalls for Alex?"

"You're in luck, Mr. Policeman. I was gonna have an assistant for such a long time that I keep stuff for him in the van, just in case."

"OK then. We are all set."

Jake went to get the stuff out of the van.

"This situation really reminds me of so many things." – said Michael wistfully.

"What? You want to revive your career of a Polish plumber?" – asked Alex.

"No, not really, although now I look at it quite fondly. Unfortunately we are missing our real plumber."

"Yes, we certainly are. You don't have to remind me."

Chapter 39

.

There were all kinds of strange ideas flying through Alex's mind as he was being driven by Jake Sylvester towards the Hawkins ranch. The road was pretty bumpy, the van jumped up and down, and all the tools and cables in the back rattled incessantly like a haphazard version of an Electric Light Orchestra instrumental number. Alex was wondering whether he actually had a realistic chance of mapping out the computer equipment at the compound, given very limited time. He thought about his friend Kazik, tried to mentally reconstruct all the events of his Polish trip with Michael, and worried about Jimmy's task of keeping a woman captive in Janice's basement. But most of the time he was asking himself repeatedly the same question over and over again: "What in the name of god are you doing here, you stupid jerk?"

A bit earlier a call came through to the police station. Betsy, who dutifully plunged Wakarusa into darkness at 3 pm, informed the chief that someone from the ranch got in touch with her and wanted to know when power was going to be restored. She told him – as instructed – that Jake would have to pay them a quick visit to have a look at 'circuits'.

Just a few minutes later Alex, dressed in somewhat oversized overalls, attached a strange, two-wire contraption to his laptop. Both wires were connected to a single jack at the side of the computer and were attached at the other end to long, thin, metallic probes. Although all of this looked highly professional, almost like a mobile colonoscopy testing kit, it actually had zero functionality – it did absolutely nothing.

For the purpose of this trip Alex was actually no longer Alex. Willard, in his infinite folk wisdom, pointed out that the guards at the Hawkins ranch might be checking the identity of people coming in and out, and - based on Albert's story - it was fair to assume that Alexander Malak was on the 'kill asap' list and needed to travel under an assumed name.

To everybody's amazement Chief Thompson whipped up a blank, fake drivers' license from very deep recesses of his desk, 'transferred' Alex's data to it, and managed to copy and paste the appropriate photo. Alex was now Andrew Kuhlman, a happy inhabitant of Elkhart, Indiana.

"Here, Alex" – said the chief, handing him his new identity – "this will probably earn me a few years in prison, but it's going to be like a life sentence for me, because I'll probably have to share the cell with Willard."

The van was getting close to the point at which it needed to turn right into a gravel path leading to the ranch. Alex's traveling companion was in a very good mood. He listened to a country music radio station, whistled cheerfully some of the tunes, and was totally oblivious to the fact that they were just about to enter potentially dangerous territory. Alex decided that he needed to temper Jake's enthusiasm, at least just a bit.

"Listen, Jake" – he said – "I know that you've been to this place before, and you never had any problems, but I got to tell you - this time around it is a bit different."

"What d'you mean?"

"Well, first of all, we're faking it. We are fooling these people, and you need to know that these guys are a pretty dangerous lot. So please be very careful and if at any point you get the impression that they are on to us, don't hesitate to retreat. Just pack your stuff, grab me, and we are out of there."

Jake looked a little puzzled.

"Sure thing, boss."

"And please, never call me boss. Remember, I'm your newly hired apprentice - Andrew."

"Right boss. Sorry, I forgot."

"That's OK."

The van continued on its bumpy way for a few minutes more. Then Jake took a right turn into the path leading to the compound. It wasn't long before Alex noticed some pretty disturbing things. Although technically they were still on a public road, he could clearly see armed men in full camouflage gear lying out in the field and watching the terrain. Even before they reached the entrance gate, they could see two weird armored vehicles parked at a distance. They looked like campers clad in iron sheets and equipped with turrets – perfect vehicles to take on a tour of Yellowstone Park during an armed conflict.

The ramshackle gate, which Chief Thompson had visited with Willard just a couple of days earlier, was still very much there, except now it was guarded by a bunch of men – all in combat fatigues, all armed, and all looking very determined. Some of them were constantly saying something into their shirt sleeves, which made them look like Secret Service agents securing the perimeter during a presidential visit. Two of them were standing on both sides of the gate, on platforms positioned slightly above it, and were aiming their guns straight down the road.

Jake took the van as far as he could – a man with something like an AK-47 slung over his shoulder motioned them to stop about a 100 yards away from the entrance. He approached the vehicle on the driver's side. Jake rolled down the window.

"Hi, I'm the electrician." – said Jake – "Apparently you guys are having some problems with power. Betsy from the substation sent me."

The sentry came up close to the car and peered inside through the open window.

"What's your name?" – he asked.

"Jake Sylvester."

"Who's the other guy?"

"Oh, that's Andrew. He is our new hire."

"Wait here." – said the man and walked a few paces away from the van.

259

Jake and Alex could see that he was once again talking to someone hidden in his shirt sleeve, although the conversation wasn't very long, because he returned to them very quickly.

"All right, I need both of you to step out of the van."

"Why?" – asked Jake to Alex's horror.

"Just do as you are told. Step to the side by the edge of the road".

When Jake and Alex complied, the man went up to them.

"I need to see your IDs."

"Sure." – said Jake.

They both handed him their driver's licenses, and he looked at them very carefully, glancing at their faces every now and then. Alex had a pretty uncomfortable feeling of abruptly ceasing to be Andrew, being discovered as Alex, and being shot expeditiously in the face. However, they were both handed their IDs back.

"Any firearms in the van?" – asked the man.

"Firearms?" – exclaimed Jake – "Oh, no boss. Just tools, cables, and such."

"I'll take a look, if you don't mind."

They didn't. He opened the back door of the van and jumped in. They could hear him rummaging through Jake's collection of electrician's gear. And then they heard a loud yelp and an even louder 'Shit!' from the inside of the vehicle.

"He must've touched the bar?" – whispered Jake with a wicked leer on his face.

"What bar?"

"The bar with 240 volts and 15 amps on it?"

"What?"

"Shhh, just keep quiet."

The man got out of the van, staggered briefly while clutching his hands together, and then nodded his head to suggest that they should get back to their seats.

"All right, listen carefully" – he said when he reappeared by Jake's window, still clutching one of his hands – "go straight to

260

the inner gate, which is down this road about a quarter of a mile away. Do not stop anywhere and do not get off the road for any reason. You'll be met by our janitor who will lead you to where you need to go. Is this clear?"

"Absolutely, boss."

The gate opened and Jake drove through it rather quickly, almost afraid that the guards would change their minds. Alex tried to scout the terrain as they were moving deeper into the compound, but he could hardly see anything, because the road past the gate was lined on both sides with dense vegetation. He spotted a couple of wooden shacks at a distance and small groups of uniformed people standing around them, but it was impossible to make out anything in detail. Suddenly they entered a large clearing at the end of which they saw an iron gate topped with barbed wire. Whatever was past that gate couldn't be seen – a 6-foot wooden fence surrounded the entire area.

As they were approaching the gate, a short, balding figure stepped outside and waved to them to approach. The man was in some sort of a uniform, but appeared to have no weapons.

"Hello, you must me Jake." – he said.

"Right, boss."

"My name is Rich and I'm the janitor. If you don't mind, I'll squeeze in with you and tell you where to go."

"Sure thing. I need to get to wherever your main electric wire goes into the main building." – said Jake.

"No problem."

Rich hopped into the car, the gate opened, and they drove on. The sight that presented itself took Alex by surprise. He expected to see frantic activity of some sort, with people scurrying to and fro, vehicles moving, and loud commands being issued. Instead an eerie peace greeted them. The main compound building was right in front of them and it looked more like a forest retreat for retired vacationers than a paramilitary command center. In front of it there was a gravel parking lot where Alex saw a row of pretty expensive cars from several different states. There were two armed guards at the front door and a sharpshooter on the roof, but otherwise nothing betrayed the fact that something pretty ominous might be happening inside.

"Ok, go to your right, along the side wall of the building." – said Rich.

Soon they saw another guard standing by the generator which was making quite a lot of noise.

"You can stop by that earsplitting piece of shit – that's where our main electric hookup is. I hope you can get us our power back, because this thing is driving me nuts." – said Rich.

"We'll give it our best shot, boss."

The van stopped and Jake got out to talk to the guard. Alex immediately opened his laptop, with its fake electric probes hanging lifelessly down around his knees, and ran a quick test which was supposed to show him all the routers in the vicinity. He quickly found one – 150 feet way. "Got you, you stupid schmucks!" – he said to himself.

Jake was ready to start on his fake electrician's mission.

"Hey, you do what you need to do, and I'll start gettin' out my tools – as slowly as possible. How will I know that you're done?"

"I'll come up to you and tell you that I ran all my tests and the circuits are good to go."

"That'll work. Hope we get outta here in one piece".

With these wishful words Jake got out of the van, opened the back door, and started dragging all kinds of things out onto the ground. Since he had no real repair job to do, he grabbed stuff in a totally random fashion, making sure that there were more or less equal numbers of cables, probes, and meters. Rich was still talking to the guard and pointing something out to him, but they couldn't hear a word because of the generator noise.

Alex stayed in the van a bit longer, setting up his stuff on the laptop and starting all kinds of computer scripts which needed to be running while he would be doing his bogus tests. Once he saw that Rich was done talking to the guard, he too got out and walked up to a large electrical panel which was mounted on the wall, to the right of the generator. It was immediately obvious to him that the guard was not in a cooperative mood.

"Please stand back!" – he yelled at Alex as he pointed his machine gun at him.

"Hey, wait a second. Put that thing down. I need to get to this panel, and so does my boss over there."

"The panel is padlocked."

"Who has the key?"

"Rich will unlock it. You just stand back, and I need to see what you're doing at all times."

"All right, all right, calm down – we're just electricians."

"I don't give a shit who you are."

Rich and Jake approached them together.

"What's up, Hermann?" – asked Rich.

"Nothing. Just open this damn thing for them and leave the key with me."

"OK."

Rich unlocked the panel, handed the key to the guard, and turned to Jake.

"I'll leave you to it now. When you're finished, just get in your van and leave the same way you got in here. Nobody will stop you on the way out."

"Great. Thanks Rich." – said Alex.

Rich walked away towards the front entrance of the building while Jake started to unroll a large coil of black cable, pretending that he was making a direct connection from the panel to some mysterious equipment inside the van.

"Andy, you need to clamp them probes to the Phase I and Phase II connectors, up there yonder, in the corner. That should give you reliable readings."

Alex almost missed the fact that he was now Andrew and that Jake was talking to him, but he reacted quickly enough not to raise Hermann's curiosity. And Hermann was certainly curious – he was standing just a few paces behind both of them and watching their every move. He was also in constant contact with someone somewhere, talking to his shirt sleeve frequently in a very hushed way. Alex attached his 'probes' to two large screws, hoping they were not holding live wires. Then he watched intently the screen of his laptop. His scripts were running and they were cryptic enough to fool Hermann into believing that he was indeed measuring something. In the meantime Jake was staging a major performance, touching all kinds of tangled wires in the panel, both with his hands and with imposingly looking pieces of equipment. All along he was whistling happy tunes and occasionally murmuring to himself such gems of electrician's wisdom as 'get in there, you stinkin' piece of crap' or 'oh, how twisted you are, my darlin'.

The problem for both of them was that Hermann seemed to be getting increasingly impatient and started talking to his superiors more and more frequently. Alex could only see him as a reflection on his computer screen, but he had absolutely no doubts that their time was running out, and he still needed at least a few minutes to try to inject the zero-day virus code into their computers. And then his worst fears suddenly materialized.

"All right, boys, you need to wrap this up." – said Hermann.

"We ain't done yet." – replied Jake.

"Doesn't matter. If you can't fix it, we'll just use the generator until you figure it out. My orders are to get you out of here now."

"You aren't understanding me, my friend. I got to finish this, 'cause otherwise you'all be screwed. I need to get the dikes to get to the scotch lock and follow homerun to test your horse cock."

"What?"

Hermann was visibly flustered.

"Listen son, I ain't gonna stand here and explain to you my terminology. If you want your juice back, just gimme some more time and space. I'll be done soon."

The guard hesitated.

"OK, you have two minutes."

Jake looked at Alex with a bit of desperation in his eyes, but Alex was too engrossed in trying to give a bunch of computers a serious case of cyberflu. He was close, very close, but not quite there.

"OK, boss" – he said – "I'm almost finished with the circuit tests". His statement confused the hell out of Jake, not really accustomed to being called 'boss' by anyone, and he almost asked why Jake was calling him that. But before he had time to commit this potentially lethal blunder, Alex had something else to say.

"Great, all circuit tests completed. We're ready to go."

Jake reacted to these words with great speed. He told 'Andrew' to disconnect his probes, rolled back all the wires, packed random gadgetry back into his van, and told Hermann to padlock the panel again. Then he whipped up his cell phone and was just about to call Betsy, but Hermann intervened again.

"What are you doing?" – he asked menacingly.

"Relax, I need to call this in to the substation, so that they can try to give you your power back."

"Be quick about it".

Jake called Betsy and told her that the 'fault' had been fixed and that she could go ahead and 'run with it'. And she did just that since about 30 seconds later the generator automatically shut itself off, which was a clear signal that electricity was back on. Jake waved merrily to Hermann showing him two thumbs up, but that didn't seem to impress the guard too much.

"Let's get the hell out of this joint." – said Jake to Alex as they both got back into the van.

On the way back to Wakarusa Jake couldn't resist asking Alex the obvious question.

"So, did you get what you wanted?"

"I hope so. I'll know when we get back to chief's office. By the way, what was all that baloney you said back there?"

"What baloney?

"I thought you were going to use some electrician's crap to delay things, but you suddenly started sounding like a vulgar veterinarian."

"You lost me, boss."

"Well, what was all that about horse's cock or something."

"Oh, that" – said Jake grinning – "don't worry, it's still very much what people like me say on the job."

"Oh yeah? What exactly did you say then?"

"That I needed to use side-cutters to get to the twist wire connector, so that I could follow the wire going straight to the back panel in order to test the explosion proof flexible conduit."

"And what does that mean?"

"Jack shit. Just a bunch of electrician-speak which you asked for."

"Great. One more thing. What's that bar with 240 volts of electricity in the back of the van?"

Jake smiled slyly.

"Just a bit of protection against thieves. If you ever get in there, don't touch anything."

"Thanks for the warning, but I think my days as an electrician are over."

Chapter 40

While Alex was totally engrossed in his stint as a clueless electrician, back at the police station Michael had to deal with a completely different set of difficulties. Almost as soon as Jake and Michael had left, he got a call from Jimmy who told him about Linda's ravings concerning the possibility of a total and automatic self-destruction of the compound and a massive bomb attack on the town of Wakarusa.

"Do you think she's bluffing?" – he asked Jimmy.

"It looks that way, but what if she isn't?"

That was indeed Michael's worry. And Chief Thompson certainly shared that concern with him, because as soon as he had been told about Jimmy's call, he marched into the back room and sat down in front of Albert who was still licking his wounds while lounging on a tattered loveseat which looked like it remembered the times of the Civil War.

"Albert, did you ever hear anybody at the Hawkins ranch talking about rigging the compound with explosives or having some sort of a self-destruct plan B in case of a total failure?"

"Well, yes..." – said Albert hesitantly – "but it was all just pie in the sky... you know, things which might be done in the future. I don't think anybody did anything to implement something like that."

"Are you sure?"

"Chief, I can't be 100% sure. I just heard speculation about it, but nothing concrete. Why are you asking me about it?"

"I'm not sure you're going to like it. It is your daughter who claims the entire compound and all kinds of places in this town are going to be reduced to shreds if at 11 tomorrow things will not go according to plans."

"My daughter! Well, how the hell do you know?"

"We know, because we're holding her captive in a basement in Fort Wayne." – said Michael. He sneaked in behind the chief and was standing quietly in the corner of the room during this entire conversation.

"Holding her captive? Jesus, what's going on?"

Michael decided that Albert needed to know a bit more than he did.

"Listen, Albert. We already told you that Linda tried to kill us. It didn't work and we sort of captured here. We couldn't just let her go, so we decided to keep her until all of this is done, one way or the other. She's perfectly safe and well taken care of, and – regardless of what happens - we'll release her tomorrow. The person who is taking care of her has just told us she claims the compound will self-destruct. Do you think she is telling the truth?"

"How could I possibly know that? It sounds like a desperate bluff, but these people could've done something like this a long time ago and no one, except for the 'big wigs', would know anything about it."

Further discussion was suddenly delayed by an electrical event – the power was back on. This could either mean that Betsy got really angry and acted on her own or – more likely – that Jake and Alex did what they needed to do at the Hawkins ranch and signaled it was OK to switch electricity on. A few minutes later both of them walked into the police station. Alex wanted to immediately talk to everybody about what happened at the compound, but the chief waived him off, asking everybody to sit down, take a deep breath, and relax.

The truth was Chief Thompson was getting increasingly worried about all kinds of things. His office had gradually become an odd 'command center' of its own, with people coming in and out and plotting things that were mostly illegal or at least very risky. He was also stuck half way between his deeply rooted belief that law and order took precedence over anything else and a nagging feeling that this was perhaps one of the few situations in his life which required extraordinary measures, legal or otherwise. In short, he didn't know what to do, and the idea that his town could be in some way mined and targeted for destruction wasn't helping his general mental condition one bit.

Alex almost read Chief Thompson's mind.

"Hey, chief" – he said – "I know you are worried, but we're half way there – I think I got the info we needed."

"Great. Except you don't know about the info we certainly **didn't** need." – replied the chief. He then proceeded to tell Alex about the call from Jimmy. At this point Michael – sensing a possible confidence crisis - intervened and asked everybody to gather around the table in the back office. He did not exclude either Willard or Jake – he thought that one way or the other they could prove useful. As the six of them were slowly taking their seats, he couldn't help thinking that it was utterly ridiculous to imagine that this strange collection of characters could in some way stop a plot which had been in the works for decades and which had been commissioned by Hitler himself. And yet he felt somehow in charge, as the person who decided to react to an anonymous letter sent to him from a foreign land. He also felt absolutely obliged to go on.

"All right, gentlemen" – he said - "we have very little time, let's start."

He seemed to have everybody's attention, so he continued.

"First of all, Jake and Willard, you don't really know what's going on, but there's no time to explain, so I'm asking you to just go along with us and offer any help you can. I hope we can count on you?"

Both men nodded, and Willard even managed not to say anything.

"Good. Alex, what can you tell us about the stuff you've discovered?"

"OK, basically their computer setup is fairly straightforward. They have one big server, as expected, 4 other PC's, one laptop, a wireless router, and a UPS connected to the server."

"UPS?" – asked Willard.

"Don't worry, sergeant, it's not a brown truck. It's a battery backup called Uninterruptable Power Supply. Anyway, I think I successfully infected all of their machines with the zero-day virus, which means I can shut them down any time I want over the Internet and - once I do – they won't be able to restart them until they remove the virus. Basically these machines will be in a startup loop, which renders them useless."

"You **think** you successfully infected the machines?" – asked the chief.

"Yes, I do. I can't really test it, can I? We can only test this when America will be on the line, so to speak. As for the server, we still need to get its electricity cut off. Shutting down all the other machines just eliminates possible backup plans."

"All right, go on."

"So our task for tomorrow is to get into the compound and cripple the generator before 11 am. And before anybody else is going to say anything about it, I'll be the person doing it – by myself. I started all this shit, and I need to finish it. Now, there is a possibility that the nuts we are fighting are suicidal and that they rigged all kinds of things with explosives which will go off tomorrow if we successfully stop them. I'm going to be very frank with you – there is nothing we can do about it in the time we have left, and we should just ignore it. If we blow, we blow."

"There is only one little problem with that, Michael" – said Chief Thompson – "I don't mind being blown up, and maybe you don't either, but if various places in this town will get destroyed, we may be looking at hundreds of casualties."

"I realize that, chief, but there's simply nothing we can do about it right now. But I'm glad you spoke, because I was just about to say that you should take over this meeting and the entire operation."

"I'm not sure I understand."

"It's simple. You are the local, legal authority, and we are on your territory. And the people who are planning to wreak havoc on all of us are operating just outside of your town. If anybody should be in charge, it's you."

Chief Thompson was both surprised and a bit moved, although he fought desperately to hide it. He then stood up, turned towards Michael and made a hand gesture which could only mean one thing – 'thank you'.

"Now then, since I've just become a dubious commander of an even more dubious force" – said the chief - "I'd like to first of all suggest that we make this room our base of operations. Willard, you'll be in charge of making sure that nobody gets in here without our permission. The back door is locked, so all you have to do is to keep an eye on the front office. Jake can help you with that if he wants to."

"No problem." – said Willard.

"Albert, I don't think you are fit enough to actively help us, however I want you to try to draw a diagram of the area surrounding the generator, possibly identifying best routes for Michael to get in. If you could start on that immediately, it would be great."

"You got it."

"And Alex, please use the table in the corner over there to set up your ridiculously illegal gear. I'm sure you'll need some space, not to mention peace and quiet, to do what you need to do."

"Thanks."

"OK, before we start working on a detailed timetable for tomorrow, let's talk about the two main tasks: getting Michael to the generator, and disabling it".

"I would insist on adding a third task." – said Alex – "Getting Michael out of that damn place."

"Right, I agree. So what's the quickest way of screwing up the generator?"

"Water, baby." – said Jake.

"What?"

"All you have to do is to pour a small bottle of water into the gas tank. Water is heavier than gas, so it'll sink to the bottom and start cloggin' the shit outta the engine almost immediately. The thing will start sputterin' and will eventually totally die. But even a sputterin' generator engine is great for us, because it ain't makin' juice reliably."

"Can they repair it?" – asked Michael.

"Sure they can. But they would have to drain the tank, clean out fuel valves, and so on. It would take hours."

"I like it." – said Michael. So did everyone else.

The next hour or so the entire crew spent on discussing various logistical details. In particular, Alex told everyone that although he neither had time nor opportunity to examine the generator, it seemed to him to be a relatively standard piece of equipment, with automatic 'switch on/shut off' functionality. Jake concurred. There was also some discussion about the guard positioned just by the generator. The prevailing view was that normally there was probably nobody there and that his presence was the result of the fact that there was a power outage at the time Jake and Alex were around.

"How about communications?" – asked Alex – "How are we going to communicate with Michael once he's out there?"

"You're not communicating with me in any way. First, we don't have the necessary equipment, and second, even if we had something, it would be too risky to use it."

"Well, in that case, take this." – said Alex, reaching into his bag and handing Michael a small USB pen drive.

"What the hell am I going to do with this?"

"Well, it's not only a USB key, but a GPS locator. Just put it in your pocket, and I'll be able to at least see where you are at any given moment".

Chief Thompson was again somewhat disturbed.

"Tell me, Alex, what else do you have in this bag of yours? Miniature hand grenades? Pershing launch pads? Or perhaps a small nuclear device? That could really come in very handy."

"Information technology people need to be prepared for all kinds of eventualities, Chief Thompson." – said Alex, betraying a bit of uneasiness.

"Really? So the guys back at your rubber factory in Morton Grove carry this sort of crap routinely, just in case they get hopelessly lost in the sea of vulcanized parts and need to be found and rescued?"

"Chief, I'm just trying to help. I admit some of the stuff I have and use is on the fringes of legality, but perhaps we can discuss this some other time, like when we are all alive and still living in America that we know."

"All right, all right... I guess the next item on the agenda is weapons."

A total silence welcomed Chief Thompson's words.

"Michael, do you want a gun?" – asked the chief.

"No, I don't. I never had one and I don't know how to use it".

"I can teach you how to use it in five minutes. Listen, I'm not saying you should be going in there and shooting people, but what if your life is threatened? What if shooting someone is actually the only option?"

"I guess I'll take my chances."

"Really? But why? If you are dead before the generator is out, we are all totally screwed."

"And if they catch you, they'll shoot you on the spot." – said Albert.

"Well, thanks, I feel much better now."

"Think about" – continued Albert – "this is their big day, the final 'hurrah' for which they were waiting for decades, so they'll wipe out anybody who stands in their way tomorrow."

Michael didn't really know how to respond to all of this, nor was his general frame of mind conducive to rationality. In a number of ways he felt totally overwhelmed by the rush of events over which he had absolutely no control. After all, he still was a city desk editor at 'Chicago Tribune' and he really wished he could just get back to his desk and talk bullshit with his odious colleagues.

"All right, I'll take the gun." – he finally said – "Just tell me how I avoid accidently shooting myself."

With the weaponry problem solved, the discussion veered towards probably the most important issue – getting to the generator just at the right time. Albert produced a rough sketch of the area and explained to everyone that although there was a fence at the back of the compound, it was lower than the one upfront and it ran through dense bushes. It was routinely patrolled, but to a much lesser extent than the terrain leading from the front gate to the main building.

"Do you think there are any cameras back there?" – asked Alex.

"I doubt it. I certainly never saw anything like it. Michael, you should probably try to jump the fence right in the middle, here."

Albert was using his diagram to point things out as he went along, and everybody formed a tight circle around him to have a better view.

"Wait, how will I even get to this area?" – asked Michael.

"There is a narrow road in the woods at the back. I think Jake should take you there in his van. Even if they somehow see the vehicle, which is unlikely, it shouldn't raise any suspicions. In fact forestry guys and firefighters travel down that road quite frequently. The closest you can get by car is about a mile away from the back fence, but that mile is all wooded, so you'll have good cover. There is also an outer fence, pretty close to the road, but it's this low 'country style' thing which shouldn't be any problem."

"What should I expect on the other side of the inner fence?"

"I'm not quite sure, but I think you'll land in tall bushes and from that point on you'll have about 150 yards to cover before you reach the edge of an open field. If Willard is right about the generator, it will be right in front of you, about 50 feet away. But that 50 feet will probably be the hardest, because you'll have to be totally in the open."

274

They spent a lot of time hammering out all the details, both in terms of the sequence of events and their exact timing. Alex checked the weather forecast for November 24th, Thanksgiving Day, and discovered, to his excitement, that it was supposed to be quite foggy in the morning, which could be a big advantage for Michael. The discussion continued for a while, but it was getting late, and everybody was getting tired. Chief Thompson decided it was time to review the detailed plan, so that everybody understood what was supposed to happen on Thursday morning.

"Let's go over this again." – he said.

"Wait, chief" – said Alex – "Are we all staying here overnight?"

"I would say that's the best option. I have some cots which we can use, so make yourselves at home and I'm sure Willard will make coffee for us first thing in the morning."

"I can even cook some scrambled eggs." – boasted Willard.

"Great, Willard. Please do. I knew you would be useful someday. Anyway, as we agreed, at about 8 am tomorrow Jake takes Michael to within a mile of the compound, to the spot identified by Albert, and then comes back here. Michael walks towards the back fence and lays low, waiting for the best moment to get in. Alex, Albert, Jake and myself will remain here, and hopefully we'll be able to track Michael's position via GPS. Then at 10 am, if everything goes well, Michael gets to the generator, pours water into the tank, and retreats to the wooded area to observe what happens."

"Shouldn't he just get the hell out of there immediately?" – asked Alex.

"No, I won't." – responded Michael very forcefully – "I have to verify that when the power goes down, the generator is fucked up and doesn't do its job."

"OK, then" – continued the chief – "at 10:15 Betsy pulls the plug on electricity, which will automatically start the generator, and – assuming the water in the tank works as expected – it'll sputter or die in just a few minutes. At 10:30 Jake shows up in his van at the main entrance to the compound claiming that he needs to do more repair work. The idea is to create as much commotion and chaos as possible to make Michael's exit from this hellhole easier, but also to find out, if possible, whether the generator is actually broken. Fifteen minutes later our chief cyber-criminal, Alex, switches off all the remaining computers at the compound. At 10:50 Jake arrives at the spot where he earlier dropped Michael off and waits for him. Hopefully he'll collect a live person, and not a guy full of bullet holes. Then they'll race back here, and we'll either celebrate our success or wave one another fond goodbyes as we fly through the air, due to a bunch of powerful explosions. Did I miss anything?"

"There is of course another possibility." – said Michael – "No explosions and no celebrations, because their plan somehow works and we all become inmates of some 're-education center' where they connect our brains to large electrodes in order to clean our thoughts of bad shit."

"I prefer explosions, if I were to choose. Plus there is no bad shit in my thoughts." – said Alex.

"All right, everybody" – said the chief – "time to get some rest – I'll wake you up tomorrow at 7 am. And I certainly hope this will not be the last time we all wake up."

"Amen to that." – said Jake.

Chapter 41

For once meteorologists were right. Thanksgiving morning turned out to be murky, damp, and foggy. Michael got up first, even before Chief Thompson's 7 am alarm. Having had his coffee, he started preparing himself methodically for his escapade – he chose dark clothes and planned to wear a short, black coat. Chief Thompson joined him at the table, bringing his own coffee and a small gun which he placed right in front of him. For Michael it certainly was not his typical morning as normally what accompanied his coffee were just cream and sugar.

"This is Ruger LCP 380." – said the chief.

"Am I supposed to be impressed?"

"No, you are supposed to say – 'wow, it's really small.'"

"Wow, it's really small, chief."

"It was designed for 'conceal carry' and it's very light and easy to use."

"Easy to use? You mean easy to kill people with."

"You can use it as a door stop if you want, I don't care. But just in case you need to use it in its intended role, you probably should know a couple of things about it."

"All right, I'm all ears."

"It's a seven-shot semi-automatic."

"Holy shit, I can wipe out seven people with this thing?"

"Theoretically, yes. But in your case you'll be lucky if at least one of your bullets hits someone or something. Anyway, right here, by the trigger, there is a little push latch which is now in the locked position. The gun can't fire until you unlock it by pushing this latch in the other direction. It's not loaded yet – go ahead and try it."

Michael picked up the gun cautiously, almost like a piece of delicate glass. He looked at it from all sides and then gripped it in his right hand. He was surprised by the fact that it was tiny and extremely light.

"Go on, unlatch it. Then point it at the wall and squeeze the trigger in one, smooth motion."

"You're sure there're no bullets in this piece crap?"

"I'm sure."

Michael pushed the latch and pointed the gun at a picture hanging on the wall. He suddenly thought about Linda pointing the gun at him and his friends, and could hear in his mind the loud clicks of her broken weapon. A moment later he heard a very similar click, as he mock-fired his Ruger.

"I assume that my having this gun is illegal." – said Michael, putting the gun back on the table.

"Yes. It's my private weapon, and I have a license for it, but that doesn't mean I can lend this to people. But that's OK, I already got used to the prospect of spending years with Willard in some smelly jail cell."

"How do I carry this thing?"

"I'll put a holster on your back, just below the collar line – you'll be able to draw the gun just by reaching behind you neck. If you get into some kind of confrontation, people will typically tell you not to put your hands in your pockets or to put them up. The gun will be within almost instant reach regardless of the circumstances. In fact, let's go and put that holster on you right now – you can practice drawing the gun a few times."

Chief Thompson's office was suddenly full of bustle, as everybody got up, drank some coffee, and ate Willard's scrambled eggs. Alex arranged his equipment on the table in the corner of the room and tested the GPS tracking device – it was working very well. The only person who didn't get up was Albert – he was awake, but decided to stay in his cot. In fact everybody noticed that he didn't look too good, but there was no time to do anything about it.

By about quarter to eight Michael was more or less ready to go. He watched Chief Thompson load the gun with seven bullets and place it in the holster that was already on his back. Jake went outside to start the van. For a while there was a bit of awkwardness in the air as Alex went up to Michael and embraced him briefly.

"Good luck, my friend. See you soon." – he said while handing him a plastic bottle of water which Michael put in his coat pocket.

Everybody else shook Michael's hand. As he was just about to walk out, Chief Thompson stopped him.

"Wait, I know you are all going to hate me for saying this, but let's synchronize our watches. I don't care about seconds, but let's make sure Michael is not on Pacific Time or something."

And then Michael was gone. Chief Thompson sat by Alex and watched the GPS dot moving around the laptop screen, although there was nothing particularly interesting about it since Michael was just traveling down a public road towards the Hawkins ranch. After a while the dot stopped moving, at a distance of about a mile from the back fence surrounding the compound – a clear indication that Michael was dropped off in the woods and was preparing to make his next move. A quarter of an hour later Jake got back to chief's office.

"Everything all right? – asked Alex.

"Yep. It's damn foggy out there, which is probably just as well. I'll tell you – Michael is a weird dude."

"Why do you say that?"

"Well, I offered to go with him all the way up to the fence, but he just kept saying he needed to do this by himself."

"Don't worry about it, Jake" – said Alex – "he's just being who he really is – a totally anal jerk."

Although things were already put in motion, Alex was still thinking about the possibility that Linda had been telling the truth and that both the compound and the town had been in some way rigged with explosives. If that was indeed the case – he thought - someone had to know something about it. And there seemed to be no better person to ask than the only electrician in town.

"Jake, how long have you been doing electric stuff around here?" – he asked.

"Oh, must be about a dozen years now."

"Did you ever have to deal with some totally weird installations or repairs – you know, stuff outside of the usual crap you have to deal with?"

"Not that I can think of. Well, a few years ago reverend Whaley was absolutely convinced that someone pissed into his fuse box at the back of the church, and I had to prove to him that he was wrong."

"How did you do that?"

Jake grinned.

"There's nothing better than a good smell test." – he said.

"Anything else?"

"Let's see... The only other thing I can think of was that weird request to install a satellite amplifier at Ms. Goral's house."

Chief Thompson, who was quietly sipping coffee at his desk, suddenly put his mug down and turned towards Jake, showing both interest and urgency.

"When was that, Jake?" – he asked.

"Oh, maybe a year or so ago."

"So what exactly happened?"

"I don't know all the details, but apparently Ms. Goral was always bitchin' and moanin'... I mean... complainin' about her bad Internet service. One day someone overheard her talkin' about it in the grocery store and told her he owned some sort of an electronics company that could provide her – free of charge – with a better satellite dish and a special signal amplifier. She immediately agreed and then called me to see if I could install that for her, because that company didn't do installations. So I did."

"What did you install?"

"It was just a regular satellite dish, although larger than what she had, and a green, sealed box, hooked up to the dish. It had some sort of a power supply and a backup battery".

"Did you put that green box inside the house or on the roof?"

"Inside, by the satellite modem. But what's with all these questions, chief?"

"I'm not sure yet. Do you know the name of the guy who gave the dish and the box to Ms. Goral?"

"Hell no, I don't remember that. But I have it written down in my log which is in my van. Do you want me to go and check?"

"Please".

Alex didn't quite understand chief's sudden interest in all of this.

"Chief, who the hell is Ms. Goral and what do we care about the quality of her Internet access?"

"Alex, we found the body of your Polish friend in Ms. Goral's field which is just a stone's throw from the Hawkins ranch."

"Wait, wait... I'm not sure I understand what you're saying. Do you think there is some connection between Kazik's death and this satellite installation?"

"No, I don't. At least not directly. But let's wait for Jake's news on that."

They didn't have to wait long – Jake came back with his notebook in hand, opened it on the page that he had clearly bookmarked before, and uttered words that had an astonishing effect on Chief Thompson.

"It was Travis Prescott. That's the guy who donated the equipment to Ms. Goral."

Chief Thompson stood up with amazing alacrity, as if he had just accidentally lost a ton of pounds. Without saying a word, he walked up to a locked cabinet at the back of the room, opened it, took out an imposing looking rifle, and loaded it.

"I need to go" – he said – "please stay in touch with me by phone."

"Where the hell are you going?" – asked Alex.

"To Ms. Goral's house. I need to save my town."

Chapter 42

After he had been dropped off by Jake, Michael sat down in thick underbrush at the edge of the woods. He had plenty of time, so he decided to first have a good look at his surroundings before venturing towards the back fence of the compound. The trouble was he could see very little – it was a bit foggy, and large trees obscured his vision on all sides. He listened for any noises suggesting the presence of other people, but the only thing he could hear were branches fluttering in light wind.

He started walking south, directly towards the Hawkins compound. This was no easy task – he didn't have a compass or any other navigation device, like his cell phone, so he had to constantly confirm his direction by watching a faint glow of the sun hidden behind pretty heavy clouds. The terrain wasn't particularly easy either – he advanced slowly through tall grass, fallen trees, and lots of leaves. On top of all that, he felt distinctly uncomfortable and somewhat incongruous. The gun on his back started feeling like it weighed much more than he originally thought, and the bottle of water in his coat pocket now seemed to him to be a pretty pitiful weapon against a sophisticated terrorist plot. "Who told you to leave your damn office in Chicago, you moron?" – he asked of himself philosophically, but was unable to find any rational answer.

It was nearly 9 am, and Michael still couldn't see anything other than the woods. After a while he started hearing noises – not of people, but of moving vehicles, somewhere at a distance, probably within the compound. He trudged on and was beginning to have doubts about ever reaching the fence, but then it suddenly showed itself, right in front of him, about 100 yards away. He dropped to the ground and waited to see if there was any movement around the perimeter of the compound. There was none. He got up and moved on, this time as quickly as he could, reaching the fence and dropping to the ground again.

It was a pretty chilly day, but Michael felt sweaty and tired. The wooden fence seemed to be about 5 feet high. Unfortunately there were no gaps between the slats, so he couldn't take a look inside. He raised himself off the ground very slowly, staying in a relatively crouched position until his eyes were level with the top of the fence. He peered over the barrier. "Shit, Albert was right" – he thought when he saw tall, dense bushes on the other side. He could also see a silhouette of a pretty big, flat building which had to be the main part of the compound.

Michael waited for about five minutes, listening for any signs of life and surveying the landscape in front of him. However much he dreaded the next part of his mission, it was time for it. He jumped over the fence in one, smooth motion, surprising himself with his own agility, which at his age was spotty at best. According to Albert, there was now about 150 yards separating him from the open field by the side of the building. He started plodding through the bushes, going diagonally to the left.

Although initially time was on Michael's side, his progress was now very slow, not only because of the density of the surrounding flora, but also because of the fact that he had to be extremely cautious. He stopped frequently to scrutinize the terrain. When he finally reached the edge of the woods, it was 9:45. He had the generator in sight, but another object in front of him was much less welcome. There was a tall man in full combat gear standing at the side of the building, about 10 feet away from the generator. He had a machine gun in his hand and seemed to be just looking around, as if checking if everything was in order.

"Fuck, I'm slightly outgunned." – thought Michael, remembering the 'weapons' at his disposal, i.e. a handgun for Lilliputs and a bottle of water. He was lying on the ground, behind a tall, dense bush, so he was fairly certain that he couldn't be seen, but time was running out and any move on the generator was obviously doomed as long as the man was there. Michael could see that the 'soldier' was in communication with someone, because every now and then he would whisper something to a walkie-talkie. At about five minutes to ten, after another yakking session with his comrades, he suddenly started walking away from Michael, along the side of the building. He then turned right and disappeared round the corner, presumably going towards the front door.

Michael waited for a couple of minutes to make sure that the enemy's disappearance wasn't just a temporary fluke. He took a deep breath. "OK, let's roll the stinking dice." – he whispered to himself.

Chapter 43

On the way out of his office Chief Thompson grabbed his reluctant partner Willard and together they raced to Ms. Goral's house in his sergeant's private car – going there in a police cruiser with flashing lights seemed to him potentially risky. While Willard was driving, the chief got on the phone with Alex who still had no idea what was going on.

"Listen, Alex, that guy, Travis Prescott, is a phony major in the ranks of the nitwits at the ranch. If he really had something installed at that house, it cannot possibly be anything good."

"So, what are you planning to do?"

"I'll have a look at that green box, but I'll need your help, 'cause I don't know too much about this shit. I'll call you back when I get there. How's Michael progressing?"

"Very slowly, which kind of worries me. He seems to be right at the fence now, but he's been sitting there for a while. Hey, chief, one thing – don't cut any wires over there until we discuss this."

"You got it."

To say that Ms. Goral was surprised by her unexpected visitors would be a major understatement. She visibly gasped at the sight of Chief Thompson and Willard, fully expecting that another mangled body had just been found in her field.

"Ms. Goral, please calm down, there's nothing to worry about" – hastily said the chief – "we just need to have a quick look at your satellite installation."

"Why?"

"I'm afraid there's no time to explain. Where is your modem?"

"My what?"

"The black box which is connected to the dish on the roof."

"Oh, that's in the basement, but..."

"Thanks. You stay here with Willard and I'll go down there."

Chief Thompson rushed downstairs and quickly got to the wall at the back of the house. It was time to call Alex again.

"All right, so what I see is a large black box with blue lights blinking on it – I'm guessing that's the modem. It says HughesNet on it."

"You're right."

"Next to it on the same wall there's the green box. Nothing on that one – no lights, no symbols, just nothing. It's connected to the power supply and to the modem."

"Connected how?"

"With a short yellow cable, almost like phone cable, but thicker."

"Good. That's a network cable. Don't unplug it. Just take this unit off the wall and see if there's any way to open it."

Chief Thompson did exactly as told, but when he flipped the box over, he couldn't see any screws or latches. He noticed, however, four tiny dimples at the corners of the bottom cover. When he scraped these areas with a small knife, he saw screw heads.

"Willard, come down here for a second!" – roared the chief. He instructed his slightly frightened underling to bring him a flat-head screwdriver, which he did with astounding dexterity. The chief got rid of the screws and opened the plastic cover.

"Are you still there, Alex?"

"Yeah."

"First of all, there is no ticking bomb in here, and no visible timer of any kind. The box contains a weird device with some lights and has a model or serial number on it. It's X-WR-1R12-1I24-I."

"Crap, I know what it is." – exclaimed Alex.

"Could you perhaps share your knowledge with me before something blows up in my face?"

"Nothing is gonna blow. It's a ControlByWeb WebRelay switch."

"I'm already feeling much better." – said the chief sarcastically – "Does it make strong coffee?"

"It's basically an Internet device which allows you to switch things on and off via the Web."

"Wait a second, does that mean someone sitting in Acapulco or Vladivostok can control shit in my town?"

"Yes, that's pretty much it. But the good thing is that if you unplug this device, it disappears from the net and all the control capabilities are lost. And nothing will explode."

"All right then, I'm going to do just that."

"No, chief, don't! If you unplug it now, the jerks at the compound will immediately notice it and may send someone to Ms. Goral's house to see what the trouble is. It's 9:50 right now and Michael seems to be ready to do his thing with the generator. Stay put until 10:15 when Betsy cuts the power off. The green box will still function, because it's probably a low voltage thing that can run on a backup battery for at least an hour. But by that time the people in the compound will know that their operation is being screwed up, so your unplugging this thing won't matter in the larger scheme of things."

"No problem. I'll wait. But do you think this green box is here to set off explosions in case of their failure?"

"I have no idea. It certainly has that capability if someone knows what he's doing. And if all of this is rigged properly, someone can set the bombs off from any place on the planet."

"That's just great. I'll destroy this thing as soon as I can."

"Good, but be careful and disconnect the box in stages, one cable at a time."

"Got it. Where's Michael now?"

"Inside the compound, within striking distance of the generator."

"All right. Keep me posted."

Chapter 44

It was true that Michael was within 'striking distance' of the generator, but Alex didn't quite understand what was going on. His friend seemed to be staying in various spots for quite a long time, which could mean he was running into all kinds of issues. There was absolutely no communication between them, so the only thing he could do was to stare at a little GPS dot on his laptop screen. At 9:57 the dot started moving again and stopped at the coordinates roughly designating the generator. "God damn it, Michael, it's about time." – muttered Alex.

He couldn't have known that his friend had encountered a major problem. Michael ran across the open field towards the generator and then sat by the side of it, shielding himself somewhat from anybody's view. When he unscrewed the gas tank cap and looked inside, he suddenly realized that there was one scenario nobody had ever predicted or discussed – the tank was totally full and there was no way he could pour any water into it, at least not enough of it, so that it could sink to the bottom. "Shiiiiiit....! We're so totally screwed." – he thought.

Panicked and unsure of his next move, he sat there for a few minutes trying to figure out what he could possibly do. There was no way of pouring some of the gas out, because the generator was a massive piece of equipment and was bolted to a concrete slab. All kinds of ideas rushed through Michael's head, mainly centering around some distant and pretty dim childhood memories of his dad syphoning gas out of a camper's tank by sucking it out through a plastic tube.

"Right, I need a fucking tube." – he told himself. He looked around, but could see nothing that even resembled a tubular object. In fact, there was nothing at all. He stood up and circled the area, even though he knew perfectly well that he could be spotted at any moment. In growing desperation and anxiety, he sat down by the generator again and peered behind it – although, to his disappointment, there were no hoses or tubes back there, he did see a relatively long piece of thin cardboard, like a torn off flap of a box. He picked it up. It looked miserably inadequate and way too thick, but he started rolling it into a tube which he then fashioned, not without difficulty, into a moon crescent shape. "If this works, I should get a Nobel prize in some bullshit science." – he mumbled to himself.

He stuck about half of the length of his 'tube' into the gas tank opening, and started sucking the air out of it. A whiff of gasoline fumes attacked his face, but it wasn't followed by a rush of actual ethylene. Michael was acutely aware of the fact that his window of gas siphoning opportunity was closing down rapidly – the cardboard would soon get completely soaked in fuel and would become even less of a tube than it was initially. He tried his sucking prowess again, and then again. On the third try gas started flowing out, trickling steadily to the ground in a sickly, slow sort of way.

It was difficult to gauge how much gas was siphoned off, but Michael looked at his watch and realized that he only had three minutes before the power cutoff. In other words, he was already 12 minutes late. He yanked the 'tube' out of the tank, poured nearly the entire bottle of water in, and put the cap back on.

"Freeze!" – said a loud voice to his left. Michael looked up and saw the same tall guy in combat fatigues standing about 30 feet away from him and pointing his gun straight at his head.

"Stand up slowly, put your hands above your head, and step away from the generator." – the man said.

Michael more or less assumed that his life was just about to end in a remote compound in the middle of nowhere. His worst fears were quickly confirmed.

"I'm going to shoot your brains out in just a second, but perhaps before you die you'd like to tell me who the heck you are and what you're doing here."

"Sir, I'm sorry, but I just wandered in here by mistake." – said Michael lamely.

"Oh, don't give me this bullshit. I'll tell you who I am, so that you know who killed you. I'm Major Travis Prescott. Who the hell are you?"

Michael decided that he no longer had anything to lose.

"All right, if you must know, I'm Private Michael Riedle."

Major Prescott briefly stopped in his tracks.

"Riedle? So you are that poor sucker who went to Poland in the hope of screwing up our organization? Well, I'm glad I found you at last. I could spare your life, because in just a few minutes your existence or non-existence won't matter one bit to anyone. But I won't."

As Major Travis Prescott raised his gun to send Michael to hell, the generator suddenly started, making a horrible, grinding noise. Startled Prescott turned briefly towards the machine that had undoubtedly been kicked into action by Betsy. This gave Michael the only chance of survival that he could possibly have. He reached behind his back, pulled out the gun, unlatched it, and fired three quick shots, aiming roughly at Prescott. He had no idea where his bullets went, but they certainly had the desired effect, because the major suddenly grabbed one of his buttocks and fell to the ground yelling 'you son of a bitch'. Michael didn't wait for any further developments. He rushed back into the woods, trying to follow more or less the same path as before, except this time around he was running, brushing aside branches and stumbling every now and then over things scattered on the ground. He could hear animated voices behind him, but he never looked back until he reached the fence over which he jumped immediately, landing awkwardly on a pile of pointy twigs.

Michael sensed instinctively that he needed to get as far away from the fence as possible, so he continued towards the dirt road where Jake had dropped him off earlier. When he reached it, he had no idea whether that was indeed the spot from which he was supposed to be collected. He crossed the road and lied down in a shallow ditch running along it. It was 10:20. "Damn, how am I going to survive here for 25 minutes?" – he thought while shivering with fear and agitation.

He started doubting the possibility of his survival even more just a few minutes later, as soon as he heard a distant but fast approaching car engine. Since it was way too early for Jake to show up, Michael was more or less certain that he would soon be confronted by angry Major Travis Prescott, clutching his hand over a bullet hole in his ass. He clung to wet grass trying desperately to disappear as much as possible. The engine noise was becoming louder, and Michael's life expectancy was getting shorter, at least in his own mind. But then the car went quickly past him, never even slowing down, and he had just enough time to look at the back of the vehicle. It was an open jeep with three men in it. Two of them were wearing semi-military uniforms and both brandished automatic guns. Whoever they were hunting for, it wasn't Michael. And he had another 20 minutes to wait in the ditch.

Chapter 45

Shortly after the lights went out at Ms. Goral's house, courtesy of Betsy, Chief Thompson carefully, and not without some foreboding, unplugged the network cable from the green box. Nothing happened, which in this particular context was good news. He then unplugged the power cable running to the box. Still nothing. Emboldened by his success at not blowing anything up, he got rid of a couple of screws and took the box completely off the wall. Once again it was time to call Alex.

"All right, I got this thing all disassembled." – he said – "Now what?"

"Chief, just stay there for a while. I'm watching Michael's progress. He got to the generator all right, but I have no idea if he succeeded."

"Well, so where is he now?"

"That's the problem. He said he was going to stick around for a while to see if the generator would fail, but he didn't."

"What do you mean?"

"At around 10:15 he started moving quickly away from the area, back towards the fence. He now seems to be over it and still moving fast."

"You think he's being chased."

"I wish I knew. At least it seems he's alive, but he may have failed. I don't know."

At this point Willard ran down the stairs into the basement and started flailing his hands wildly, apparently trying to attract Chief Thompson's attention. He succeeded.

"Alex, I'll call you back. My personal calamity named Willard wants something from me."

"Chief, we may have guests." – blurted out the sergeant.

"Great. Put the kettle on."

"It's a jeep with armed men in it."

The chief paused for a brief moment.

"How many and where are they?" – he asked.

"I could see two guys and a driver. They are about half a mile away – coming this way."

"Is your gun loaded?"

"What?"

"Is your damn weapon loaded, Willard?"

"I guess, but..."

"You guess?"

"Well, the thing is the last time I used this gun was about 2 years ago, and even then I was just testing it to see if it still worked."

"And did it?"

"Yes."

"Great, let's hope it still does, because your life may hinge on it."

Willard was thoroughly confused, but he was just about to get confused even more, because his boss suddenly put a green box on the concrete floor and stepped on it, thus applying the entire mass of his police body to it and reducing it to an electronic pancake. He then grabbed his rifle, armed it with a fast back and forth movement of his hand, and started on his way back upstairs, inviting his bewildered assistant to precede him.

Ms. Goral was sitting quietly in her front room, and her confusion was very much in sync with Willard's. Chief Thompson's next move did not alleviate the situation in any way.

"Ms. Goral, I'm going to have to ask you to go down into the basement and to stay there until I tell you that it's OK to come up again. Please don't do anything, no matter what happens or what noises you hear. And don't be alarmed – everything is going to be all right."

Ms. Goral was obviously at the end of her wits.

"Chief, you keep telling me not to get alarmed, and yet it's the second time I see you in just a couple of days, and on each of these occasions all I can do is to get more alarmed."

"Yes, I know. I'm sorry, but there's no time to explain right now. Please go downstairs."

As soon as Ms. Goral complied, Chief Thompson told Willard to draw his gun and stand by the window left of the front door while he took position at the side of the room, by the other window, overlooking the road and the driveway leading to the house.

"What exactly are we doing, chief?" – asked Willard who was holding his gun gingerly and looking at it furtively every now and then, as if he wanted to convince himself that after many years of mundane police work, largely consisting of doing absolutely nothing, he was suddenly facing a real firefight.

"Don't panic, Willard. We'll see who this is. Perhaps it's just a bill collector who likes driving jeeps."

The theory about the bill collector fell flat on its face a few moments later when the jeep drove up to the front door and discharged two young men in camouflage outfits with guns in their hands. They stood at their vehicle for a while, discussing something among them, and then they started walking slowly towards the front door. Chief Thompson opened his window slightly.

"This is Chief Thompson!" – he shouted – "Please stop, turn around, get in your car, and leave".

The men stopped, clearly startled by police presence in Ms. Goral's house. Nobody said anything for a while, which gave Willard some time to regret the fact that he never got around to having his testament written up.

"Chief, we don't want any trouble." – said one of the men – "We're from the Hawkins ranch and we just need to check on a piece of equipment in this house."

"What, you forgot to turn off your hair curler? Don't worry, I can do that for you."

"Please, it's important."

"It is? Then perhaps I can help you."

Chief Thompson opened the window a bit more and tossed the flattened green box out of it, so that it landed just at the feet of the two intruders. They looked at it for what seemed to be a very long time. Then one of them murmured something to his companion and they both started approaching the house again. The chief aimed at just above their heads and fired his rifle. It produced a very loud, menacing bang. Both men dropped to the ground instantly.

"All right, boys" – yelled the chief – "if you make another move towards this house, my next shot will be right between your eyes. Once again, leave your guns on the ground, stand up very slowly, and walk back towards your car."

While the two men were weighing their pretty limited options, the driver of the jeep suddenly showed up just in front of Willard's window, armed with a revolver. Before Chief Thompson had any chance of saying or doing anything, he heard a single shot. The driver dropped his weapon, grabbed his arm, and issued a very loud, but semantically hollow yelp: "Shit, I've had it with all this shit!"

Chief Thompson, sensing some weakness in the ranks of the enemy, told all three men to return to their vehicle immediately. He was a bit surprised to see that they actually gathered themselves up, dusted their pants off, and obeyed his order meekly, climbing back into their jeep and driving off.

"So why the hell did you shoot at him?" – asked the chief, looking sternly at Willard.

"Well... I don't know, chief.... Sorry. He just suddenly showed up and I reacted."

"Good job."

"What?"

"Good job, sergeant. I don't get to say it too often, but you did just the right thing."

"Thanks."

"Did you aim at his arm?"

"No, at the legs."

"Close enough. And I'm glad your gun fired after all these years."

"So am I, chief."

Chapter 46

Jake arrived at the compound gate right on time, just a couple of minutes after 10:30. Even before he got to the 'Berlin Wall', he saw that things were not good in the kingdom of Nazis. There was a lot of commotion, and people were running nervously all over the place, yelling at one another and frantically conversing with higher authorities via the ever useful microphones hidden in their shirt cuffs. The sight of his approaching van caused even more tumult, and one of the armed guards started running towards him waving his hands.

"Stop, stop!" – he yelled.

Jake stopped his vehicle and waited.

"What the hell are you doing here?" – asked the man as soon as he got to the car.

"Well, you guys seem to have power problems, right?"

"None of your business."

"None of my business? I'm the stinking electrician, and Betsy sent me to..."

"You'll be a dead electrician if you don't turn around and leave."

"Listen, son, don't threaten me. I'm just doing my job. Why don't you blow into your magic shirt cuff and consult with your bosses about this. I know you have a generator, but I may be able to help anyway. If they say they don't want my help, I'll leave."

"They're kind of busy right now."

"What? Mending fuses?"

"As I said, none of your fucking business."

Jake saw that the guard was clearly nervous and a bit hesitant. He also noticed, to his alarm, that a number of other armed goons started approaching his van and soon congregated around it. They had a brief, animated discussion about something, but Jake could only hear disjointed words. Finally one of the men separated from the group and talked to his invisible superior somewhere inside the compound. The conversation must have been difficult, because at times the man was punching the air angrily with his hand. Finally he approached Jake who was still sitting in his van, with its engine running.

"All right, we need your help with something, so we'll let you go to the main building. There'll be people waiting for you there."

Jake panicked. All along he was counting on the fact that he would not be let through and that he would simply find out if the generator was working and then leave. He obviously had no time to work on anything, as his rendezvous with Michael was just minutes away. The guards waved him on. He put the van in first gear and started moving slowly towards the gate, watching all the people around him carefully. He was waiting for the best moment to perform what he thought was the only possible maneuver. When all the men were slightly behind him, he suddenly swerved sharply to the left, made a very tight 180 degrees turn and raced away from the gate, passing the startled guards. He didn't look in his rearview mirror to see what was happening behind him, but he didn't have to – he heard a series of shots, and then the sound of shattering glass. It took him a few seconds more to feel a sharp pain in his right shoulder. "Damn, they hit me" – he thought as he continued on his way towards the dirt road where he was supposed to pick up Michael. He took his right hand off the steering wheel and let his arm dangle by his side. This diminished the pain a bit, but meant he had to steer the car with his left hand only, which - on a bumpy narrow road - was a bit difficult.

When he got to the place where Michael should be waiting, it was 10:40. Jake stopped by the side of the road and looked over his right shoulder. He could see blood dripping down his shirt, but there was nothing he could do about it. His prospective passenger was nowhere to be seen, so he grabbed his cell phone and called Alex, wincing with pain as he punched the numbers.

"Alex, I'm at the pickup spot. Where's Michael?"

"He's right there. I can see the GPS dot on that road."

"Something ain't right then – I can't see him."

"Just hang tight – I'm sure he'll show up."

"I can't hang tight too long, boss. I got shot."

"What?"

"I'll explain later. It's no big deal. And I didn't find out if the generator got busted."

"That's all right. Just come back here safely. I need to hang up now and shut down all their computers."

"OK."

Neither Jake nor Alex could have known that Michael was still in the ditch by the side of the road and had the van in clear view, at a distance of about 100 yards. Unfortunately he was in no position to do anything – there were at least a dozen men combing the woods on the other side of the road, clearly looking for him. Luckily for Jake, they couldn't see the van from where they were, but their presence meant that Michael was the prisoner of his ditch cover.

"To hell with this crap" – he said to himself after a while, and started crawling in the ditch towards the van. His progress was very slow – there were patches of mud and standing water every now and then, and he had to constantly monitor the movements of the people on the other side of the road. After about 10 minutes he reached the car, but it was parked on the other side of the road. He found a small rock and threw it at the driver side window. Jake was slow to react, but then waved to Michael and opened the door.

"Come on, just get inside." – he said in a hushed voice.

Michael stood up and darted towards the vehicle.

"You're late." – said Jake.

"You're bleeding." – said Michael.

301

Michael knew immediately that his driver was hurt, so he told him to move over and then jumped into his seat.

"What happened?" – he asked as he was speeding off towards the main road.

"Them jerks shot me."

"How bad is it?"

"Don't know. Did you get the generator?"

"Don't know."

"That's just great. Can't wait until 11".

Chapter 47

Back at the police station Alex used his hacker powers to shut down all the computers at the compound at exactly 10:45. A minute later he got positive confirmation of the shutdown, so he was almost certain that at least that part of the entire operation ended up to be a success. As for all the other parts, he wasn't so sure. Michael's movements and his successive locations were puzzling, to say the least. He had no idea why his friend left the generator location at 10:15 and why he remained in the same spot in the vicinity of the dirt road for over 20 minutes. And then he watched with growing anxiety the GPS dot representing Michael moving ever so slowly along the road, as if crawling to nowhere.

Alex knew that if everything had gone according to schedule, the situation at the compound would have to have been chaotic. He tried to imagine the panic of the people responsible for the successful operation of all the computer systems – backup batteries drained, all the workstations mysteriously switched off, and the server down because of the erratic operation of the generator. Yet he had no idea whether that was indeed what the crew at the Hawkins ranch was facing.

His thoughts were abruptly interrupted by Chief Thompson and Willard who burst into the office through the front door. They both seemed to be somewhat agitated.

"Are you all right?" – asked Alex.

"Yeah, we're fine. We had to scare off a couple of thugs who wanted to fix the green box."

"Really? Wow, I didn't really expect them to attempt that. How did you stop them?"

"By shooting at them. But don't worry, we didn't kill anybody."

"Frankly, I don't give a shit about that. I'm more worried about Michael and Jake. I have no idea where they are and on top of that..."

Alex abruptly stopped talking and looked at his laptop screen.

"Wait, they are moving again. Or at least Michael is."

Just a few minutes later Michael entered the room with Jake hanging precariously on his shoulder. Neither of them was a pretty sight. Jake had a large bloodstain on the back of his shirt and was clearly struggling to stand on his two feet, while Michael, all covered in caked mud, had bloody cuts all over his face and looked like he had just returned from a failed attempt to capture Iwo Jima. They all steered Jake gently onto a cot right beside Albert and Chief Thompson immediately started cleaning and bandaging his wound.

Once that was all done, they all sat down in half circle around the two cots. It was 10:56. There was nothing else to do but wait and watch the clock.

"Michael, did you manage to put water into the tank?" – asked Alex quietly.

"I did, but I had to leave, so I have no idea whether this actually worked."

"I guess we'll know soon. No matter what happens, thank you all. We did what we could."

And then all of them just sat there, looking tired and apprehensive. The minutes kept ticking away. They knew that they wouldn't know what happened unless Wakarusa suddenly exploded which, unfortunately, would mean that they both won and lost. At one minute to eleven Willard accidently knocked a paper punch off Chief Thompson's desk. It landed on the floor with a loud bang. Everybody visibly twitched. The chief looked at his sergeant with scorn, but he didn't say anything.

At 11 am absolutely nothing happened. And nothing happened for the next two minutes. But then the good news stopped. A huge blast rang out somewhere in close proximity of the police station, blowing out one of chief's front windows and sending shards of glass flying all over the place. Everyone dropped down to the floor, fully anticipating further explosions. None came. Chief Thompson got up first and surveyed his office. It was all messed up, with shreds of paper floating in the air. His desk lost a leg and was tilting dangerously to one side, threatening to discharge a year's worth of police bureaucracy to the floor.

"Everybody OK?" – he shouted.

He got muffled responses from all the people in the room except for one - Albert. The chief went over to the cot Albert was lying in and he saw immediately that they had lost one comrade. There was a large splinter of glass lodged deeply in Albert's chest and he was staring at the ceiling with glassy eyes.

"Albert is dead." – announced the chief.

Nobody said anything. In fact nobody knew what to do or say next. They were more or less cowering all over the office expecting the worst.

"Willard, pull yourself together and meet me outside. I think the explosion was in the vicinity of the school." – shouted the chief, although he did not sound too sure of himself.

"I'm going with you, chief." – said Alex.

The three of them went out to the street. There was nobody around, and all they could see was a plume of black smoke hanging over an area just a couple of blocks away. It took them about a minute to drive to the site of the Wakarusa Elementary School. Except it no longer existed. The building was totally leveled and various parts of the rubble were on fire. There were also distant sounds of approaching fire engines.

"I think we'll need a new school." – said the chief with quiet resignation in his voice.

Slowly people started emerging onto the street from the surrounding houses most of which had windows blown out. The nearby grocery store was missing a part of its roof, and a damaged hydrant was spewing water all over the sidewalk. It was a scene that no Wakarusa resident had ever seen before.

"Anybody hurt?" – yelled the chief.

"I think we're all right." – answered a young man who started shepherding people away from the smoking debris.

"Willard, stay here and wait for the firefighters." – said the chief to his clearly panicked subordinate.

"All right, chief." – he said.

Alex jumped back into the chief's police cruiser and they raced back to the station.

"What the hell has just happened?" – asked the chief.

"I have no idea. But it might actually be good news." – responded Alex.

"Really? You must live in some other universe, because in my world blowing up school buildings is never good news."

"Think about it, chief. There's been so far just one explosion, which probably means that we've successfully screwed up their plans. And, because no other parts of Wakarusa seem to be flying through the air, including your office, their ability to blow things up around here seems to be gone."

"So why did the school explode?"

"I have no clue. They could've had another green box somewhere else. But I'm sure the building was totally empty, because it's Thanksgiving, so at least we don't have to worry about that."

"But we do need to worry about the possibility of other bombs exploding. They could've spaced the timing."

"True, but I doubt it. It's already ten past eleven, and nothing is happening. As far as I remember, Linda said bombs would go off immediately after 11, and that was supposed to include their own compound. We didn't hear any sounds of an explosion coming from that direction."

"I hope you're right. I've had enough of demolition stuff for today.

Chief Thompson and Alex ran back into the police station to find everyone standing over Albert's body covered with a piece of white cloth. There was a long moment of somber silence, but it was also obvious to the entire group that they needed to somehow move on and find out whether everybody still lived in the same country they knew so well.

Chapter 48

As they were standing over dead Albert, Michael couldn't stop thinking about the fact that he was looking at the second victim of the venture that he himself had started. It wasn't a pleasant thought, but he knew he couldn't dwell on it.

"I'm sorry, everyone, but we need to get on with it." – he said, breaking ruthlessly the silence prevailing in chief's office.

Nobody reacted to this in any way – the entire gang of four seemed to be totally immobilized, seemingly transfixed by whatever occurred or did not occur. Michael picked up his cell phone, lying amidst assorted rubbish on the floor. To his surprise, it still worked, even though it was covered in dust. He dialed a number.

"Hi, Rick." – he said to his co-worker, Mr. Weigert.

"Michael? Holy crap, where are you man?"

"Doesn't matter. I'll be home soon, I think."

"You think? Listen, there were some FBI agents looking for you, and..."

"Rick, shut up. I need to ask you an important question."

"You can't just keep calling me to tell me to shut up. What the hell is going on with you?"

"Where are you now?"

"What? This is your important question?"

"No, but first tell me where you are."

"I'm at home. It's Thanksgiving, you know."

"Yes, I know. Where do you live?"

"Jesus, Michael, I think you've finally flipped. What difference does it make where I live?"

"Holy fuck, can't you just answer my question?"

"All right, suit yourself. My apartment is just west of downtown, on North Halsted."

"OK, did you hear any explosions or loud booms of some sort in the last 15 minutes or so?"

Although Weigert couldn't shut up prior to the last question, now he did.

"Rick, are you there?" – asked Michael impatiently.

"Yes, I'm just getting my smelling salts."

"That's not even funny. Answer my question, please."

"No, I didn't hear any stinking explosions. Shall I produce some for you?"

"Any police sirens blaring?"

"The only thing that's blaring is your brain. It's Thanksgiving. The streets are almost empty, and all the policemen are probably at home cooking some festive shit and stuffing it with doughnuts. Which is what you should be doing."

"Great, thanks. I'll be in touch."

Michael abruptly ended the call and turned towards the people gathered anxiously around him. For a while he didn't really quite know what to say, because he thought there were no adequate words to express what he felt. The truth was he just wanted to go home. He eyed briefly all the eager faces staring at him, and slumped into an armchair, resting his head in his hands for a while.

"Well, gentlemen, I think we did it." – he eventually mumbled almost to himself.

"What?" – asked Alex.

This time Michael was ready for a louder pronouncement.

"God damn it, I think we've successfully screwed up Hitler's plans, although unfortunately the stupid schmuck will never know about it."

There was a palpable sense of relief in Chief Thompson's office, but nobody was doing high-fives and nobody was celebrating. They seemed to be stuck in the middle of chief's totally trashed room, not saying anything, just savoring the fact that it was all over. Finally the chief took over as the local commander.

"Listen, there are two things we need to do immediately." – he said – "Let's get medical help for Jake. I'm kind of tired of having this makeshift hospital in here. Michael, call 911 and tell them we have one person wounded at the station and one guy dead. If they ask, and I'm sure they will, tell them that one of them has a gunshot wound, and the other suffered a fatal injury to the chest."

"Got it, chief. But what if they ask who did the shooting?" – said Michael.

"Oh crap, I don't know. Tell them Willard did it in a fit of rage provoked by me. We'll sort it out later."

Michael quickly alerted the authorities, but he really didn't need to do this – all the agencies in the area were already aware of the fact that something dramatic was playing out in Wakarusa.

"The second thing we need to do is to call the feds." – said the chief.

"I don't think that's going to be necessary." – said Alex, pointing to one of the windows.

Everybody turned around and looked outside. There was at least a dozen black SUV's rushing past the police station at breakneck speeds and going in the direction of the Hawkins ranch. All had flashing lights on and all were adorned with large yellow lettering on the doors. The FBI has just arrived. A minute later they could hear a low hum which was steadily gaining in intensity until it presented itself as three military helicopters heading in the same direction as the SUV's, flying very low and fast.

"They are late by 27 minutes." – said Michael.

Alex went up to the chief and asked him if he and Michael could have a private word with him. Chief Thompson led them to his desk at the back of the room.

"What is it?" – he asked.

"Chief, once this is over, the FBI guys will be here asking you all kinds of questions. We both want you to come out of this whole thing as the local hero – you know, the person who suspected something and acted to trip up their plans by cutting electricity."

"But they'll be asking questions about you too."

"Sure they will. Just tell them we were passing through and volunteered to help. Obviously they'll get in touch with us, so let's agree that this is our version of the story and let Willard know about it too. As for Jake, he knows nothing anyway. In other words, sell to the FBI the story of two accidental Chicagoans."

"Are you sure?"

"Absolutely."

"Under normal circumstances I would probably refuse, but this gives me a rare opportunity of avoiding anybody telling me in the future to quietly fuck off and not bother them."

"What?"

"Nothing, never mind. Just squaring off with my past."

"OK, then. Michael and I are going back to Elkhart to check out of the motel. We're not going to wait for the feds to show up here."

"Fine with me. Before you go, what exactly happened back at the compound, Michael?"

"It's just as well you reminded me" – said Michael, pulling the gun from behind his back and handing it back to the chief.

"Did you use it?"

"I'm afraid I did. I shot Major Travis Prescott in his behind."

"You shot that pompous bastard in the ass? Hallelujah, I'm so proud of you!"

"Well, it was an accident."

"No, it wasn't. The gun didn't fire by itself, did it?"

"No, but I fired three times in the general vicinity of the target, and two of my bullets might now be in someone else's ass."

"Who cares. I hope this idiot will not be able to sit in his prison cell for weeks. Anyway, I may have said a couple of untoward things about both of you, but I really need to thank you – Wakarusa is still standing, and America is still more or less the same as before. I'd call it a win, by whatever standard."

"Agreed. But all the thanks should go to you. Without your help we would've almost certainly failed. So, thanks chief. I would hug you, but my chances of reaching all the way behind your back are slim to none."

"Get the fuck out of my face." – said Chief Thompson, chuckling happily.

"And a happy Thanksgiving to you too." – responded Michael.

Michael and Alex started on their way back to Elkhart. It was a short drive and they didn't really say anything to each other, mostly because Michael was not only dirt tired, but also covered with dirt. As they were approaching the town, Alex picked up his phone and entered a text message which he sent to Jimmy.

"Telling Jimmy to let Linda go?" – asked Michael.

"How did you guess?"

"I'm a reporter. Or at least I hope I will be one again soon if it turns out I'm still employed."

"I'm sure you are. Listen, are we going straight back home or should we stop by Jimmy's house, just to thank him or whatever."

"Your call."

"Why don't we stay one more night in Elkhart, which will give you the opportunity to clean up and look like a half decent human, and then we swing by Fort Wayne. We should be back in Chicago on Saturday morning."

"No problem. Let's do it."

Chapter 49

At the Klonowskis' house things were in full Thanksgiving mode. Stuff was being cooked, baked and prepared, assorted relatives from Chicago and various other places were slowly gathering, drinks of all descriptions and strengths were being poured and quickly consumed, and a huge turkey was inching towards its intended state of perfection in the oven, filling the entire house with a wonderful aroma. It all looked perfectly normal and calm, even though it wasn't.

In the midst of all this commotion Jimmy was bravely fighting to appear his normal self, but he was extremely nervous and kept checking his watch about every five minutes. Shortly after eleven he slipped out of the kitchen and went down to the basement to have a quick look at a few TV channels. This was easily justified to the rest of the company since he was known to disappear periodically from various family functions to check on the latest Chicago sport teams' scores.

Jimmy flipped quickly through a bunch of channels. Nothing suggested any major, catastrophic events. It was just routine everyday stuff interrupted regularly by totally useless commercials. "Since they're still peddling Viagra, we should be in good shape" – he thought. He rejoined the crowd upstairs and had a few beers with cousins, uncles and aunts. His wife was very busy with all the festivities, but he could see she kept a keen eye on him, expecting some news – whether good or bad – at any moment.

And then shortly before noon his cell phone beeped loudly. He picked it up with a totally phony air of indifference and looked at the screen. As he expected, he got a text message from Alex:

Release the bitch. We won. Albert is dead. Will call later.

Jimmy didn't display any emotion. He just went over to his wife and showed her the message. They hugged briefly, in an innocent sort of way, which could not be interpreted by anybody as anything more than an expression of holiday spirit.

"Would you do the honors, Mairéad?" – asked Jimmy quietly.

"What do you mean?"

"Would you release the bitch with me?"

"Gladly. Let's go."

They announced to everybody that they needed to run a quick errand and that they would be right back. As they were going down the stairs into Janice's basement, Jimmy was wondering whether Linda knew what time it was and whether she was aware of the fact that her fascist comrades didn't pull anything off. She was sitting on the couch as usual, and she stared at both of them, in a decidedly hateful sort of way.

Jimmy approached her and ripped the tape off her mouth, fully expecting to immediately hear some revolting ideological crap. However, she remained totally silent and seemed to be somewhat befuddled.

"I have good news and bad news for you." – said Jimmy – "The good news is that my wife in a just a moment will personally cut all your restraints and will set you free. I hope she'll control herself and not cut anything else, but no guarantees. The bad news is that your bunch of crazies in Wakarusa failed miserably at creating the Fourth Reich and is probably in the hands of federal authorities. So I would say your stint as an FBI agent is more or less over, and so are any hopes of government retirement when you are old and ugly, which will be soon."

"You're lying." – said Linda, although her voice noticeably lacked conviction.

"No, I'm not. You **will** be old and ugly. Prison dampness does that to people."

"You know what I mean. I'm sure we've succeeded."

"Your opinions on this matter don't mean shit to me. I'm sure you'll be able to find out for yourself whether I'm lying or not once you are out of here."

"Where am I supposed to go?"

Michael was visibly shocked by the question.

"Where you're supposed to go? Are you kidding? Go to hell for all I care. Just stay out of our lives. Perhaps you can get to Germany to see whether it would be possible to engineer another firestorm at the Reichstag, killing a few additional Jews in the process. Or how about a quick visit to Dachau to reminisce fondly about good old times while sitting by the crematorium? Although I rate your chances of getting anywhere other than to prison pretty low."

Mairéad took a pair of scissors from Janice's art desk and cut the tape binding Linda's hands and legs.

"Bon voyage, my darling." – she said with a wicked smile.

"In other words, get the fuck out of here." – added Jimmy, translating pleasantries into stark orders.

As Linda started going upstairs into oblivion, Jimmy had one more thing to say.

"By the way, your father Albert is dead. Unlike you, he was a decent human being who helped us a lot. I just wanted you to know that, so that it weighs heavily on your non-existent conscience as you rot for years in a cold jail cell."

"How did he die?" – asked Linda quietly and without any emotion.

"I don't know, but I would bet your deranged pals had something to do with it."

Linda hesitated for a moment and it looked like she was just about to say something. But then she just continued up the stairs and disappeared without a word.

Jimmy turned to his wife.

"Mairéad, let's go and have our damn turkey." – said Jimmy.

"I'd say it's about fucking time." – replied his wife.

Chapter 50

Once they reached their motel in Elkhart, Michael and Alex showered and feasted on a couple of Big Mac's that they bought on the way into town. Alex also called Jimmy to tell him that they were going to visit him briefly the following afternoon. They had lots of time on their hands so they decided to go for a couple of drinks to a bar which was conveniently just across the street. This was the so-called 'sports' establishment, which meant that the place had a bunch of television screens showing humans engaging in all sorts of weird activities, typically centered around hitting, kicking or throwing a ball, and trying to legally kill their opponents.

They were on their second drink when suddenly most of the screens switched to 'breaking news'.

"I knew this was going to happen." – muttered Alex.

The TV just in front of them, although technically showing NBC's soccer channel, inexplicably switched over to the network's newscast. They saw a serious looking anchor guy who informed the nation that federal authorities had just thwarted a major terrorist plot by raiding a rural compound in Indiana, home to a 'hate group' called National Socialist Brotherhood. The anchorman continued:

According to preliminary reports, as a result of a massive operation FBI agents arrested more than 50 people and confiscated weapons as well as computer equipment. Further arrests in various parts of the country are expected. Additionally, 17 arrests warrants have been issued for rogue FBI agents who apparently aided the terrorists. The group was reportedly in the final stages of preparing a major, nationwide attack.

"Final stages, my ass! How about minutes away from total disaster?" – said Alex?

"Hey, shut up - let's listen."

The FBI agents on the ground acknowledged the help of the local police chief, Oliver Thompson, who suspected something was wrong and engineered a power outage that made executing the criminal plot difficult. According to some sources, he also managed to disarm an electronic detonation trigger linked to bombs placed at various places in the town of Wakarusa, including a police station, a local school, a church, and a fire station. One charge did explode and destroyed the school building, but there are no reports of casualties. The local police chief was aided by two volunteers whose identities remain undisclosed.

"I like being undisclosed. How about you?" – asked Alex, grinning mischievously.

"Same here. I'm glad the chief is going to get a lot of accolades."

They had a few more drinks, looking at a slapdash collection of local drunks who congregated around the TV screens to watch latest reports about how their country had been saved by 'undisclosed' people.

The following day, at around 3 pm, Michael and Alex showed up at Jimmy's house. Mairéad cooked and served her world-famous gumbo which normally would have been based on duck meat, but this time around it was all turkey, since there were pounds of Thanksgiving leftovers stuck in the fridge. They were all sitting around the dining table, sipping wine, and talking about trivialities. Strangely enough, it almost seemed like absolutely nothing extraordinary happened in the last couple of weeks. They had all kinds of successive toasts and, since the

Klonowskis' daughters were present, they refrained from recounting any of their recent adventures, especially the ones concerning tied-up women in basements.

Half way through the proceedings Michael got up, excused himself, and went upstairs. When Alex started looking for him a while later, he found him sitting in front of the house, clutching the envelope they brought back from Poland.

"What are you doing, Michael?" – he asked.

"I actually don't know. It seems all so bizarre. I'm holding this thing in my hand and all these images are racing through my head, but none of this makes any sense any longer. Other than the fact that two people are dead."

"Let's just go back home."

"Sounds like a good idea."

"What do you think would've happened if you'd immediately given your Belize letter to the police?"

"No clue. It's actually funny - it could have ended up in the hands of Linda who would have - of course - 'investigated' by waiting until all their plans had fired off. After all, they apparently had at least 17 'implants' within the Bureau."

"Right. And also, if you'd given this stuff to the authorities, you would have never had a chance of playing a Polish plumber, and I know how much you liked it".

"Alex, sometimes I really wonder why I hang out with someone as weird as you."

"Easy. You must think that being friends with a Polish guy atones for your rough and profoundly sinful Teutonic soul."

"Right. That must be it."

At that point Jimmy emerged from his house with his two dogs.

"Let's go for a walk, guys." – he said cheerfully.

They went down the street towards Janice's house. It was eerily quiet, as if nobody actually lived around this neighborhood. Jimmy told his two companions that earlier he had called Janice and Archibald to tell them that they could safely come back home on Saturday without encountering any women in their basement.

"Do you think Linda got busted?" – asked Alex.

"I don't know." – responded Michael - "But who cares? She has no chance – I'm sure they know she was in on it."

They walked on in silence for a while.

"I thought I'd never say it, but I like the prospect of being back at my shitty job." – said Michael.

"So do I." – said Alex.

"And I like being still married – it was touch and go for a while." – said Jimmy.

"You know, Alex" – said Michael turning to his friend – "one day we should write a book about all this stuff."

"Nobody will believe us, Michael".

"If it's a novel, it won't matter. I would call it 'The Breslau Conspiracy' or something similar."

"OK, you write it, and I'll correct all the grammatical mistakes."

"And I'll just skim the royalties." – said Jimmy.

"Deal".